No Escape from Greatness

No Escape from Greatness

by

Jeffrey John Eyamie

TURNSTONE PRESS

No Escape from Greatness
copyright © Jeffrey John Eyamie 2016

Turnstone Press
Artspace Building
206-100 Arthur Street
Winnipeg, MB
R3B 1H3 Canada
www.TurnstonePress.com

All rights reserved. No part of this book may be reproduced or transmitted in any form or by any means—graphic, electronic or mechanical—without the prior written permission of the publisher. Any request to photocopy any part of this book shall be directed in writing to Access Copyright, Toronto.

Turnstone Press gratefully acknowledges the assistance of the Canada Council for the Arts, the Manitoba Arts Council, the Government of Canada through the Canada Book Fund, and the Province of Manitoba through the Book Publishing Tax Credit and the Book Publisher Marketing Assistance Program.

Printed and bound in Canada by Friesens for Turnstone Press.

Library and Archives Canada Cataloguing in Publication

Eyamie, Jeffrey John, author
    No escape from greatness / Jeffrey John Eyamie.

Issued in print and electronic formats.
ISBN 978-0-88801-537-2 (paperback).--ISBN 978-0-88801-538-9 (epub).--ISBN 978-0-88801-539-6 (mobipocket)

    I. Title.

PS8609.Y34N6 2016   C813'.6   C2016-901395-2
                                                            C2016-901396-0

To John Ruml, who lives in these pages.

To Tiffany and Sophie, who are in everything I am.

No Escape from Greatness

1.

Victory!
 Finally, after a decade of what could only be described as a Sisyphean boat tour through the nine circles of hell—an inferno so arduous that only the Fates themselves could have laid them out for me—finally, I will taste my emancipation.

My return to Greatness is at hand.

I hit the brakes and gravel dust billows through the car, stinging our eyes. I can barely see Zac in the passenger seat as he coughs.

"We're here?" he says.

"Switch on the camera," I tell him. Zac's got one of those little GoPro cameras the size of a facial tissue travel pack. He's going to film all of this and produce a documentary. It wasn't even my idea!

I begin my on-camera commentary:

"We are in a truck stop parking lot outside of Greatness, Manitoba. Population: I have no idea, but there is one traffic light. We're here to sign my emancipation documentation." As the cloud of gravel dust settles, we see the tarnished tin exterior of the Four Winds Truck Stop. Before I left this place, the truck stop was a classic diner, clad in reflective aluminum siding like an Econoline camper. Years of prevailing winds pounded dust into her hull and sanded away any protective coating. Manitoba winters did the rest. Like everything here, simply existing was reason enough for the universe to dole out its punishments. Nature herself had been kicking the Four Winds Truck Stop around like an old tin can, and seeing the corroded greasy spoon through the settling dust hits me in the stomach like an Oil Man Special with a black coffee.

This is Indian summer in Greatness, Manitoba: stinking, arid, gravel-stained, with a tinge of sulphur and a whole mess of torment. It's a special kind of hot in Greatness today. The kind of hot that Satan himself reserves for only the most deserving. Being back here is hard to swallow, but the heat makes it doubly so. Here in southwest Manitoba, October is like the worst stepdad: it starts off full of promise, but could walk out on you in the middle of the night, and more often than not, it'll leave a beating on you before it goes. The leaves could fall off tomorrow and Greatness could be under three feet of snow by Tuesday. You could be unplugging your air conditioner and plugging in your car's block heater in the span of a week. Today is a hot that sits on you until you can't breathe. If I weren't so full of victorious verve, I would be oppressed by the day itself.

I gesture solemnly through the scalding haze toward the diner. Zac pans the teeny camera over as I make a steel jaw and grimly pronounce: "Today, Gabriel Pegg will set himself free. Freedom awaits, inside the Four Winds Truck Stop."

I should probably back up.

Like so many of us Canadians, no one gave me the time of day in Canada until I made it big in America, and then Canada proclaimed "O-ho! One of ours." And like Marshall McLuhan, Neil Young, and Apa Jack before me, I became a Great Manitoban

No Escape from Greatness

Who Wasn't Really Manitoban. I mean, I spent my childhood there. So what? When you get big-time, you leave small-time behind you with all your might. Greatness, Manitoba, and any connection I had to it, has disappeared from my mind entirely. Maybe it would be more apt to say that the memories have *been* disappeared.

Under the Wikipedia entry for *Pop Culture Lowlights 1996*, there would be a picture of my face. The face would be under a top hat, of course, and that dreadful costume (you know the one), and beneath it there would be a tagline: "Gabriel Pegg, better known as Port-O-Potty Guy, from the comedy troupe Erratic Automatic." I'm not proud of it, but it's still my face.

If you're over the age of thirty, you already knew that.

The fame and the money only lasted about five years. I didn't live some Hollywood cliché and blow my fortune on entourages and substance-fuelled VIP parties. I lived a Hollywood cliché and then Manitoba itself conspired to end my career.

I had made two appearances in feature films at that point—comedies, of course, where I played cartoonish, moronic caricatures with the staying power of a fruit fly—and I may have even earned seven figures in a single year.

Then my brother showed up.

Daniel, the Chosen One. Daniel, who was so smart with money. Daniel, who was supposed to manage my fortune, but instead, invested it in such gems as Apa Jack Enterprises, the Crocus Fund, and Royal Canadian Distillers. He even sunk money into the Flin Flon medical marijuana industry, *Archie Wood: The Movie*, and a nuclear waste disposal business in Pinawa.

So that's where all my money went. Manitoba took my life savings to its own personal VIP room and then racked up an enormous tab. And yet, Daniel made enough money to buy a house in Tuxedo, the most affluent part of Winnipeg. Perhaps it was the Apa Jack royalties.

Manitoba took care of the fame, too, in the form of a woman. Her name was Marushka. The bartender introduced us at the Hotel Rockefeller on Hollywood Boulevard. She was sultry, blonde, Slavic, raised in the old Point Douglas neighbourhood of Winnipeg. Marushka knew what a Prairie Caribou was and she was willing to take me upstairs and mix me one. Marushka's smile was intoxicating, but I wanted to get mule-kicked in the soul for old time's sake, and only a Prairie Caribou had the hoofs for that job.

If you don't know what a Prairie Caribou is, I'm certainly not the one to tell you. Let me just say it's not the concoction they serve at Festival du Voyageur, the annual festival celebrating our provincial affinity for pelts and beards. Their "caribou" drink is fortified wine, used in a not-so-different way from a Catholic sacrament ... it's supposed to represent caribou blood. No, Prairie Caribou is much, much, much more potent.

Really, it's best you don't know. I had my reasons, though.

In the hungover wake of that bender I made an important and terrible discovery: Marushka was married to one of the most powerful men in Hollywood, whose private investigator sent him pictures of our dalliance. Just like that, I was ruined.

Jobs evaporated. I became *persona non grata instantanea*. Within weeks, only a handful of my so-called friends would still take my calls; they were the decent ones, the loyal ones who had some compassion for a human being and his foibles. But since those last few decent friends had such strong senses of loyalty, compassion, and humanity, they each got sucked into their own domestic penitentiaries of reproductive disappointment and suburban grass-clipping contests, otherwise known as "wedded bliss." Hollywood is no place for a family, so they packed up their families and moved away, leaving me utterly alone. If it wasn't for Erin, my Toronto agent halfway across the continent, I wouldn't have found any work at all.

No Escape from Greatness

In that loneliness, a part of me died, I think. Life wasn't exactly rich with humour, so why try to be humorous? I wanted my "*E! True Hollywood Story*" to have an up ending and tear-soaked denouement, and I vowed never to be laughed at again. It was time to let my inner artist emerge. That's what I said to myself in my dilapidated dressing room trailer eleven years ago, in front of the tiny makeup mirror whose lightbulbs had burned out. "No one laughs at Gabriel Pegg. Never again," I vowed to myself on the set of a talking hockey dog movie.

"Time to become truly great," I said.

But Destiny laughs last, and the hardest, because exactly one second after my vow to never be laughed at again, Luanne, my long-lost wife, whom I had forsaken to chase what I thought was my purpose, knocked on my trailer door.

We had been married six years previous, in a little roadside church with a white steeple and all the town of Greatness watching, the whole odious cliché, back in 1988, just a month after Erratic Automatic had played its first comedy festival.

Ah, heady times. Seemed like I was on a road to somewhere. Or, perhaps more accurately, a rocket ship to the stars. But Luanne couldn't leave her dad behind to take care of her ailing mother alone, and the Erratic Automatic tour became a pilot on the Mother Corp and a pilot became a series in Toronto, and before you knew it, it was 1994, I had "made it," and my marital status looked like a river at the bottom of a ravine as seen from the top of a mountain.

Six years after I had abandoned her to chase the rainbow, Luanne ambled her way onto the set of that talking hockey dog sequel, past the PAs and the security like she belonged there, marched up to my trailer and knocked on the door, then walked right in like I had invited her. I hurtled toward the river at the bottom of that ravine like a cartoon character, waving goodbye from midair.

I really don't want to get into the details, but Luanne and I ... yes, we had already been together for thirteen years (and married for some of them), but we conceived a daughter that night in the trailer on the set of *Grrrsky versus Howel: Shinny Shih Tzus Part Two,* and Destiny had to either hork its drink back into its glass or risk a cosmic spit-take.

One year later: no more work. Overdue bills. A separation agreement mailed to me from the Court of Queen's Bench that said I owed thirty thousand dollars a month in child support. That's how I found out we had conceived. I am proclaiming that moment my rock bottom.

I sold my West Hollywood condo and lived on my troupemate Shane's futon. It was degrading, but I made my payments and kept the other usurious leeches at bay for four miserable years. I also kept virtually clean and ostensibly substance-free.

Then I missed one little thirty-thousand-dollar payment and suddenly I was wanted for arrest in Canada. When I tried to reach out to Luanne, she was very clear: payment was all she needed from me. Which is fine, because I wasn't exactly Father of the Year material anyway, and we could both see that. Luanne didn't ever send me a photo of our child, though she did mention that her name was Petunia.

Artistically, I was in a bottomless pit. Comedy was the only thing gatekeepers wanted to hear from me, so when I pitched the studios and networks a drama starring myself as a man trying to escape a island prison to be with his family, they wouldn't return my calls. My bottom-of-the-barrel Hollywood agent fired me. My upper-middle-barrel Toronto agent, Erin, couldn't get me work anymore because I was a wanted man, which is bad for the brand.

I wasn't funny and all they wanted was comedy.

Desperate, I tried to convince Shane to bring Erratic Automatic back together. A reunion tour. Maybe a mini-series. But

No Escape from Greatness

no, the other guys couldn't get over themselves long enough to cash in on that, and Shane had made the leap to drama that made me eat my fist. It was too much for me to bear, and in 2008, Shane kicked me out of his house. I remember his ankle-biting rugrats tugging at his pant leg and his second wife kissing his cheek as I walked down their sidewalk, into the abyss.

I call 2008 to 2010 my dark years. I felt all of it. Man did I feel it. I wore black turtlenecks in summer. I found the black lining to every cloud. I didn't smile for 233 consecutive days. I know that because it broke my previous record of 207 days, which I had set the day before starting the new record. I countered all the rubber chickens and scatology of my comedy years with three years of the opposite: nihilism, self-destruction, darkness.

Screenwriting saved me. Angry with the rejection, I redoubled my efforts, placing a character that I secretly knew was me in crucible after crucible, from which he emerged triumphant again and again, armed with fresh purpose. I loved what I was writing and I knew that I had to be free from the threat of arrest. Free to shake hands with Destiny.

I got a team of the best lawyers my money could buy (it wasn't a lot of money) and we drafted my emancipation documentation, a divorce agreement that frees me of my celebrity child support payments and enables me to use my remaining residuals to fund a dramatic work that will crush all naysayers and win me the acclaim I deserve. I'll be on top. Again. This time, the right way. I'll be the toast of Toronto. Then on to the Great White Way. Movies of quality. *Time* Magazine. Then the retaking of Hollywood.

So here we are.

"The prodigal son returns," Zac says from behind his little camera.

"Do you even know what 'prodigal' means?"

"Wasteful? Squanderer? A fool who lost all his money and

now returns to beg forgiveness to all those he left behind?" Zac changes the angle to try and catch my bad side. I instinctively give him my right-side profile to avoid it.

"No one likes a Literal Lanny," I tell him as I unbuckle my seatbelt, knowing that he has nailed the definition.

"Is that even a thing?" Zac says.

I take a deep breath and open the car door, ready to smell the sweet pheromones from the nape of victory's neck for the first time in so many years.

Instead, the odour of rusty sewer pipe swats my nose. The scent of Greatness never changes. And we're only on the outskirts.

2.

The little tin bells on the door of the truck stop jangle exactly the same way they did twenty-five years ago: like they've been deadened by a layer of bacon grease vapour. It's funny how a smell can make a memory rush back. How rust and mildew can remind you of a greasy sausage-and-egg platter you had when you were twenty-five, and how carefully you wiped your lips afterward. It's jarring.

Everybody stops what they're doing when the bells jangle. Oh yes, they know who just walked through the door.

This moment deserves an address, and I know how to deliver one.

"Attention, residents of Greatness."

I spy an abnormally large man, tall and thick, sitting alone in a booth, reading *The Atlantic Monthly*. He scowls and tries to put his nose a little further into the pages. I didn't think anyone under forty read current affairs magazines made of paper anymore. This large fellow appears to be about thirty.

"I have come to seal my emancipation. Once I sign this

document, I will be rid of you all. I can finally flush you away, Greatness, and all the nuts you contain." Someone whispers, "Hey, that's Port-O-Potty Guy," but I leave it.

I shoulder-check furtively to ensure Zac is catching audience reactions as well as my farewell monologue. He's not. He's ogling some diner waitress. She's mousey and bookish with a tattoo on her forearm—just hipsterlicious enough for my nephew. She glances over at him furtively, then wipes her stained bar rag over the excoriated stainless steel countertop.

I hear a voice that makes me feel like a shrimp being deveined. Or a duck becoming *pâté de canard en croute*. I can feel my bones being pulled out of me. Can a voice spatchcock you?

Luanne.

"Gabriel," Luanne hisses from the furthest booth. "Just get over here." She's beet red with embarrassment. Perfect. I take Zac by the sleeve and pull him to the booth, forcing him to break the gaze he was sharing with the waitress. Luanne sits with a couple of lawyers. No sausage-and-eggs platter; just coffee and paperwork. The emancipation documentation. My freedom.

She looks fit. She's got some grey streaks in her hair now (don't we all) and the blonde isn't quite as lustrous as it used to be. She's aged, but she's still Luanne. Those wrinkles around her eyes—she's been doing a lot of smiling. Probably at my expense.

"I wondered why you wanted to meet here, of all places," she says. "Now I know."

"No, Luanne, you don't know," I pronounce. "You were insistent that this take place in Greatness and so I chose the site that would allow me to avoid as much of it as possible."

"A diner during the breakfast rush?"

"Okay, I did want to give my nephew some good visuals for the behind-the-scenes documentary he's producing, but this has no relation to any sentimental historical significance this place may have for you, so put that thought out of your conniving mind, all right? Where do I sign?"

A lawyer shoves a document in front of me with little "sign here" tabs jutting out from the sides. I flourish. *Victory. Victory! VICTORY!* An eleven-year odyssey is over with a single flourish of the pen.

I am free.

The documentation signed, I take a step onto the vinyl booth cushion and make another announcement, fighting a tide of hick eye rolls and exasperated yokel breaths:

"I hereby commend you to the custody of my succubinical wereshrew of an ex-wife. If I pass through here ever again, I will pass through like warm probiotic yogurt."

The only sound is of the giant-man turning the page in his magazine.

"Quickly," I say, filling in the punchline for them. "Quickly."

Perhaps it comes off as bitter, but it makes for good video.

"You're not leaving," Luanne blurts. I can't quite tell if it's disbelief, but I choose to ignore her because I am now fully emancipated and able to tweak the areolas of Destiny!

"You can't leave," Zac says. He points to the emancipation documentation. He's pointing to fine print in the documentation. My medulla oblongata quivers. "Says right here."

I examine the document. All the diner patrons seem to have their eyes on me now, burning holes in my back. I see blurs with the occasional word thrown in: "visitation" ... "charges reinstated" ... "six days per week" ...

"This is all legalese!" I bark at them. Luanne's lawyer is all doe eyes and red hair and credibility, and she smiles at me pleasantly, like a person who knows she is the smartest individual in the room.

"We think it's pretty clear," her lawyer says. "In exchange for the elimination of maintenance payments, you have agreed to six-days-per-week visitation of Petunia, here in Greatness, until the date of Petunia's eighteenth birthday."

"I need to get home before then," Zac says.

I am having some kind of near-death experience where I float beneath my body instead of above it.

The lawyer's composed eloquence slides into my ears like a snake: "Any breach of this agreement will be a contempt of court and all pre-existing criminal charges, henceforth seen as being suspended, shall be seen as in force."

The greasy ceiling fans spin ominously above my head. They wobble and chop and threaten to come down on me. Actually, the fans aren't working. The Four Winds Truck Stop Diner itself has become a spinning sardine can.

"But—," I manage.

Luanne sneers that sarcastic sneer I've seen so many times before. "My daughter needs her father and you want to be legally allowed in Canada with no child support payments. Everyone's a winner."

She gives me the energy to take back a little bit of reality. Things begin to get stable again. "You think you can force me to *live* in this sulphuric podunk? Think again, Luanne. Think again." I spring into action. Luanne continues to sneer as she sips her coffee. My phone is up to my ear and my lips may just come off, I am pursing them so tightly. Pick up, Dalton, you bush league chiseler! You've been outsmarted. I can feel the electricity of panic sliding up and down my arm. *Maybe I'm getting what I deserve*, a teeny inner voice peeps—a voice that should know better than to speak up when I'm in crisis mode.

"Who are you calling?" Zac says. Now he puts the camera close up on my face!

"My lawyer."

Dalton finally picks up.

"Dalton, you're fired … Why? What do you mean, why? The

divorce!" Luanne shares a look with her own solicitor, like they're keeping a secret from me. Like they've told a joke about me.

"This is Gabriel Pegg."

That elicits smirks from the peanut gallery. I try to shield my mouth from them so they can't hear me so well. *You get what you deserve,* the teeny inner voice peeps. Shut up, inner voice.

"But I gave you a retainer. What did you have me sign? My fault? Well, when I said 'agree to anything,' I didn't mean *anything* ... oh."

Everyone in this room is laughing scornfully at me, and Luanne is the conductor.

"Fine," I whisper, "send me another invoice and when the cash flow returns, I can pay—don't you hang up on me!"

Everyone watches for what I'm going to do next, but there is nothing left to do.

I dunk my cellphone into Luanne's coffee, causing a splash that makes Luanne squint and gasp, and I march out of the Four Winds Truck Stop Diner with as much authority as I can muster, given the circumstance. As I reach the door, I hear the innocent voice of a little girl say, "What's a podunk?"

I shoulder-check to see if Zac is marching out with me. He's not. He's answering the rugrat.

"A podunk is where Port-O-Potty Guy has to live for the next seven years."

There's some quiet laughter.

I jangle those greasy tin bells again and I run. I run and run and run.

3.

I have nowhere to run. I realize this fact after sprinting halfway down the massive gravel parking lot abutting the Trans-Canada Highway, probably twenty yards past the car. Making the "stop running" impulse doubly impactful is my current level of physical fitness. I was on the Greatness track team when I was sixteen. Somewhere beneath these folds and rolls lies the heart of a lion. Unfortunately, the lion has arrhythmia. Well, self-diagnosed. No health insurance, you see. Haven't been in Canada long enough to see a doctor. Am I even insured if I have a massive infarction from this pointless sprint?

The desert-coloured gravel crunches as I skid to a halt, right beside the car. I decide to drive the hell out of Greatness and never look back. Zac comes racing out of the diner but I pay no heed. I suppose he's concerned about losing his car.

I turn the ignition.
Then it dawns on me.
I can't leave town.
I really can't.

I get that feeling that people get when something hellish happens to them, like a sinkhole swallowing up their house. I start to move backward and forward in my seat. My arms fold and tighten around my gut. The rocking gets stronger and stronger. The steering wheel gets closer. It beckons me. I pound the steering wheel with my head. Nail it and nail it and nail it some more, with such ferocity that the horn honks.

Zac opens the passenger door and gets in. I know he's still filming, but I act oblivious. I use the horn-honks as punctuation for my lament: "*How* can *I pursue* my *art* if I *have* to *play* … *Barbie* with a *kid* I've *never* … *even* … *met?*" The timing doesn't quite work out, so I have to pause where the ellipses are. That's going to give us a powerful moment in the documentary, a part of me thinks.

"But she's your daughter," he says.

"Hipster freak. What do you know about daughters? What do you know about anything? All you care about is your vintage fixed-gear bicycle and your hobo band you discovered before everybody else and your—and your charcuterie plates with those idiotic gherkins!"

I've lost it and we both know it. Zac looks at me with those stupid inquisitive eyes, the same eyes Daniel has, that made me want to punch Daniel in the face when we were kids.

"This is your chance to get to know your only child," Zac says. "How bad can it be?"

"It can be exactly this bad, and no worse, Zac. Don't tempt fate. This is the part of the story where the hero says 'Der, how can it possibly get any worse?' and then—boom, crack of lightning and it starts raining blood. So don't ask."

The car is running and every fibre of my being wants my hand to shift this econobox into drive and leave a wake of gravel dust as we escape. But my hand won't move. I stare down at it as though trying to Uri Geller the transmission into D. And then my idiot nephew slides his hand on top of mine, which only makes me try harder to push the pain away.

Zac's trying hard for a poignant moment. He moves his face closer. "She was married to you once, man. Maybe you can find a way to be kind to each other and make the situation work."

I shake my head. "Affairs like this, Zac, you have to put in your rear-view mirror. Married women are the worst kind."

"She was married to *you*."

"I evolved."

I see faces peering out of the diner's windows. I see Luanne's face. She isn't looking at all. There was a time when we would be in an eternal, unbreakable eye-lock, a connection so strong and mystical that we could seek each other out across a crowded fairground to lock eyes. But I have outgrown this place and all of its trappings, I insist to myself.

"I have a calling," I tell Zac, but really, I'm telling Luanne. " I haven't yet become who I am meant to be …"

"Uncle Gabe, you need to be flexible, that's all. When life gives you lemons …"

"Then say enough with the fucking lemons, already."

Zac's silence fills the car as he looks out at the dusty sky. People inside the diner return to their seats. He doesn't push back. For a nephew, he's not all bad.

"Why don't you make a lemon spritzer?" Zac says.

"I don't drink soda."

"Beer shandy."

"I don't drink beer."

Zac grits his teeth.

"Just take the stupid metaphoric lemons and do something good with them, okay? Become who you truly are, but become it here in Greatness. It's not what you had in your imagination, but it can still be a launching pad."

My mind has been hard-wired for forty-three years, since I

was eleven, to escape this dusty dungeon of rusted out pumpjacks and bottomless gravel pits, and to stay away. I can't find happiness here. I can't find my purpose here. Greatness is a trap. Loving this place is a trap.

I smile and bulge my eyes out as wide as they'll go. My voice doesn't drip with sarcasm; it's more of a tsunami of condescension. "Oh sure. The quaint, amateur townsfolk could be cast and crew. Wish-granting fairies can build us a studio. And then, when the wingèd unicorn poops rainbow dust on us all, the leprechaun's gold can give us enough money to buy some movie equipment."

"I've got this," Zac raises the camera a little, "and you've got this." He points to my head. "Why don't you grow some of this." I think you can guess where he points.

"While I can appreciate your youthful naïvety and unmolested enthusiasm, Zac, what you're suggesting isn't possible. I won't do it."

Zac puts the camera down. Flicks it off. Looks down at his kneecaps and then back into my eyes. There's a new expression on his face. Suddenly he looks like a snake.

"Won't," he hisses, "or can't?"

I know he's pressing my buttons. I know he is. But the magma of determination begins to rumble beneath my mantel, causing me to quake.

"What ... did you say?"

"I just said the c-word. You heard it loud and clear. You refuse to do it because you know that you can't. You cannot do it. It is an impossibility for you. C-A-N-T, can't."

My flesh turns green and my muscles bulge until they burst through my clothing.

"Once, I locked myself inside a room at the Beverly Hilton for a whole month. Do you want to know why?"

"I imagine it had something to do with substance abuse."

No Escape from Greatness

"Because someone told me I walked like a comedian. No one was going to believe that Port-O-Potty Guy was a legitimate and serious artist if he walked around like a damn fool. But with time, persistence, and a pair of orthotics, I taught myself to walk like a dramaturge. With presence. Authority. Drama."

"Explains a lot," Zac hisses at me, looking for a rise.

"So just go ahead and tell me I can't do something. Because Gabriel Pegg can do anything. Give me your phone." I extend my hand like a dramaturge.

"Use your own phone."

"My phone is having coffee in the diner!" I wrestle the phone from the pocket of his green jeans and dial Erin.

"Go get my phone," I tell him.

"I'm not your personal assistant," Zac says.

The phone rings. "Oh, you aren't? So I should tell your parents about how you spent your RESP money?" I'm so fraught with determination and pluck that when I mimic the universal gesture for toking marijuana, my fingers make a little farting sound against my lips, which causes some sort of esophageal chain reaction and I actually cough hard on my own spit, like a rank amateur of toking. It gets the point across in spades.

"All right, all right," Zac says and gets out of the car.

"Find out about studio space," I beckon as Zac leaves.

I'm still coughing when Erin answers the phone.

"I'm busy with clients who work," Erin says to me. The din of people doing business leaks into the receiver: people doing business, making deals ... moving forward. Launching. "I need your help."

"No way. No. Never again. I told you this."

"Please, Erin."

"What did you just say?"

"Please. I'm not incapable of saying please. It's a little offensive to me that you think me so self-involved, rude and arrogant that I would somehow be incapable of saying the word 'please.'"

"But this time you meant it. What's wrong?"

4.

I would later come to discover that, while I begged for help from Erin, an important conversation was taking place inside the diner, between my nephew and the waitress he had been eyeing earlier.

I'm sure it went something like this:

"I sling pancakes and pie while my mind wanders off to a land of kitten-related internet memes."

"Duhhh, coffee-soaked Samsung Galaxy? Arcade Fire. Pinterest."

"Is this your coffee phone?"

"You get a lot of coffee phones?"

"Hashtag sarcastic quip."

Gabriel Pegg, dramatic screenwriter, writes the scene this way:

INT. (that means interior) **TRUCK STOP DINER - DAY**

JILL (polyester uniform) dangles a cell-phone with coffee still dripping off of it.

                JILL
        This the one?

                ZAC
        You get a lot of coffee-
        soaked phones around here?

                JILL
        Good point. This is Port-O-
        Potty Guy's phone, right?

Jill flips her hair to broadcast a mating signal only pre-linguistic infants or a Concorde aircraft would miss.

                ZAC
        Yeah. Port-O-Potty Guy. The
        great Gabriel Pegg.

                JILL
        Kind of a jag.

                ZAC
        He's mostly harmless.

                JILL
        Oh, you're a "deep down

No Escape from Greatness

we're all good people"
person.

                    ZAC
        I am?

                    JILL
        Yep. I'm more of an "if you
        act like a wad, you are one"
        type. So if you're chasing
        him around with that camera,
        what does that make you?

Zac touches the camera in his pocket and considers her.

                    ZAC
        Oh, no, that's not -
        I'm shooting an ironic
        documentary. The joke is on
        him. He just doesn't know
        it. Not yet.

Jill and Zac exchange a devious, evil, mean, villainous smile as he takes the phone.

                    ZAC (cont'd)
        Hey ... is there a theatre
        in town?

                    JILL
        There is, but I don't even
        know you ...

                    ZAC
          Oh, no, no, like a
          performing arts-type
          theatre, for rehearsals ...
          not like a let's-go-to-the-
          movies theatre -

                    JILL
          Oh my god. How conceited am
          I?

                    ZAC
          No, you're very ... I would -

                    JILL
          Let me give you a number.

                    ZAC
          For a rental place?

Jill walks over to the counter to jot down a note.

                    JILL
          For a rental place.

We clock Zac's anxious excitement as she glances back at him. He's like a child poking his nose over a candy counter.

INT. CAR - DAY

Zac hands Gabriel the phone. Gabriel taps it, angrily.

No Escape from Greatness

> GABRIEL
> No email ... no tappy square things. My phone is ruined!
>
> ZAC
> You should have installed a temper control app.

END OF SCENE

I evoke enough pity out of Erin to get her to spin her rolodex. Her contacts find the address of Manitoba 19800232B, Inc., registered as the single largest owner of rental property in southwest Manitoba, and she passes it along. Apparently a couple of production companies have hired Manitoba 19800232B, Inc. for shoots and they have a lot of leasable assets. Zac's foray back into the Four Winds Truck Stop Diner nets us the exact same address, so we know we're in business.

I grip the wheel and Zac beckons me to get going. I steel myself with a deep belly breath. I've tried to avoid this very moment, yet here I am. My knuckles are white.

"Are we leaving or what?" Zac says.

"We are about to cross the threshold, Zac," I whisper, "Into Greatness. Do you comprehend the magnitude of what I am about to do?"

"I know this hurts," he tells me, and he's right. This does hurt. Greatness made me what I am today. That's not a very nice thing to say, but it is true.

I shake my head: "You don't fully understand, Zac. Greatness is a menagerie of the bizarre. This is a town where dreams go to die." I push the thoughts of what my daughter might look and sound and smell like at eleven years old; push them all the way out of my head. All I want is to serve my life's purpose, I tell myself. It's not my fault Luanne pushed me away for all these years. My road was never meant to run through this place again.

"Come on," Zac says. "You're just bitter, Uncle G. No town can be that bad. Or that weird."

"Seeing is believing, my boy," I tell him, and put the car into drive.

Our tires crackle on the gravel as we pull out of the truck stop, get back on the Trans-Canada Highway for fifteen seconds, and pull into town. There's the Trans-Canada Grocery, the teeny tiny town grocer, on our left; a little further past it is the old Clayton Marvin. It just looms there, black and decaying, like a head on a stake, warning us to check our sense of propriety at the door.

Now entering Greatness.

A lot has changed. I knew from my brother Daniel that there was a traffic light; I didn't know there were three different Chinese restaurants and one of them actually offers sushi.

We pass Binscarth Drive on our right—the house where we grew up is on that street. For a split second, I wonder if it's still the same colour, white with technicolour red trim, and wild poppies growing in a white planter beneath the second-floor windows, or if there's a kid in there who's as bored as I was, wishing to escape a life that he knows was never meant for him. I replace that question with a flashback of how I got so blasted on Prairie Caribous that I stole my mother's car and did donuts in the gopher patch until I rolled the car and totalled it, and how my mother didn't speak to me for two months.

After crossing 7th Street, which, in a demonstration of the superior urban planning of the town fathers, is the main drag of Greatness, we head farther down King Street and past a water treatment plant. It can't be more than ten years old. I think back to my childhood baths and how the bathwater was always seasoned with a fine yellow sediment, like the undissolved crystals

No Escape from Greatness

of Tang in the bottom of a glass. I imagine that today's townsfolk can probably drink their tap water, have bathtubs without scratches down the centre, and even have blonde hair that doesn't turn orange.

Yet, it still smells like the inside of sewer pipe here, no doubt the work of a heritage preservation committee. Greatness would be unrecognizable without that rusty sewer smell.

Greatness was built around the railroad tracks, back in the thirties when anything was possible with a little irrigation and some pluck. They turned this desert cesspit into a town, and obviously someone thought Greatness would achieve, well, something eponymous. They should have called the town Meh.

I don't hate Greatness, because hating the town would imply that a part of me still loves it. The opposite of love, as everyone knows, is indifference.

There's an entire new subdivision past the railroad tracks now. The new subdivision is called Gopher Trails, which is a nod to how Greatness fell into oil money. They call Greatness the oil capital of Manitoba, which is kind of like calling Don Mills the salmon capital of Ontario. There are no oil tycoons in Greatness, but now there are some middle managers. There are a couple of farm families who bought nice houses with their subsurface royalties, it looks like. Maybe that's where we're headed: Manitoba 19800232B, Inc. must be some old farmer who bought up all the shacks around here with his Chevron money.

We drive right through Gopher Trails and onto a field that's been roughed out for more home construction; power lines and sewer pipes are getting dropped into the excavation. One can make out the shape of a cul-de-sac in the earth, with little neon orange stakes dotting the soil. It looks like the beginnings of a big-city suburb.

"There," Zac says. He points to a farmhouse, a sprawling bungalow with a Quonset big enough for tractors or a school bus in the back. The driveway is wide enough for a triple garage. And beside that driveway, I spy a two-hole talent trailer. It's dented and rusty, but it's the kind actors use to take naps, to feed their legion of self-destructive vices, and even occasionally run through their lines on film or television location shoots.

"Will you look at that," I murmur as I get out of the car. "I did the deed once in a trailer just like this one. Right on the fold-out kitchen table."

"Disgusting," Zac says. "One sec." He pulls out the GoPro. "Say that again."

I think about *Grrrsky versus Howel: Shinny Shih Tzus Part Two,* and how Luanne paid me a visit in one of these trailers, and then I usher those thoughts out of my mind as quickly as possible.

"She was conceived in one of these," I say to him gently. "Petunia."

"I don't think I ever heard you say her name before," he replies.

He hasn't. It hurts to say her name. I have made a habit of not reminding myself of how Luanne has pushed me away from my own daughter. Something changed, though. Why did I capitulate so easily? Over the years, I found ways to stop wondering whether Petunia had learned to walk yet, or read, or kick a soccer ball. I focused on what I was doing, not what some hypothetical person in a faraway place might possibly be doing, or how Petunia might be feeling about her absent father.

Or if Petunia even knew about me.

"Know why her name is Petunia? Know why Luanne did that? So she could never take my name. Think about it."

"Petunia Pegg," Zac says, barely withholding an idiotic guffaw. "What's Luanne's name? Welsh? Petunia Welsh, much better." Zac closes his camera in on the pain etched across my face.

No Escape from Greatness

It doesn't take much effort to summon up this expression. Suddenly Zac pans to my left, to something behind me.

As I look skyward, above the trailer, I hear that voice behind me, and my spine stiffens. "She's for rent if you're interested," Luanne says. Of course it's her trailer. Of course. She is Manitoba 19800232B, Inc. because this is the worst day of my life.

I don't even look at her. "We're leaving," I announce. I turn on a heel and march right past her.

"Are you the rental agency?" Zac asks Luanne.

"I own a few things around town."

"We—were just—LEAVING." I take Zac's elbow.

"We need a place to stay," Zac says as I shake my head at him "No."

"We need a place to rehearse, too. Maybe shoot some scenes. Like a studio?"

"Oh," Luanne says to me, "what kind of assterpiece are you working on this time?"

"Clever," I say. "Oh, did I say clever? I meant cleaver. As in, I would rather hack my kneecap off with a cleaver than rent anything from you."

Luanne smiles at Zac, and it's a smile only minor demons, harpies and gorgons can muster: the angry/sadistic revenge smile that precedes being cursed by an ancient vexation. I notice there is no wedding band on her ring finger. There's no replacement father.

Then she hisses: "You know what? Why don't you borrow it? Free of charge."

Right. "Show us the strings, o puppet master," I conjure, as though summoning a spirit through a séance that all the audience could see.

That accursed grin curls up the corners of her mouth, stretching that bee-stung rosebud lip. It's Luanne's famous 'I'm so intelligent' expression, unchanged through the years. "One string," she says. "The trailer doesn't move. It stays right here on the driveway. I can bring Petunia by around five-thirty for today's visit."

"Dibs on the hide-a-bed," my idiot nephew interjects. I'm too dumbfounded to say anything. *Today* at *five-thirty* knocks around inside of me. This is really happening.

Zac feels he hasn't done enough damage. He continues: "And a rehearsal space?"

"A couple of years ago we fixed up the chapel on the highway and turned it into a little theatre. You remember the one, Gabriel?" She glowers at me.

"I have a vague recollection." Of course I remember the chapel. I inform Zac: "The chapel is where I sanctified my union with the Devil."

"The key's in the mailbox," she says to Zac in the exact same tone as mine.

"So generous, Luanne," I seethe. "You buy up half the town with my money and then offer me a star trailer in your driveway. I'm moved to tears." I run a sarcastic finger down my cheek.

"I'm already regretting this," Luanne says to herself. "You can take the deal while you find some way to weasel out of the settlement you legally agreed to, or you can use your quote-unquote 'fortune' to rent one of my houses in Gopher Trails. And—ope—aw, shucks, the rent just doubled all across town so I guess you'll need to stay here in the trailer."

"You're the devil," I seethe.

"You're an asshat," she retorts.

"Well then I smite the hat with your own satanic flame."

"Welcome back, Gabriel. Glad to see you've changed so much."

A disappointed scowl crosses Luanne's face as she backs down her gravel driveway and goes into her sprawling farmhouse.

"It's official," Zac says. "I now believe that karma is a thing."

No Escape from Greatness

"The goddess Kali herself couldn't have this level of schadenfreude for me," I lament.

Zac opens the trailer door, which is flimsier than a storm door and sticks for a split second before releasing its grip on the doorframe, making a jarring diving-board sound. He peeks inside.

"Not bad," he calls back as my phone rings.

A ringing phone: the calling card of the working man in the business of show! I yank my coffee-stained Samsung from my pocket urgently, knowing it might be my lifeline out of here. As I press the phone against my cheek, I realize it must be Erin before she even speaks: I can hear the din of careers moving forward.

"Go for Gabriel," I say once my tongue returns to my throat.

"Stratford needs a Robin Goodfellow," Erin says. My stomach falls to my knees as I curse the timing. "It's Shakespeare ..." she trills.

"It's an imp." It's Puck from *A Midsummer Night's Dream* if you're playing along at home.

"It pays."

I peer up the trailer steps at Zac. He has no idea who I'm talking to. He's too busy checking out the troutboard walls and dining nook of our new hovel.

Shakespeare at Stratford. That is certainly a break for me, even if it is to play a lowly imp. I can start all over. I can make some connections with Shakespearean types and woo Toronto into backstopping my projects.

"I swear," Erin says angrily, "this is the last favour I ever do for you, Gabriel."

Zac is inside the trailer. I lower my voice.

"I'll do it."

"Do what?" Zac says as he pops out of the trailer.

I shake my head and slide the phone back in my pocket.

"Hm? Oh. I'll do … the film project. Here in Greatness. Let's make lemon spritzer."

5.

The trailer is hot like an oven with dengue fever. My eyes throb as I sleep. I'm so exhausted from the day's calamity that I find a way to pass out on the yellow and brown plaid loveseat, curled into and over the armrests. My left knee rubs against my chin and wakes me for a split second, then I return to my dream. Who knows what it means?

Some people have flying dreams. I have dragging dreams. I believe that experts suggest flying implies freedom and creativity, the subconscious power within to rise above it all. My suspicion is that dragging dreams, where you're so low to the ground that you're sometimes beneath it, in the dirt, imply that life has sucked you down and overwhelmed your innate creative power with the sheer mundanity of life's suckitude itself. I don't ride the wings of an eagle or gryphon in my dreams. I burrow beneath the footsteps of humanity, then scurry below the earth's surface, only occasionally looking up, never long enough to be caught by the surface dwellers.

In this particular dragging dream, I'm in my childhood back

yard on Binscarth Drive, circling a small cinder block fire pit, scurrying beneath a couple of trashcans and a recycling bin, then back into the yard and some dill weeds. The sun is way too hot. I stay in the cool peat. Something drags me to a chrome barbecue. I feel as though I'm being pulled through the ground to its edge, where interlocking patio bricks keep me from moving. I see four giant sets of man legs, reclining in lawn chairs. You know in your dreams how you know you know something? That's how I know that these towering, pasty, hairy legs belong to Shane, JD, Gord and Snorri-Stein, my troupe-mates in Erratic Automatic.

"No," I hear a voice boom through the grass, a terrorized adult voice, and I know it is my own.

A hand reaches down and picks me up by my heel, and I am removed from the comfort of the peat like a newborn is taken from the womb. My mother, with her cleated gardening gloves, has picked me up by the tail. I urge myself to twist around to the chrome barbecue and finally cop a gaze at my true face in the reflective metal. I can only see a blur, but the blur's colour is light brown …

My dream is interrupted by the sound of rapping on the door. My knee shoots up into my jaw. "Back to my hole!" I yell, then my eyes open and I am back in the trailer, the late-morning sun blaring in so intensely I have to close my eyes again and groan.

Someone raps on the door a second time. *Where is Zac?*

I tell them to wait a second and wipe the slobber from my chin. I stumble over to the door.

It's Luanne, and she's got Petunia under her wing.

The bottom falls out from my stomach. I am face-to-face with my daughter for the first time. Her face is like my face, but also like Luanne's face. She's half an adult already and I've just met her. And suddenly I am supposed to know how to be her father and raise her via time-limited daily visitations, six days a week.

No Escape from Greatness

Petunia looks like every other present-day eleven-year-old: a little chubby from too much time on the couch, plain brown hair, a backpack with a teddy bear poking out of the top. Her dress is almost like a school uniform, but there's a t-shirt or something underneath a dress shirt. Maybe Luanne has gone all churchy. "This is your biological father," Luanne says to Petunia, ushering her up the steps and toward me. "You can call him Gabriel."

"Hey," Petunia says, waving. She maintains a safe distance from me, two steps away. I catch a whiff of some kind of cosmetic, a little cloying and almost like an orange smell. It's not a bachelor smell. She looks back to her mother, uncertain.

"See you in an hour," Luanne says to her. "If you're not comfortable for any reason at all, you just come back home," Luanne says as she kisses Petunia on the forehead. Home looms not a hundred yards from my trailer door so it wouldn't take her long to run away from me.

Luanne sidles away without even saying hello to me. "Love you sweetie," she calls as Petunia scampers up the stairs.

"Ya bye."

Petunia shuts the door. She whips the backpack off and tosses it on the floor. The teddy bear rolls right out. Petunia doesn't seem to care.

This is all making me extremely uncomfortable. I am in a closed, private room with my eleven-year-old offspring. I'd rather be penned in with a rabid elk.

"Let's go," she says.

"Sorry?"

"You're here to take me away, right? Let's go. I'm ready."

"Take you away?"

"You got a place where I can change?"

I can't even respond before she spies the bathroom and goes inside. From there, Petunia keeps talking:

"I'm a big fan," Petunia says. "I think I've seen just about every sketch you've ever been in. I've seen the whole *Shinny Shih-Tzus* series, even that really dumb cop movie you did."

No one has seen the cop movie I did.

Petunia comes out of the bathroom wearing an American Apparel monstrosity. She looks like Richard Simmons with hair relaxer. Petunia's neon tank top beneath a sweatshirt—which looks like it was cut by Picasso—makes her look like a pudgy little weightlifter. Her shorts shimmer like Liberace's teeth. From her backpack she grabs over-the-knee socks that are peppered with sequins and splotches of neon shaped like scabbards.

Her outfit is entirely inappropriate, I think.

It turns out I may possess paternal instincts after all.

"So I know you're going back to Toronto or Hollywood or New York as soon as you can get there, and I'm ready to go," she says as she slips on a pair of brown leather shoes.

"You're not running away from home, Petunia."

"I hate that name. Call me Toon."

"Okay, Toon. You're not running away from home, and that's final." Those sound like father words.

"But I need to get out of here. You want that too, right?"

Right. "Why do you want to leave?" I say.

"Because this town sucks donkey balls? Der."

"Easy," I caution her. "No need for such salty language."

She sits down on the loveseat, which is still covered in my sweat and dream-slobber, and puts her head in her hands, frustrated.

"What was wrong with the outfit you had on earlier?" I ask.

"This is my big city look. Did I get it wrong?"

I look into the vanity mirror, which has only two working light bulbs, and I flatten my hair down as best I can. "What does a big city have that Greatness doesn't?" I offer, although I can come up with a thousand reasons of my own.

No Escape from Greatness

"The bus? A shopping mall to take a bus to? Everything? You know all of this. You grew up here and you left."

I did grow up here. I try hard not to remember that, and I'm usually quite successful. But I do remember staring out of my bedroom window, snorting like a horse to get the sulphuric smell of sewer pipe out of my nose, literally watching tumbleweed roll down the street. I think I had the latest high-top sneakers with pumps when I left town. That was my attempt at a big city look. At least this girl has the ability to shop on the internet.

When I was here, they played Tire Wars in the schoolyard. The "town fathers" of Greatness were still too drunk to actually get anything done, and they hadn't allowed the womenfolk to run the affairs of the town yet, and so nothing got done. As a result, the students of Ruml Elementary had nothing to play with in the schoolyard, until one resourceful teacher canvassed local farmers (including Jimmy Welsh, Luanne's dad) to donate their tractor tires to the school. And so Tire Wars was born, the white schoolkids versus the Native kids they bussed in from Maple Lake. Sometimes it took a week of recesses to play out a war. Girls and boys equally played out our own little pretend race war, every recess. While most of the wars involved pretend guns and invisible grenades, pretend swords and circular steel-belted castles, sometimes a kid did get run over by a two-hundred-pound Firestone and had to be carried off to the infirmary.

Me being who I naturally am, I had a flair for the dramatic turning point and enjoyed taking a stereotype and turning it on its head. I quite often made unholy alliances with the Maple Lake kids, turning race traitor and sticking it to our collective oppressors. I remember once I befriended the kid no one was friends with in school, Bruce Wapiti. One time Bruce ran me over with a tire and I couldn't turn my neck for a month. He laughed a lot. We both did.

Maybe the town isn't all bad, but there's no sense in dwelling on it.

Eventually the town fathers would relent and the women of Greatness held coupon redemption drives that raised enough money for play structures, and that was the end of Tire Wars. Our primitive games were gone and more enlightened times were upon us.

"We can't go right now," I tell Toon.

"Why not?" She throws this expression at me. I have a hard time quantifying it: I think it is a look of disappointment; betrayal, perhaps. It's a sour look with her mouth in a straight downward line, her little baby-fat jowls pulling to the floor, her brow shrivelled. I can't explain the expression, but it does something to my insides that is unpleasant, like swallowing a whole scotch bonnet pepper.

"Why not …" I stammer, "… is because I'm making a film. Here. In Greatness." Like any good parent, I tell my child a lie.

"Here? Another talking dog comedy?"

"No, not another comedy! Something serious. Something that says something. Something that makes people think. You could help me with that, maybe." *Brilliant, Gabriel. It's all coming together. Get everyone busy with this ridiculous* Waiting for Godot *ridiculousness and then get to Stratford by the weekend.*

Zac rumbles up the metal steps and bursts through the door.

"Hey, you're Petunia," he says, employing his keen powers of deduction.

"Toon," she says. He nods at her and says, "I'm your cousin, I guess. Zac."

They awkwardly shake hands and Zac turns to me. "I put posters up all around town for auditions. You know, see what's out there before we start writing."

I didn't say anything about holding auditions. Off my scowl, Zac continues: "I scheduled them for Saturday."

"In two days?" I drip with sarcasm. "What's the rush?" My false grin makes Zac recoil. He knows what he's done is a colossal mistake.

"Oh," Toon says with a distracted look, "I know the perfect act for your show thing. Can I invite them?"

"Of course," I say. "You're going to be my assistant, right?"

"Right," Toon says. She smiles. Maybe I can see a bit of myself in her dental structure. "I get to boss him around if I'm your assistant, yes? Or are we equals?"

"Oh, no, no," Zac says. "I'm not an assistant."

"Okay then," she replies. "No worries. I'll go easy on you, kid."

Yes, a definite resemblance in the teeth.

6.

The first visit went the full hour, but with Zac there, we didn't discuss all that much of significance. I was also a little distracted with Zac's bombshell that we would be playing Greatness Has Talent in only two days, and we'd be doing it in the building where Luanne duped me into a life of imprisonment. Also, Zac informed me that he slept like a baby on the hide-a-bed, and that made the world seem a little more red than normal.

"Gramps forced me to say hello to you for him," Toon says, referring to old Jimmy Welsh.

"Oh," I say charitably. "How is he keeping?"

"Ask him. He wants to take you golfing or something. Of course, if we're out of town by then …"

"We won't be." I might be.

Jimmy Welsh is the one person who I could always count on to treat me like the son he never had. Of course, he had plenty of friends, many of whom could have been candidates for Jimmy to treat like his own son, but for some reason, I was the one he wanted to golf with, or drink Old Vienna and watch the Bomber game with, or stare at car engines with. I always assumed I had lost him forever when I treated Luanne the way I did.

"I'd be happy to see your Gramps," I tell Toon. And before I know it, Toon looks at the clock on the fibreboard wood-grain panelling and puts her fuddy duddy clothes back on and says, "See you tomorrow."

She pauses for a second. Am I to embrace her? Do we shake hands?

Zac just nods once with his hipster dingleberry nonchalance, and then Toon is out the door and it doesn't matter what she's expecting anymore.

"Now what," Zac says.

"Let's get drunk," I tell him, but Zac knows I don't entirely mean it. Instead, he rinses off an ancient Tupperware cup and pours me a glass of lukewarm water.

"I hear you can get drunk off this if you drink enough of it."

"You don't drink tap water in Greatness." I show him the bottom of the cup. Full of yellowish ultrafine gravel. It smells of sulphur. Some things never change, treatment plant or no.

Two quick raps on the door and suddenly Luanne is in my face. "Go for a walk," she says to Zac. He turns and leaves as though compelled by The Force. Luanne immediately commences a round of pokey-chest with me. "Get this straight," she hisses. "You are to visit with Petunia only. She is your daughter, not your sidekick or personal assistant. Just spend quality time with her, all right?"

"What on Earth are you on about? All time with me is quality." Luanne's hair, streaked with greys, is mussed and some of it flies into my face. She smells exactly the same as when we met, when we married, when we conjured up Toon: like candy and the beach and a vanilla cigar of victory and everything that isn't Greatness. Excitement. An ancient feeling yawns and stretches in me.

No Escape from Greatness

"She told me your so-called plan," Luanne seethes. "Pretending to make a movie while you try to dodge your commitments once again? You would never stoop so low as to make Greatness a place for your high-fallutin' *art*. You're getting her hopes up already and I won't let you smash them all to hell."

"I didn't sign my life away, Luanne. You don't get to tell me what to do. Who says I'm pretending? Maybe I really want to make the best of being here. Maybe art can happen in Greatness."

I know it can't.

"This kind of crap is what got you in trouble in the first place. You can fool yourself all you want, but you can't fool me," Luanne says, and I know that I can't fool her. Stratford awaits and somehow she's intuited it.

"Toon wants to leave Greatness. Did you know that? She wants to leave here."

Luanne's face registers unease for a flash. "She's a kid. One week she wants ponies and next week she'll want a motorcycle. Why don't you try getting to know her for more than a day before you tell me what my daughter wants?"

"So how is all of this working for you, Luanne? Since I'm here, I presume everything is not quite tickety-boo." There's no uneasiness on Luanne's face now. I'm ready for Luanne's full thunderous rage. Instead, she gets all quiet, like Dirty Harry.

"Petunia needs a father in her life. But if you're not going to take this seriously, you can go ahead and weasel your way out of this. Just run on back to La-La-Land and rot, Gabriel." There's that pang again, when Luanne says my name.

At this point I have a choice. I can let this … feeling … fully awaken and once again take over my life, like riding a rollercoaster of excitement and pain that draws me back into situations that will only damn me to Greatness for all eternity. Not Luanne, and I know it's not Luanne, because the opposite of love is indifference and there's nothing indifferent about this.

So I can choose to ride the rollercoaster or I can keep being the Gabriel Pegg I currently am. Whether I like it or not.

"No, Luanne. What you need … what you need is a good rogering." I've come up with better comebacks. "That's why I'm here, isn't it. I'm not here for Petunia. I'm here for you."

"When you see Roger, tell him I said hello," Luanne says. She makes her way to the door. Then she turns back and we take our masks off for a split second. "If you break her heart, I will break your face. Know this," she tells me.

"I know it, I know it," I reply, and she finally lets me be.

I have to take a seat on the hide-a-bed to catch my breath.

INT. TRANS-CANADA GROCERY - DAY

In Greatness, this is what passes for a supermarket.

TOM (20s and in charge) stands on a step stool, stocking a shelf. KARL (40s and mute) carries a box of coffee cans from the back.

                    TOM
          What took you so long? I was
          thinkin' you got lost in
          there.

Karl shrugs and plods over to the shelf where coffee goes.

Toon enters, quite chipper as is her wont.

                    TOON
         Hey Karl. Hey Tom.

No Escape from Greatness

Karl rips open the box.

          TOM
What can I do you for, Miss Toon?

          TOON
Boys, I found my ticket out of here.

          TOM
Well that's great, I guess. Because your dad is Port-O-Potty Guy, right?

          TOON
Right. He was. But now he's a real serious artist. That's why I need you to ruin his audition thing so he's convinced he can't stay here and then he'll take me to Toronto or L.A., where every school has an anti-bullying program and people know that Thai food isn't from Taiwan.

Tom gestures to Karl to toss him a coffee tin.

          TOM
Ruin his audition thing? We can't do that.

Karl tosses three cans of coffee, rapid-fire, up at Tom. One can hits Tom in the face and all three cans go flying and Tom performs an unintended pratfall from the stool.

A single can from the fiasco rolls up to Toon's feet.

Yup, these two will be perfect for Toon's evil plot to undermine her father.

                    TOON
          Karl, your wife is a welder, right?

Karl nods.

                    TOON (cont'd)
          Think I got an idea.

Toon rubs her fingers together, wishing she had a handlebar moustache she could twirl deviously.

END OF DEVIOUS SCENE

7.

I wake up with the smell of outhouse stuck in my nostrils. My forehead has made contact with my shoulder—the armrest has forced my neck into a ninety-degree angle, just like a sponge mop with the wringer stuck in the closed position. When I roll off the loveseat, my forehead remains fused to my shoulder. This is the proper meaning of unhinged: a joint, which was once hinged, no longer moves. I am officially unhinged.

"Help," I call out to Zac, or anyone. "Help."

"Mornin', guv'nah!" he says in a terrible false Cockney as he traipses over to the living room with a cup in his hand and the camera in his other. "A great morning, idnit? Should I brew you a cup of delicious instant coffee, boiled with the delicious waters of Greatness?" He sips the coffee and gives me a wink. He's poking the bear for the benefit of the camera.

"Screw you. Help me straighten my neck."

"If you're gonna be like that, forget it. I'll just stand here and record your stupid-looking discomfort." He breaks into narrator voice: "So, Gabriel Pegg, tell us how you got your neck and head to bend like that. Is it your Cirque du Soleil training, or that you have no spine at all?"

"There's nothing loveable about that loveseat. I think my Atlas has melded to my C-5."

"You are an old, brittle man, aren't you?" Zac says with a smirk.

"Is this funny to you?" I cry, projecting my torment into the lens of his GoPro.

"How about we make a deal? You release me from the terms of my blackmail and I release your subluxations so blood and oxygen may someday return to your brain."

The camera is still on.

"Blackmail? What are you talking about?"

I know exactly what he is talking about. Three weeks earlier, having been finally allowed to cross the Canada-U.S. border, I visited my brother Daniel's house in Winnipeg. Perhaps I didn't have a lot of options in terms of places to live, but still, it was a pleasant visit and I had every intention of leaving as soon as I had worn out my welcome.

At any rate, Zac was a University of Winnipeg student and I had heard their film and theatre department may be looking for faculty (judging from the faculty list, I believed myself qualified to be the head of the department), so I visited the burgeoning downtown campus. And that's when I saw Zac, hanging out at Vimy Ridge Park with doo-ragged Birkenstock girls, smoking at ten in the morning near the wading pool.

I did nothing. But the next day, I overheard a conversation between Zac and my brother—Zac said he needed cash to pay for lab fees. Daniel, pushover that he is, simply wrote him a cheque, no questions asked. So I followed Zac the next day, right to Vimy Ridge Park and his klatch of footbagging philistines. Sure enough, Zac pulled out a giant bag of something leafy from his backpack. Boys with dreadlocks joined the party. Zac bought everyone burritos.

Concerned for Zac's well-being, I visited the admissions department and told them I was Zac's father. They gave me his full student records. His full records would have fit on a business card: registered for four courses; voluntary withdrawal on four courses three weeks later. Zac had registered for university long enough to access his RESP money, then promptly dropped out and shared his bounty with his hippie communist share-the-wealth peer group, which I'm sure was happy to accept any handout Zac was offering. So yes, I know what he's talking about when he refers to blackmail.

"I'm not blackmailing you. This is a mutually beneficial arrangement."

Zac sighs and puts the camera down. He counts to three and wrenches my neck. Six cracks, all in succession, like stepping on a stack of twigs. Zac could have given me a chiropractic stroke and I wouldn't have cared, it is such a relief. He twists my skull the other direction, probably two hundred and seventy degrees, and as I'm looking backward I see our trailer door swing open.

A silhouette fills the doorway, a hulking man's silhouette. A hulking man wielding some kind of club in his meaty hands. He steps forward.

"Don't kill me," I say. "Please."

"Tee time is in five minutes," Jimmy Welsh tells me. He offers me the 3-wood in his hand. "Let's boogie."

Jimmy has aged poorly, but he still looks like he could still crush me like an aluminum can. From the first time Luanne and I got together, I feared he would do exactly that: crush me. But instead, inexplicably, we bonded and he became my number one fan. To this day, I still don't get it. Maybe our shared inability to understand humanity is what we see in each other. I'm not sure.

A youth spent on the oil rigs and football fields made Jimmy tough. At one point, he was the undisputed King of Greatness, retiring from the farm to town. He bought the local "fine dining" establishment (i.e., a Rooster Hut that offered several off-the-menu items, like chicken Kiev, "oink 'n' cluck," and a Sunday smorg that fed half the town), while at the same time serving as the alderman for the RM of Ruml. But once the Pump & Pit came to town, his restaurant floundered. And when Greatness incorporated as a town and withdrew itself from the municipality, Jimmy resigned from public office—or, rather, slipped into the shadows to run things without the burden of public accountability. He and the town fathers went to war: Jimmy worked a trenchline of business buddies and called-in favours, while the town fathers passed by-law and ordinance after by-law and ordinance, like volleys of mustard gas into the trenches, all in the name of making Greatness great.

Luanne, despite never speaking to her father, keeps that tradition alive to this very day. The town fathers are like illuminati with nothing to illuminate: they like to think they are in charge, but Welshes are the ruling family. They're the Borgias of Manitoba's oil capital.

The one traffic light in town (not counting the one traffic light on the Trans-Canada, which is on the edge of town and not actually town), to hear Jimmy tell it, was a symbol of Luanne's supremacy over the town fathers. Under her dominion, and with my financial backing via usurious maintenance payments that assumed my income would be exactly as much money as I made in my best year of income in perpetuity, Greatness has Gopher Trails. And one traffic light, not counting the one on the highway.

It also meant Jimmy's career as a politician was over. His own daughter had made him obsolete.

No Escape from Greatness

Jimmy and I get into his golf cart and he floors it, spitting gravel from beneath his little tires as we hurtle at thirty kilometres an hour through the mean streets of Greatness, run the only red light in town as we get to the back highway, swoop down a ditch, get enough hangtime coming out of the ditch to make us honorary Knievels, and stop at the first tee box of the Owl Point Golf and Country Club. We scare a cluster of garter snakes as we skid to a halt and they zip away in all directions.

I pick a mosquito carcass out from beneath my eyelid.

"You're looking well," I say.

He gets and pulls out a pitching wedge from the ancient golf bag he's got strapped to the back of his cart, then stares out at the first hole. I stand beside him and pretend to warm up with the 3-wood he gave me.

"Look well? I'm on a steady diet of beef jerky and French Vanilla ice cream, Sunshine, and the only water I put in my body is the frozen kind I mix into my rye," he says to me with a wink and a grin. Sunshine is what Jimmy always called me. I think maybe it's as close as either of us could come to having him call me his son. "I look like shit," he says with a chuckle and waggles up to the tee box. "So do you," Jimmy tells me, halfway through his backswing. His pitching wedge tee shot goes about two hundred yards and spooks three garter snakes as it rolls up the sod patch they call a green around here.

"I ... I fell on hard times," I say to him.

"Fell on hard times? Fell on your head, more like," Jimmy says as he ushers me to the tee. I try to remember how to hit a golf ball as he continues: "I haven't been able to figure out Luanne since she was a kid, but you? You, I never had a problem figuring out."

I swing and hit the ball on the first try! Its trajectory is shaped like a candy cane as it slices to the right, landing on the wrong fairway. "Oh, I see it, on the fairway," I murmur. Jimmy doesn't look. Instead he's scanning the grass … and he stomps a little to his left.

"You're like this snake here when I put my foot down on its tail." I notice there's a garter snake thrashing and writhing underneath his orthopedic shoe. "Lulu got you pinned down and now you're gonna try to bite anything you can and cover everything with your stinky snake piss."

As if on cue, the snake coils back and bites the top of Jimmy's foot. Jimmy doesn't flinch. "But you got no venom." He lets the poor snake slither off. "And you can keep your piss to yourself."

I nod. It was a classic Jimmy Welsh threat, and my cowardly overreaction to his subtle threats has been a cornerstone of our relationship from the time we first met.

"I want to give you some advice on how to deal with a daughter." I give Jimmy every iota of my undivided attention. "I want to give you advice … but I got bugger-all. I learned nothing. It was hell from day one until the day she stopped talking to me. At first, it was easy. Even after Joyce got sick, the whole town was happy to help me raise Lulu. She was cute and there was lots of pity to go 'round. Sorry I don't have more for you."

We golf the nine snake-infested holes of Owl Point, him shooting under forty and me not keeping score after two ten-stroke holes and three lost balls. I golf all of it with the 3-wood, even the chip shots, and I borrow Jimmy's putter to finish up. He gives me his best poker face every time I duff one, only a teensy curl of a crow's foot on his right eye betraying him—he wants desperately to laugh at me, but he knows my temperament and keeps his delight in a jar.

It's just like old times.

After the humiliation is over, he scoots us on his golf cart back through town—but not to Gopher Trails and my hovel. Instead, we go north, up to the Trans-Canada Highway, and stop at the nearby Trans-Canada Grocery. Greatness used to affectionately call this place the Highway Robbery. I see no reason why they wouldn't still.

"What are we doing here?" I ask Jimmy. He just grins.

"You're back. This calls for a special celebration."

He gestures for me to get out and leads me into the store, which hasn't changed in thirty years. Tom introduces himself and shakes my hand with enthusiasm.

"I'm a big fan, Mr. Pegg," he effuses. "We're rehearsing our auditions lots and lots. You're not gonna know what hit you on Saturday!"

"Good for you," I tell him. "Maybe you're the Bugatti in this cultural used car lot."

Tom doesn't know what to make of that statement. Then Jimmy leans over the counter and pulls out a fifty. "Time for the Blue Boy," Jimmy says to Tom. With an excited smile, Tom snatches the red bill from Jimmy's fingers and marches to the back room.

"Dutch Chocolate or French Vanilla?" Tom calls back.

"What do you think, dummy?" Jimmy shouts back, and I know he means French Vanilla.

"It's good to see you," Jimmy says to me. "Not a lot for a fella like me to connect with around here. Not when you been excommunicated by the town pope."

Tom pops back out from an unseen freezer with a one-gallon paper bucket in an orangey-mustard-gold colour I haven't seen in thirty years. Mustard gold and a purple lid that was supposed to be royal blue. And that ridiculous English portrait of a dandy in blue knickers that was, at one time, more ubiquitous in these parts than dogs playing poker. Blue Boy ice cream. The one and only.

"Oh my god," I exalt as Tom hands me a spoon. He has to put the bucket between his knees to pry the lid open, and it makes that pleasing lid-opening noise that only paper containers stuffed with goodness can make. Jimmy holds up his spoon like he's about to perform surgery on the ice cream. He scrapes off a layer of freezer-burn frost an inch thick.

"Wait," I say. "Is this ice cream thirty years old? Isn't that …"

"Don't wuss out on me now," Jimmy says. "It's been frozen. Suspended animation. Dig in."

Surely dairy products that are thirty years old would kill you, frozen or no. Surely. But Jimmy expects me to do it, and Jimmy can crush me.

With a shrug to Tom, I dig in. I follow the trail Jimmy's spoon has left and slide the ice cream in my mouth.

Despite the faintest soupçon of wet mop, it is still divine, thirty years past its expiration date. There has never been, nor will there ever be, an ice cream as good as Blue Boy ice cream.

Jimmy smiles at me with a mouthful of melting ambrosia. "Welcome back," he utters, his tongue yellow from the ice cream.

I can't help but smile back and allow myself to feel a little bit welcome. Who gets to eat Blue Boy ice cream anymore? Who says you can never go home? Then a pang of guilt shoots through my lower abdomen as I remember the Stratford job I just accepted. The pang becomes more of a gurgling queasiness, and then morphs into magma-hot lactose intolerance.

"What is it?" Jimmy says.

I double over in pain as my intestine becomes a poodle-shaped balloon animal, then a giraffe, then a motorcycle with a sidecar, then a scud missile. "My stomach …" I manage. Jimmy doesn't think I can see him rolling his eyes, but I see it.

"The ice cream is killing me! You guys have—urk—poisoned me with toxic ice cream!"

"You really are a delicate flower, aren't you? We just re-use the ice cream pails, doofus."

I look up at Jimmy, betrayed and yet not surprised, and wincing in gastrointestinal agony all the same. "He can't be sick in here," Tom says, and Jimmy ushers me out to the golf cart as all the blood rushes from my brain into my digestive tract. I fall into a hallucinatory fugue state, and like everyone who edges near the untraveled frontiers of the afterlife, my subconscious goes to war with itself, playing out thousands of scenes all at once and over and over, like some kind of subconscious death spiral:

EXT. GRAVEYARD - DAY

ROSENCRANTZ and MARLON BRANDO AS A LONG-SHOREMAN stand at Gabriel's gravesite.

> BRANDO
> Such wasted potential.

> ROSENCRANTZ
> How did he die?

> BRANDO
> He died the same way he
> lived. Completely by
> accident.

> ROSENCRANTZ
> At least he gave the world
> Port-O-Potty Guy.

> BRANDO
> That's something, I guess.
> Damn. Hey, is that Yorick in
> your hand?

Rosencrantz holds up a tiny rodent skull.

Jeffrey John Eyamie

> ROSENCRANTZ
> Naw, it's a gopher. I didn't know this one all that well, but if you talk to one gopher, you talk to them all, get me?

END OF SCENE

When I emerge from this fever-dream, I enter my nightmare. I am back inside the trailer. Zac nudges me with his foot.

"Audition time," he says brusquely.

I'm so exhausted. I look up and see his camera obscuring his face. "Not 'til Saturday," I groan.

"Don't worry, I opened the door for Toon and you got your visit in."

"Wait, what?"

"It's Saturday. Audition time, let's go!"

I was nearly comatose for a full day. Thanks, ice cream. Thanks, ex-father-in-law. Zac drives the car as I try to regain my senses.

We arrive at the little white chapel on the Trans-Canada, just a mile east of Greatness. It's in between the two strips of divided highway, with a tiny graveyard and a steeple, as clichéd as it could possibly be. Except the ancient sign that was there when I was betrothed has been replaced: "WELSH COMMUNITY THEATRE," it reads. Luanne has used my money to buy this theatre and name it after herself. Fair enough that we use it for free, then.

Inside looks cleaner than I remembered it. The stained glass is immaculate. The pews have been replaced by rows of theatre seating. The hardwood is restored and there's a stage instead of a pulpit. The stage is shrouded in rich, crimson velvet tapestry. Only old churches make you feel like this, with their antique cedar aromas and stiff, ghostly airs. I don't know how holy it is or isn't, but spirits fill the little white chapel up to its rafters.

Zac sets up his tiny camera on a giant tripod that he had in the trunk of his car.

I sit here and wait and do my best to avoid thinking of my wedding day, which took place here, in this very room, where that very stage is. I avoid thinking of it even harder.

"We should get organized," Zac says.

"Organized?"

"Sure. What do you need to make this project happen? Do you have a script?"

"I have some ideas."

"Maybe you should do a checklist."

"A checklist?" I make a scoffing *pfft*. "Art isn't about stroking off some checklist."

"Maybe not a checklist, no," Zac says. Zing.

Toon arrives, alone. I guess Luanne doesn't want to come in and reminisce. You know what they say about perpetrators and crime scenes.

"Hey," Toon says and sits down. No costume change today. "The first two are here—I just sent them on stage with scripts."

"Scripts?" I say.

"Yeah," Zac says with a sly grin. "I left some audition script sides around town." He gets up and runs around to adjust the camera one last time. I take a deep breath, still not totally sure I plan to go through with this project or find a way to get to Stratford. It's about to become a lot clearer.

Two women take the stage. One is thin and pretty with a pink daisy set in her curly blonde hair. Her sundress has pink daisies too. I immediately check for marital status. Drat—big white gold ring on her finger.

The woman on the right is squat, heavy-set with a crew cut

and durable work slacks. She's got a lip ring. She wears a very similar white gold wedding band.

"That's Misty on the left," Toon says. "And that's Beth."

"Are they?"

"Farmers? Yep."

Misty clears her throat daintily. From a purely superficial perspective, Misty could be something, if we were actually going to produce something.

We wait for them to begin.

Beth elbows Misty and Misty reads from her script in a tone more wooden than Archie Wood: "This folk festival is the greatest." I recognize the dialogue instantly and implode with rage.

"I will kill you for this," I whisper to Zac. Zac eases back into his satisfaction, grinning at me as his camera records my explosion. Beth jerks and over-enunciates like William Shatner trying to parody William Shatner. "You bet! It's fan-tastic! But where—do we go—to do our business?"

The women look hither and yon.

"Is this what I think it is?" Toon whispers. Zac nods. Toon golf-claps gleefully. I believe the noise she makes is "squee."

I bury my face in my hands.

"What-ho!" Beth over-proclaims. "A blue outhouse! It smells so fresh!"

"Next please," I call out. I'm not looking at this for another second. Port-O-Potty Guy in the place I got married. This is Judge Wapner's brand of poetic justice.

"Um, we're not done yet," Misty tells me. *The audacity!*

"It's okay," Beth says to her sheepishly, taking her wife's elbow.

"No. No, it's not okay," Misty says, her pink daisy falling from her hair as she takes centre stage. "It's not okay, man! I been working my keister off to get my wife a part in your movie. She wants to be famous and so you're gonna be quiet and listen to our little scene. Then you're going to give her the part, capiche?"

"She's got the part," I say. Why not. I'll be in Stratford, after all.

"She got the part?"

"Next please," I tell them. I study the cedar floorboards, just as I did the day I took Luanne as my wife those years ago. I avoid thinking about the wedding day.

On hearing the news that she has a part in a dramatic piece that won't actually exist because I'll be gone to Stratford to perform real works of art, Beth coils like she has just won American Idol. Misty embraces her and they walk arm-in-arm off stage. I have made them so happy.

"Aw, but I wanted to see Port-O-Potty Guy," Toon pouts.

"I don't do that anymore."

"It's beneath him," Zac tells her.

"That's right. It's beneath me."

The gigantic fellow from the diner strides onto the stage. He must be seven and a half feet tall, and nearly as wide.

"Do a proper slate this time," I tell Zac.

"Say your name for the camera, please," Zac says to him.

"Shoelace," he says. I'm sure he says Shoelace but that can't be right.

"I'm sorry?"

"Shoelace! Does anyone want to crack wise about my name?" He glares at Zac and me—we both automatically avert our eyes and shake our heads. *Who, us? Nope. Nobody here.*

"I will be auditioning for the part of the Proper Englishman."

More giddy golf-claps and squeeing from Toon, despite the fact that there was no mention that we would be auditioning for specific parts, nor would there be any hope in hell that I would re-create a Port-O-Potty Guy sketch for any reason whatsoever. I suddenly crave a Prairie Caribou.

"Read away," I tell Shoelace resentfully. He clears his throat and rolls up his script. Closes his eyes for a moment. Gives himself a dramatic stance. An air comes about him. His sheer massiveness gives him a presence that is undeniable.

"I need you to help me ... think of England!"

It's tragicomic. Toon laughs. Zac applauds. Shoelace becomes Shoelace again.

"Frankly, I find this material to be hackneyed and sophomoric."

"We're going to be friends, Shoelace," I tell him.

"I hope you realize how fortunate you are," he says to me. "To live the life you live."

What would this man know about how wonderful the life I live ought to be?

"Next please," I call out.

"I mean there but for the grace of God go you," he has the gall to say.

"Next! Please!"

Shoelace tosses his rolled-up script and trudges off.

"This is like trying to get Perrier from a stone, but when you pick up the stone, you realize it's just a dried-up turd." I know I need to get out of here. There's nothing for me here. Never was.

"Maybe they just need direction," Zac says.

"No," Toon says, "he's right. They suck. We need to leave town."

"Why don't you audition, Toon?" Zac asks her. It makes Toon and me equally uncomfortable.

"I wish I had a talent of any kind."

"Maybe you just haven't found yours yet," Zac says. Usually his rosy-lensed idiocy makes me laugh and shake my head. But this time, I allow it.

"No. Truly. I suck at everything I try. Everything. Ask around."

"Everything?" Zac says.

"At school they call me Suckatollah. Like Ayatollah, except of suck."

"Thanks for explaining that."

"I had to search the internet to figure out who that was, but I eventually learned there's no I in Ayatollah," Toon says. "So yeah. There's nothing. We should give up. Making a movie really isn't an option in this town."

Enough. "Is this an audition or would you like conical hats and balloon animals for your pity party? Next audition please!" I shout.

Toon gives me an odd look, like a "you asked for it" look. "Come on out, guys," she calls. Two men and a woman enter, wearing welders' masks, of all things, and carrying machetes.

I think about fleeing.

One of the men flips up his mask. It's Tom from the Highway Robbery, purveyor of toxic ice cream. "Hey Toon, hey Mr. Pegg," he says. "That's Carol and Karl, Mr. Pegg. They're big fans, too."

"How pleasant."

"We all hope your diarrhea is better," Tom says.

"You don't have to say that twice," Zac interjects.

"What scene are we seeing today, Tom?"

"Actually, Mr. Pegg, we're just gonna show you our talent for high-performance juggling." Tom flips his mask down. Somehow, as though drifting down from heaven itself, the opening strains of "Flight of the Bumblebee" play through hidden overhead Dolby 5.1 speakers.

The knives start to fly.

"Cool," Zac says. I look over at Toon. She just shrugs like she doesn't know what's going on.

The knives fly for about thirty seconds before one hits Karl on the mask and clangs to the floor.

"Thank you, that's enough," I bellow over the music.

They don't stop.

Three people. Five machetes.

Suddenly Carol and Tom pivot and exclude Karl from the juggling.

"No juggling in my films!" They can't hear me over the amphetamine blur of the music.

"Now, Karl!" Tom shouts and Karl produces a blowtorch, which roars with blue-coloured flame the length of a forearm.

"No way!" Zac says.

"No way," I say, like a man who has just said "it can't get any worse than this."

Toon tries to conceal a smile.

Karl shoots flame between Carol and Tom. The machetes alight and suddenly, there are three hillbillies from Greatness juggling flaming swords about twenty feet from my face. The jugglers start shouting guttural signals at one another—"Hep!" "Ho!" "Hoyah!"—and start to manoeuvre. Spins, hops, an under-the-leg move. I am getting nauseous, but not from ice cream. I have to stop it.

"This isn't a talent show!" I march to the stage, shouting, "Stop it! Enough!" while waving my hands maniacally, trying to get their attention.

"What are you doing?" Zac calls.

Tom turns to look at me. A sword flies past him and hits the rich crimson velvet curtain behind him.

Church on fire.

Tom flips up his mask and looks behind him.

Another sword whizzes past and nails the curtain.

"Stop throwing fiery swords when he's not looking!" I scream at Karl. Then the entire red velvet curtain becomes a curtain of flame. I do what anyone with decades of showbiz experience would do.

I squeal and run for the door.

No Escape from Greatness

"FLEE! FLEE! CHURCH ON FIRE! DAMNATION IS REAL! FLEE!"

Once my natural, uncontrollable flight instincts guide me a safe, reasonable distance from the chapel, I turn to see what I expect will be a full immolation, and five souls behind me, escaping the complete destruction with nary their lives and perhaps some charred body hair.

Instead, I am alone in the ditch, two hundred metres from the chapel as cars zoom past in either direction. Not so much as a wisp of smoke emanates from the building.

What if Toon and Zac burned to death? What if they all succumbed to smoke inhalation? It must be thick and noxious in the building if none of it is escaping. I make a serious consideration of re-entering the chapel to rescue them. I strongly ponder it. Mull it over in its all its facets and aspects.

After several minutes, Zac emerges from the church, followed by Toon and the three sword-juggling arsonists, still wearing their welding masks. Zac has his camera. Everything appears to be all right.

"You owe my mom a new fire extinguisher, a stage curtain, and a buttload of white paint," Toon says with a look of displeasure etched on her face. This day has been an unmitigated disaster, but I quietly thank my lucky stars that no one got hurt.

"The way I see it, these three imbeciles are responsible," I retort. "Send the bill to them."

"Either way, I don't see how you can go on with some kind of movie production in Greatness," Toon says, overplaying her hand. "I mean, you can't."

There it is again, like a dare. Like a big chalice of Prairie Caribou. And so, even though I plan to be on a flight to Toronto in three days, I raise my hand to her and pronounce:

"No one tells Gabriel Pegg what he can't do."

8.

We drop Toon at home and climb inside the trailer. I await Luanne's pounding on our door, her demand to be compensated for the destruction of her property, but she never comes.

We eat macaroni and cheese because it's all we have to make. We eat in silence.

After an hour, Zac disappears into the bathroom with a novel. I stare at the MDF ceiling and ponder what to do next. My ruthlessly detailed imagination overcomes me and suddenly, I'm thinking of the future. I write it as part of the screenplay:

INT. TRAILER - DAY (FUTURE)

TOON (18, Eddie Munster hair, black from head to toe) makes perogies on the kitchenette counter using an APA JACK PEROGYMATIC.

GABRIEL (60 ... 60?! How the hell did I get

to be 60?) slumps over on the loveseat, a tumbler of blood-red beverage in his hand, his eyes darkened by the monotony of Greatness living.

              TOON
      You're a disappointment to me. You know what the sum total of all your life's ambitions is? Squat. You taught me that this place can suck you down and turn you into nothing. So yay, I got you up close and look what it did for me. Now I make you perogies with our dreams inside them, rolled up and cut up and ready to digest in a pleasant shape. Our lives are these perogies.

Gabriel takes a sip of his drink.

            GABRIEL
      I stayed for you.

              TOON
      You stayed 'cuz you were chickenshit. You coulda shown me how to be great. Instead, we're a couple of losers making pre-fab perogies in a trailer.

No Escape from Greatness

Gabriel looks down at his feet, which are covered in brown fur.

END OF SCENE

I break from my screenwriting meditations and inform Zac that I plan to take a job in Stratford, damn the consequences. Damn Luanne. I'll do it for Toon, I tell him. Even I can't buy what I'm trying to sell him.

"Like you've done anything for anyone else ever in your life," Zac says.

"If I'm going to be coerced into fatherhood, the best I can do for her is to model successful life paths," I pronounce, and I know I'm right. I rise from the loveseat, slap the rickety door aside, making it three steps along Luanne's gravel driveway before I stop.

"Why are you stopping?" Zac says from the bottom step of the trailer.

I'm too busy looking at the house to reply to him—the house, with its harvest gold siding and maroon trim, its two bedrooms on the split level and bay-windowed living room. The light of the television bathes the living room in an electric blue. Luanne sits on the puffy leather couch, her legs curled beneath her bottom, sipping some tea, lost in a program. Her hair is up in a bun, except for a few straggles of greying blonde. Her face is a prosaic blue.

Toon sits on the floor, her back pressed up against the middle of the couch, near Luanne's feet. She reads a book; it isn't a novel, but I can't make out what it is. She peers up occasionally at the TV screen. Toon's in her pyjamas, but her expression looks exactly the same as the moment I told her I would not be abetting her escape from town: the pained scotch bonnet look.

There's a big empty space on the other side of the chesterfield, beside Luanne and behind Toon. I wonder if anyone has ever occupied that space.

"Let's rest our swords and shields for today, Zac," I manage to tell him. "We'll take that hill tomorrow."

"Or not at all," he says as I climb back into our hovel. "You need to be here for visits six days a week, Uncle G. You miss one, you're going to jail. So let's say you leave on Tuesday night after a visit. Wednesday's a freebie, you miss Thursday ... you will be in the poke by next weekend. Super."

"My lawyers will have to find a solution Monday during regular business hours," I say as I ready my bed. "I can't afford them to work overtime." I can't afford them at all.

"What about me?"

"As soon as I can manage it, Zac, I will get you to Stratford. It's an important part of the documentary, isn't it?"

"Right ..." Zac doesn't sound enthused.

We bed down. My back and shoulders meld into the loveseat more easily now.

"Gabe?" He calls from the other end of the trailer.

I don't answer.

"I think I'm okay with you just ratting me out to my dad. I think I need to go home."

I shut my eyes as hard as I can shut them and force my way to morning, which doesn't want to come.

At 5 AM, the sun is merely a suggestion. I uncrinkle myself and make instant coffee boiled with the waters of Greatness.

At 6 AM, I am on horrible coffee number four. The sun beams into this tin can like a hymn played on Led Zeppelin's sound system. God is overdoing it.

At 7 AM, I attempt to go back to bed. The coffee wrings my guts like a washcloth.

I hear a car start up. Peering through the window, my eyes

sting as I watch Luanne's car pull out of the driveway with Toon in tow.

I get my farewell trousers on and leave the shitcan.

At 8:15, I arrive at the schoolyard of Ruml Elementary, just as Zac catches up to me with his camera a-blazing. The yard has a new perimeter of chain link fence and I march along the sidewalk, trying to find an entryway.

"Oh, good, you're shooting this," I tell him. "This is going to be a very difficult, very dramatic conversation, but it's an important turning point in my return to greatness. The state of being, not the town."

"You can't break her heart like this," Zac says huffing and puffing. He must have run some distance to catch up with me.

"Watch me," I pronounce saltily like Pierre Trudeau or Bette Davis, and equally as macho.

"You told her that you were staying. The courts told you to stay."

"Are you worried about what this will do to her, Zac?"

"No, G. I'm worried about what this will do to you."

I avoid picturing what Zac suggests. I don't imagine what it will do to Toon and when I might see her again. Now where the hell is the damned entry to the schoolyard? Finally, a hundred yards down the sidewalk, I find a z-shaped entryway through the fence. Zac continues his pursuit, now offering narrative for the documentary:

"We are outside Toon's school and the once-famous Gabriel Pegg is pulling the plug on his much-ballyhooed comeback," he says.

"That's not what this is at all," I hiss. Children stop and stare as we march onto the grass.

"That's right, folks. He's bailing," Zac says. "This looks like the end of our documentary."

"Not the end. A turning point." I spy Toon in the middle

of the field. She's with two other girls—perhaps twins—both slightly taller than Toon and considerably more fit. Toon and one girl exchange shoves while the other screams at Toon. My stomach falls into an abyss.

"Stop that this instant!" I call out and run to Toon's aid.

The crying girl cries "Stranger danger!"

"That's my super famous biological ... father?" Toon's in disbelief.

"Suckatollah doesn't have a Dad," the bully sneers.

"Teacher!" The crying girl calls out. "Pervert on the schoolyard! Perv! EEEE!"

Both girls screech.

"Stop it!" Toon hisses.

The bully girl kicks Toon in the shin.

The other girl looks up at me. "Looking to go to jail, perv?" She kicks me in the shin. I cry out.

Zac has lowered on to his belly to get a good shot of the fracas.

The bully girl swings round to me and kicks me in the shin, to give me a matching pair.

"Will you help?!" I bark at Zac.

"Oh, yeah," he replies. "Kick the first one again, but this time, grunt. Gabe, more feeling. Action."

"What?"

"Unh!"

"Awwwwk!"

"Great. Once more for safety," Zac says.

Meanwhile, as the bully girl pushes Toon to the ground, that mousy waitress Jill comes pedaling by on (surprise!) her vintage blue bicycle. She hops off and runs to the fence.

"Hey! Enough!" she calls. "Destiny and Hope, your mom is gonna hear about this."

The girls stop.

No Escape from Greatness

Toon is crying.

As Zac trains his camera on Jill, I tend to myself. Toon straightens herself up, brushing dust from her tartan leggings.

"Why are you even here?" she says.

I prepare myself for what may be the greatest monologue I will ever deliver. I'm about to crush my own daughter's heart. I think of the sheer magnitude of this moment, avoiding the dystopia I'd envisioned in my screenwriting fugue, sending Toon on a path where she, too, will be certain to find her destiny outside of this oily gravel pit, where she, too, will find a life larger than Greatness and its sewer pipe leading straight to banality. This goodbye is what's best for everyone.

She will likely never speak to me again. She will have problems with her male attachments, never able to trust a man ever again, after this moment. She will stink at math and sports. She won't know what a healthy risk is and how to avoid unhealthy ones. She will become vulnerable to casual charmers with dependency issues and a flare for the dramatic. I will have created a person who could fall victim to a person like me.

"I need to talk to you," I say to her. Get out of my throat, blasted lump.

Toon looks into my face with Luanne's eyes and my frown. She knows exactly why I am here. "Take me with you," she pleads to me. She says it twice. "Take me with you."

I kneel to her level and put an arm on her shoulder, as though I had blocked out this scene a thousand rehearsals ago. The Greatest Monologue I Shall Ever Deliver:

"I lied. Not to you. I lied to myself, Toon. I'm not going anywhere. You and me, we're going to make the biggest comeback anybody's ever seen. We'll make that movie and it'll be the most fantastic, awe-inspiring, award-winning movie ever. And we'll do it right here, in Greatness, Manitoba." That wasn't how I had rehearsed it.

The tears well up in Toon's eyes again. Her face reddens. "You …" she wants to swear here. I can feel it. She can't. Instead, Toon lurches toward me like she wants to shove me, but then we both take a step back. She turns her back to me. I watch her sprint back into the school, disgusted with me, hating me, and I smile to myself.

9.

INT. WELSH COMMUNITY THEATRE - NIGHT

Jill stands on stage, lit beautifully, dressed simply. She looks at Zac, who sits in the seats, as though she were an angel above him.

The curtains are burned and the once-white walls have streaks of char on them, making mountain-shaped black patches, as though Jill were standing amongst the Alps.

After a beat, Jill breaks out in a stunning aria: something like "O Mio Babbino Caro." Her talent is staggering.

```
Zac smiles, immersed in the sound. His eyes
well up with emotion.

Jill's song is the siren's song to him. His
heart already belongs to her.

She has stolen Zac's soul with a single
aria.

Zac reaches for the video camera resting on
his lap, blinking standby.

He switches the power to "off."
```

END OF SCENE

"Something's come up," I tell Erin on my lobotomized smartphone. "I need to stay here for a while. How long can we stall the Stratford people?"

Silence on the other side of the line. I stare into the little marquee mirror above the vanity. I'm in the living room of the trailer. God this place is cramped.

"Erin?"

"This was your last chance, Gabriel. I can't do this anymore." Her voice cracks a little. She's really upset.

"I just need you to delay for a few weeks … three. Three weeks. I have … a project to do here … and that would give me a week of rehearsals, right?"

"No! No more! We're through, Gabriel. It's finished."

She's really mad this time. I play a card I've been holding on to for the better part of a decade.

"Why did you do it in the first place, Erin?"

She pauses.

No Escape from Greatness

"Why did I do what?"

"Help me. Why did you stick by me when everyone else ran for their lives?"

We both know the answer to that question. It's been the elephant in the room making kissy-faces at me since before the Marushka incident.

"I'm not saying I didn't deserve your undying loyalty, but you're no idiot, Erin. I'm not making you a penny. So why bother with me?"

"I don't—don't know," she stammers. "But now it's done. No more."

"It's because you love me, isn't it?" I smile to myself. "Secretly, you always wanted to fix me, like *Beauty and the Beast*. Is that right, Erin? Well we can talk about it if you call Stratford and stall them for three little weeks."

She doesn't say anything.

"I'm flawed, Erin. You can make me whole again."

"You self-righteous moron," she says. "When I was new in this business, people thought I had some kind of magical power over you. Back when you could earn for us, I made my career on keeping you signed with this firm. It was the thing that built my reputation as an agent. People thought it was me, and some days I even encouraged them to believe it was me. But really, it was because you were too inebriated to realize you could leave and cut your fees in half. So excuse me for having a sense of loyalty, since I made my career off of you and our agency fleeced you for twenty years. I will never make that mistake ever again. Love you? To think I would stoop so low."

No one can stoop that low.

I reply with the most profound and eloquent response I can launch.

"Oh."

"Goodbye, Gabriel. You are no longer my problem … at least

no more than any other member of humanity. Perhaps you should try to keep your membership from being revoked."

Click.

I could use a drink right now.

As if on cue, Jimmy walks into my trailer. He's the biggest drinker I know. The impulse to ask him for one drink strikes me suddenly, but I don't act on it. Anyway, he walks into my trailer without knocking, as only Jimmy could do.

"How's the lactose intolerance, Sunshine?"

"It wasn't … it's better. Tom and his cronies set the church on fire."

"I heard. That's why I'm here."

He's here to kill me.

"I got a proposition for ya," he says, to my relief. "You tell me what you need for your little movie project and I'll make it happen. Only catch is that you have to see it through to the end. So I'll be a director."

"Producer. You'd be the producer."

"Sure. Producer. Just tell me what you need and we'll make Gabriel Pegg's big comeback movie. How does that sound?"

It sounds like a trap.

There's a knock on the trailer door. That would be Toon.

"Daddy time?" Jimmy smiles at me and opens my door. Toon looks severely displeased.

"Mom told me I had to come or she was going to put parental controls on my tablet," she says as she stomps in.

"Petunia," Jimmy says as warmly as he can muster. He opens his arms a little, almost sheepishly, hoping for an embrace.

Toon plunks her butt into the loveseat and folds her arms. She looks at Jimmy silently.

It's a pregnant pause that goes past its due date. Jimmy waits for a reply expectantly. And waits. And waits. I think about interjecting but I don't dare, as Toon's eyes bore holes in the wall of the trailer.

No Escape from Greatness

"Gramps," Toon finally says, acknowledging his existence, but only barely.

"I'm gonna help your father make his movie," Jimmy offers. I nod with added enthusiasm, as though that would help his cause somehow with Toon. Toon examines her fingernails and bites her cuticle. She starts to bounce her crossed leg like she's waiting for something. It pushes Jimmy into a temperament I've never seen in him before: he gets almost gentle. After some time, a pained smile curls across his lips.

"I should git," Jimmy says to me, and slinks out the door. I look at Toon, dumbfounded. She turns her scowl toward me.

I decide to fix Toon a drink. I reach into the minifridge and pull out the only thing in it: a plastic bottle of orange drink with one percent real juice. I offer it to her.

"My little plan didn't work," she seethes at me.

"Beverage reminiscent of oranges?" I say. "I think Zac only had one sip."

"I'm sure you figured out already that I was the mastermind behind Tom, Karl, and Carol's performance."

"What?"

"And that's why you won't leave, right? Because you think it was all a set-up and there is actually a chance to make something good here. Well I'm here to tell you, Gabriel, that I will personally sabotage anything you attempt to make here. Greatness is going to be like a jar full of angry wasps for you. If you stick your hand in the jar? Bzzz bzzz bzzz yow yow sting anaphylactic SHOCK." She makes her index fingers like little stingers and stabs toward me with them repeatedly. It's only natural that I would flinch at every stinger jab.

Toon has some problems expressing her emotions, I surmise. It reminds me of someone.

I look at the label on the plastic bottle. "There appears to be some real juice in here." I know better than to take the bait, whether she actually betrayed me or not. She waits for me to react, but I know better, or at least I try to know better. "Less than two percent of the following juices … it's set up just like milk," I say. "This is like skim juice."

Meanwhile, I can feel the magma of rage bubbling up in my deepest chasms, nearing the parasitic cone. Toon smiles at me. Her eyes move to my hand and her smile widens; I look down to see what's making her smile and I see I have squeezed the plastic bottle, throttling its plastic throat until it drips corn syrup-based goodness onto my best pair of no-iron chinos.

"I know it makes you angry," she goads, "but you don't want to make this movie. You don't want to test me."

With ample dignity, I place the crushed bottle of skim juice on the twenty-inch-by-twenty-inch MDF kitchen table and I brush my pant leg. I disregard the fact that it looks like I've wet myself, and I straighten my shirtsleeves.

Time to be a parent, I tell myself. Tough love.

"Toon," I say, "Threatening me is unacceptable behaviour. You must treat me with respect."

Toon makes a scoffing *pfft* exactly the same that I do.

"That's it! Go to your room."

"Room?"

I gesture to the house across the driveway.

"Your room. I'm sending you to your room."

With her fists clenched, she stands up on the cushion on the loveseat. We're eye-to-eye. Toon's eyes are a stony sky blue with a thick grey border, just like her mother's. They can fire laser beams through your psyche and reduce you to a quivering mess of eviscerated entrails and existential regret. They are quite distinct. And beautiful. Like a bull considering which organ to gore, Toon snorts through her nose and I can feel her breath on my neck.

"Don't tell me what I can or can't do," she says to me. To me!

No Escape from Greatness

"Toon, I am making the movie and we are not leaving Greatness together, and we can either try to be nice to one another or I can send you to your room, six days a week."

"You can try. But you will fail, Port-O-Potty Guy. If the apple doesn't fall far from the tree, guess which tree Suckatollah fell from?"

As though by sheer paternal instinct, my next move flows from me like brushstrokes flow from a master painter: "Fine," I tell Toon, "let's see what your mother has to say about this."

Toon bounds down from the loveseat and holds the door open for me. We march-race along the gravel driveway to Luanne's front door and Toon rings the doorbell.

"You're not welcome inside," Toon says, explaining why she didn't just open the door for me here. After a moment, Luanne opens the door, a dishtowel dangling from her hand. She looks me up and down.

"I sent Toon to her room."

Luanne shoves the dishtowel into Toon's chest. "Go dry the dishes," Luanne says to her, and Toon merrily scampers into the house, shouting "See you tomorrow, *Gabe*," each word dripping with disingenuousness. I'm left staring Luanne dead in the eye.

Somewhere in the back of my mind, I swear I hear a twelve-gauge being cocked. I expect to receive both barrels from Luanne for my audacious attempt to discipline her—our—child. Instead, she does something far, far worse.

Luanne moves toward me and I back up. She pulls the door shut behind her and it's just the two of us, a couple of feet apart, talking on her front step. Her hair's in a bun, with little straggles zig-zagging all over her head. She's wearing a plaid flannel shirt that is probably a man's size, with the sleeves rolled up to the elbows. Cut-off jean shorts. Bare legs and feet. She is like the opposite of so many women: she doesn't clean up well. Makeup and fancy clothes make Luanne look as awkward as a tomboy in a ball gown, and when Luanne has to do herself up like that, she feels twice as awkward as she looks.

No, this is Luanne in her most fetching state, and her most natural: rugged and a little wild without a stitch of pretense.

"So how's it going so far?" Luanne asks me. "Everything all right?"

"Oh," I sputter. "Tremendous. Held here against my will with a half-feral pre-teen who wants nothing to do with me. It's all I ever hoped for."

"Toon expects a lot from you," Luanne says. "Since you were never around, you're kind of like a myth to her."

"Well whose fault is that?" I tell her.

"It was a mutual understanding," Luanne says. "Since you are this imagined thing that has become real, she holds you to a different standard."

I recall how I had to placate Toon with a promise to stay in Greatness and make this infernal film, and how it could never work.

"I'm not meant to be here, Luanne. I have … things to do that are bigger than this town can offer me. It's not fair to keep me here."

"How is it not fair?"

"Artists don't live in Greatness, Manitoba. Please, Luanne. You know this."

I didn't mean to make this into out-and-out pleading, but here it is. Luanne knows full well that I had planned my escape from this town since I was a child. Someone interested in arts and stagecraft and intellectual pursuits was not exactly embraced here. If the heaviest thing you could lift was a Norton Anthology, you might not be a redneck. And you might need to leave town or be labelled some kind of fancy lad, which was a problem in those days. I'm sure Greatness has become enlightened since then.

No Escape from Greatness

I remember saying that very thing to Luanne when we first got together, all those years ago, before I got famous and lost any chance at being an authentic artist. Was it thirty-five years ago? Years are like drinks; you start with one and suddenly thirty-five go by, each doing less to you than the last, but filling you with the same amount of regret all the same. Thirty-five years ago, there used to be a drive-in just on the other side of the Trans-Canada Highway. We had just watched *Star Wars* and Dudley Moore's *Arthur*, and we were in the midst of trying to stay awake long enough to understand why a dirty movie would be called *Meatballs*, when Luanne gave up and took me into the back of the boogie van I owned at the time. My van had this bright pink shag carpet on the inside of it. I bought it from a weirdo in Brandon and it was the talk of the town. Pink shag! The old bigots at the Four Winds Truck Stop Diner whispered all kinds of gossip about me—I guess it was a sort of fame. Anyway, after Luanne and I missed the opening credits of *Meatballs* with our amorousness, I remember feeling this awful, sick feeling in the pit of my stomach.

Thinking it was from my inability to digest popcorn, I ignored it and told Luanne that I loved her. Again, I did not realize at the time that I wasn't capable of knowing what love was, nor did I realize that the awful, sick feeling in the pit of my stomach may have been guilt. I remember stroking her hair all the way down, in long straight lines, past her shoulder and away from the shag that threatened to thread itself into her locks like pink polyester tentacles. I had to tell her that this was impossible, even though that corn allergy was probably telling me to fall, to let go and be in love and be happy with what I had found. For some people, hindsight is twenty-twenty. For me, hindsight is a damned oracle.

Despite my feeling of loving her, I couldn't be with her, because I would do anything to leave. As I told her this, a tear leaked out of the corner of my eye. It was soaked up by the pink shag as I looked up at the carpeted ceiling.

"I know who I am," I said to her, tenderly and tearfully, my insides wringing like a corn-intolerant washcloth. "I'm the one who leaves. If I don't leave, then who am I? I'll never know. I'll never know."

She pulled me in close and I buried my head in her breast. The popcorn cramps got worse and I told her how my whole life had brought me to this moment and now nothing could keep me from being who I was meant to be; and who I was meant to be had absolutely nothing to do with living in the oil capital of Manitoba and everything to do with leaving it. So it was nothing personal.

In Lu's embrace, I felt safe and at ease, and after a few moments I heard myself telling her my dreams, every single one, and my secrets, every single one, and even some of my innermost fears; I felt like it was okay with her. She just held me, and every muscle in my body warmed and eased, and for a moment I thought maybe I could dream and I could leave and I could still love her and it would be okay. I felt like a baby robin in a pink shag nest, coddled by its mother, while on a distant drive-in screen, Bill Murray told us it just doesn't matter.

Back in those days, before she was Luanne Who Ran Greatness and after she was my childhood friend Lulu, I called her Lu.

At her front door, I give it a try.

"Can we work something out, Lu?" I offer, and Luanne's face gets stiff. I just stepped on a landmine. "What if I took her with me, to Toronto, or Hollywood, or Winnipeg? Just once in a while so I can work?"

"I think I am being more than fair with you, Gabriel. I know you've fallen on hard times. Now you don't have the burden of these massive payments you can't afford."

"You mean the ones you used to buy up half of Greatness?"

No Escape from Greatness

"Stay on topic, Gabriel. I've been reading up on twelve-step programs …"

"Do not go there, Luanne. Do not."

"I need to give you clear boundaries. This is all in your best interests, just as it is with Toon."

I should have known. "And this, Lu, is the time when you say, 'Gabriel, now that you have a clear mind and control over your compulsions'—"

"—Addictions."

"—'Compulsions, now you are sober and rational enough to love me.' Am I right?"

Luanne laughs, but there's no joy in her laugh. "I wish I had never met you, Gabriel. Don't you see?"

Don't I know.

A dish crashes somewhere inside the house. It silences us. Did Toon hear what we said? Luanne puts her hand on the doorknob. "I should get back inside," she says and turns away from me.

"Jimmy's going to help me with the movie," I tell her. It makes her freeze. "Whatever I need, he says he'll get."

Luanne turns and throws a pained smile at me. "Well. That's all you need, then. Because I'm certainly not providing any places for you to work if you're going to torch them like the chapel."

"Luanne, please. This six-days-a-week requirement is not fair. It's too much. Just one more day a week so I can leave town."

"No. Focus on what's here, not what might be out there."

"You know, I told you from the very beginning that I can't be here. You never listen to me."

"Not true, Gabriel. I've heard more than enough, and I know what you're going to say before you even say it."

"Piffle."

"I knew you were going to say piffle. Tell me something: who knows you better than I do, Gabriel?"

I reel through my mental rolodex, interrupted by the sound of Zac driving back up the driveway.

"Shane," I proffer.

"Erratic Automatic Shane? Goodnight, Gabriel." Luanne goes back inside.

"Are you going to send Toon to her room?"

"This is for your own good," she says, and closes the door in my face.

Zac stands at the steps of our trailer. I stand across the driveway at the front step of Luanne's house, staring at him as he looks back at me. I have no idea where he's been, but he's got a furtively giddy look on his face as he makes his way into our home. He's up to something.

10.

"So what are we going to shoot?" asks Zac, clad in a kilt made from a motel-grade terrycloth towel, as he gives himself a sink-wash in our sorry excuse for a bathroom.

"I'm working on it," I tell him as I stare at the blank page. We're going to do this film quickly and it's going to be the single greatest piece of dramatic art in the history of humankind. It has to be if I'm ever going to get out of this place.

Zac has a bar of cheap-quality hand soap and he lathers his armpits with it. The soap smells vaguely of meat.

"I changed my mind about this town," Zac says. "I think I want to stay for a bit."

"Came to your senses, eh?" Of course he doesn't want to catch hell from my brother. Of course.

"No, it's not that … I just … let's see what Greatness has to offer, 'kay?"

"Once you're done making yourself smell like a lemony butcher shop, grab your camera. I have something to say."

"Just use the tripod."

"You are my tripod, Zac. You run the camera. And keep it dynamic, floating around me to see all my facets. But mostly the facets on my right side."

With a sigh, he hikes up his terrycloth kilt and grabs the GoPro. I prepare to give a confessional for the documentary he's shooting. Zac turns the camera to himself and whispers something into the lens.

"What are you doing?"

"Nothing! Nothing," he says, and starts to dance around me. I get him to stop, but as soon as I open my mouth, he starts gyrating again, whirling and bounding like an epileptic ballet dancer.

"Will you stop?!" He stops. "All right, now let's begin. I have grown accustomed to my state of exile and I am now prepared to create a drama the likes of which you have never seen before. I know it'll be a big departure for the people who ... expect a certain type of character from me, so I want to explain why. While I appreciate your unending fealty, Port-O-Potty Guy was a superficial, vulgar comedy character, and not me. It was comedy, and sketch comedy at that. You comedy fans want to laugh at something, but you won't laugh at me anymore. This film will leave a lasting impression on anyone who views it, because it will come from my innermost place."

"Your intestine?" Zac says. I make him reshoot.

"This film will explore emotional worlds and the human condition in ways that will make us all shed a tear and nod knowingly. It will be about existence, and the pure folly of everything that exists, and the heartbreaking unimportance of our place in the universe. We'll embark on a journey through fate and determinism, beyond our mortal failings, and we'll come out on the other end with the golden fleece of knowing the nearly unknowable. I will make you weep like a newborn."

Yes, that is exactly what we'll do, I think.

Zac coughs. Was that a real cough?

No Escape from Greatness

"Friends, fans, historians: what I'm about to produce will be the story of my life, just as it will be the story of all our lives. After gruelling auditions that nearly ended in death, I am ready to cast our lead characters and write the screenplay. Nothing will be the same after tonight."

"One sec," Zac says. "Memory card is full. That's it until I download."

"Memory card is full? But that was a short clip. What else is on there?"

Zac doesn't say anything. He just heads over to the hide-a-bed, where he's got a charging station for his computer, phone and camera set up.

"It's just as well. That was perfect, print it," I tell him, and set about writing the greatest drama ever told.

The night proves to be long and fruitful. I forget about everything around me and write; the muse fills me up like a chalice and spills my dramas out on to the page. None of it is comedic. All of it is compelling, from what I can see. It is my story, but it is the story of everyone—Gabriel Pegg's portrait of the human condition.

By dawn, I have written forty pages of script, more than enough to begin shooting some early scenes with key characters. Somehow, by the prairie moonlight, I have managed to come up with a premise and characters that sing to me, like heralding angels melodizing hymns. On this first night, without warning and from out of nowhere, I write this:

EXT. LIONS WAR MEMORIAL CEMETERY - DAY

GABRIEL, dressed in a tremendous double-breasted blazer with a turquoise scarf, stands at the foot of a gravestone. The stone reads "Danielle Pegg - 1939-1999."

> GABRIEL
> Mother. I've returned.

Gabriel tosses his scarf back over his shoulder and looks out to the prairie horizon. The sky looks like an exploded blood orange on an azure tablecloth.

> GABRIEL
> I'm sorry I didn't come for your funeral. But I assumed you would understand.

Danielle's tombstone doesn't reply, which somehow surprises Gabriel.

> GABRIEL
> I mean, funerals are for the living, right? I was fine. Really. Thankfully, your voice will always be inside me. Nattering. Criticizing.

Gabriel searches his pockets as though he forgot something. He looks around - sees a ditch across the gravel driveway into the cemetery.

No Escape from Greatness

MOMENTS LATER

Gabriel plucks a couple of wild daisies from the ditch.

MOMENTS LATER

Gabriel walks back to the gravesite. He holds the flowers between his fingers and looks down at where his mother is buried.

Gabriel slides the stems of the wild daisies into the lapel of his blazer.

>   GABRIEL
> You told me I can't be
> taken seriously. You told
> me I can't have it all. You
> told me I should always be
> careful and always have
> a Plan B and never walk a
> tightrope without a safety
> net. Well guess what,
> mother? It worked for Daniel
> but it never worked for me.

Gabriel adjusts the flower's petals; he straightens them delicately.

>   GABRIEL (cont'd)
> You always hated flowers.
> You thought it was a waste

>   of money - frivolous
>   vegetables, you called them.

The tombstone stares back at Gabriel, weathered and neglected. The stone is chipped.

>   GABRIEL (cont'd)
>   I'm not listening to you
>   anymore. I like these.

Gabriel shrugs, as though wondering why he's even there, and begins to walk away.

Then he stops and turns.

>   GABRIEL (cont'd)
>   Oh, and by the way? I will
>   have it all.

END OF SCENE

I'm amazed at my own achievement. At dawn, I summon Zac and we go to the cemetery. Synapses begin to fire in my mind, making connections and developing plot points at the speed of light. I can barely keep up.

As Zac brushes the sleep from his eyes, he asks, "So you're gonna play yourself and be the director at the same time?"

"Good point," I muse. "I am the only non-amateur actor in town. I should, probably. I'll need to do something about these grey sideburns for some of the scenes."

"Actually, I hear Shoelace was enrolled at Juilliard, so … not the only non-amateur."

"Where did you hear that from?"

"Oh, just … the diner."

No Escape from Greatness

The diner? My mind begins to draw a connecting line between Zac and the diner waitress, Jill, but my mind is quickly distracted by the cinematic tour de force being screened just behind my eyes. "Maybe we'll use him," I murmur absently.

"What about Beth?"

"Hm?"

"Beth? The farmer lady? You said she got the part. What part did she get?"

"Oh," I said. "Maybe she can be L—, maybe she can be the malevolent succubus who ruins my life and tries to sabotage my creativity at every turn." In this moment, I decide the film must be at least partially fictional, and names will need to be changed. The last thing I need is a libel suit added to my current list of legal woes. Besides, what I'm making is art, not a documentary, like my man-child nephew is attempting.

"Muhhhh this so early," Zac whines as we reach the Greatness Lions War Memorial Cemetery before the first rays of sunlight can catch us. Suddenly, a pang of nervousness erupts within me. I'm about to see my mother's tombstone for the first time ever.

My mother, Danielle, was a sturdy, plain woman, who worked for every single thing she ever got and she never got very much at all. In fact, she was a pariah in Greatness, because the gossip klatches and town fathers didn't take kindly to single mothers in the early eighties. No one ever accused Greatness of being progressive.

I didn't know my father. He could be alive or he could be dead. My mother never spoke of him, other than to say he had heart disease in his family and Daniel and I had a good chance of dying from heart disease. When I was a teen, the identity of my father was a great mystery that clouded my life. But then I grew up. Now it is so inconsequential to me that my reaction to discovering his identity would probably be the same as discovering that high levels of vitamin A are in the cereal I'm eating. Knowing who my father is would garner a cereal-box "hm."

My mother raised me and Daniel, and she was tough as nails. If my destiny was to be a hockey player, or a salesman-cum-shyster like Daniel, or an oil man, I suspect we would have got along fine. But I was to be an artist, and worse yet, a comedian. A sketch comedian. Port-O-Potty Guy is what probably killed my mother. To my knowledge, she didn't see me perform a single time. But she knew about it, and that was enough for my mother to die of humiliation.

She lived a long life, which was all she really wanted. She didn't care if her life was a good one, because being lucky enough to survive was all she asked for. I often wonder if I was cursed with some kind of supernatural self-awareness, as though I've reached the next level of Maslow's Hierarchy, which is a need for the specific actualization one has identified they are destined to attain; not just any old actualization will do.

Comedian as a calling? It got me out of here. I suppose there were moments when I believed it to be my purpose. In my more rose-coloured moments, I thought I was giving the world the gift of laughter. Usually I believed they were just laughing at me. Some purpose.

For my mother, I'm sure that raising two boys may have lowered the bar in terms of her own sense of purpose. We weren't easy children and she was all alone. How could happiness even have been a dream for her? I'm speculating, though. My mother and I didn't have those kinds of talks. We didn't go deep. She did enough to keep me alive and she didn't approve of my life choices.

I wonder what she'd make of my return to Greatness. I wonder if she'd roll out the welcome wagon for me. If she were alive today, I guess it wouldn't bother her that I haven't been back to see her grave in all these years.

Hm.

A cold, sweaty wave of fear sweeps over me, as though my mother could reach out and swat me. I am a hundred yards from her grave when I come to the realization that I'm not ready to see it.

"It's too soon to start shooting scenes," I say to Zac as I press myself into the driver's seat.

"You got me up this early, you better believe we're shooting something," Zac says.

"Okay, how about this. Here's what we'll do: I'll shoot my lines right here, so you get the lighting and background to be consistent. Then you go shoot the cutaways of the gravestone. All right?"

"What? Why?"

"Just do it! Why do I have to go into every niggling detail with you?"

"I think maybe the details don't niggle as much as you claim," he says. Then he produces the stupid camera and trains it on my face, while we're still in the car.

"We're at the place where your mother was laid to rest. Tell us how you feel, Gabriel." He shoves the GoPro in close. Dick.

"I'm hungry," I tell him. "Are you hungry? Want an Oil Man Special?"

"Want a couple of eggs with that ham?"

I become apoplectic. "No comedy allowed! No comedy! Not even in the documentary." I nearly break the key off in the ignition as I start the car. I speed us to the Four Winds Truck Stop, which quietly pleases Zac.

When we enter, the place is empty save for the gigantic Shoelace, the waifish Jill, and a short order cook clanging around in the back.

Today, Shoelace reads a copy of *The Economist*. He glances up at us walking into the diner and turns his page at me, very loudly. We sit at the other end of the diner and Jill is there to meet us, practically bounding right out of her loafers when she spies Zac sliding into a booth.

"You two are going to be a thing, aren't you?"

Zac looks at me like I'm speaking a foreign language.

"Hey," Jill says as we sit down. She says it to Zac, not me.

"Hey," he says back. I'd like to say their exchange is fraught with subtext, but I think they just don't know any two-syllable words. There is a lot happening with their eyes in this moment, though.

"Can I …?" So intimate they no longer require complete sentences to communicate.

"Yeah … I'll have the Oil Man."

"Two, please," I interject, and Jill scribbles something but her eyes never quite depart from Zac's, their smiles an identical match—that wry, Mona Lisa smile. This is making me ill. Once my order is placed, I find an excuse to leave: casting.

Jill doesn't move as I get up, and I need to sidle around her on my way to Shoelace's booth. It's as though I'm cleaning a wax museum exhibit entitled Staring Contest.

I escape their eye-lock and sit myself down across from Shoelace.

"Shoelace, right?"

"One second." With his glasses down at the end of his nose, Shoelace studies the article and I wait patiently. I watch Jill and Zac exchange a giggle and Jill touches him on the shoulder. Yes, they are going to be a thing. While disgusting, I immediately see how this could play to my advantage.

"Done," Shoelace says. "Yes, Mr. Pegg, good morning."

"Good morning … er, I was wondering if I might cast you in my film."

"If it's as asinine as the audition sides, I'll pass." Shoelace prepares to embark on the next article in *The Economist*. He sniffs a condescending sniff.

No Escape from Greatness

"No, I assure you, I've been up all night working on a draft and—well, it's going to be about my life, and there's nothing funny about that."

Carefully, with fingers the size of sweet potatoes, Shoelace places his magazine flat on the table and squares. Then he pushes his spectacles back up his nose and looks me dead in the eye.

"I hope you've taken to heart what I said to you after my audition," he says. His voice is thick and heavy, like his tongue is slightly too big for his throat. "Greatness is my adopted hometown. I choose to be a part of this community and I count my lucky stars every day that I am able to live here, in this amazing place with its amazing people. So when you tell me that you've concocted some narcissistic thinkpiece about your own sordid life, I hope you're going to make us all proud to know you, Gabriel, and not ashamed of the caricature you've become in your old age."

It occurs to me, in this moment, that Shoelace's left hand is the size of my skull.

"I hope you'll be respectful to my friends, as well," he says to me.

"I hear that you've studied at Juilliard. Is that true?"

"That is beside the point."

"*The* ... Juilliard?"

Shoelace takes a sip of his tea and rolls his eyes. Jill pours two coffees at my table while hanging on every monosyllabic word my nephew can conjure up.

"What's the part?" Shoelace says.

"Why, you'll be me, of course," I tell him. "Dramatized."

Shoelace purses his lips and rolls his tongue around inside his mouth. He eyes me up and down and directly through. My spleen feels like it is being examined. When Shoelace ponders you, it feels like the earth itself is placing you up for scrutiny.

Finally, he gives me the tiniest nod. "I'll review your little script. If it isn't self-aggrandizing autobiographical tripe, I will do it."

"Of course it isn't!" I lie.

Jill gives Zac the address to Beth and Misty's farm and I drive us there after we finish our bacon and eggs.

Whether you're a hack putting together a movie with hockey-playing dogs that talk, or Oliver Stone putting together his next epic, one thing remains the same in the movie biz: you take a meeting. That's what Zac and I were going to do. We were going to hold meeting after meeting until we had a critical meeting mass, and suddenly, magically, our project would be up and running, with me as producer/director/auteur and Zac as director of photography. I had elected not to star as myself, but perhaps I would find a cameo for myself later on. Shoelace would be our Gabriel. It was time to cast Beth in the role of Louise, who is not meant to bear any resemblance to Luanne at all, your honour, I swear.

In Los Angeles, all meetings involve lots of false pleasantries, awkward hugs, promises and optimism, and then you hope a tenth of what you get promised actually comes to pass. The best meetings are always outdoors—a patio, poolside in some magnate's backyard, etc.— and they always involve some kind of intoxication. If your meeting includes drinks, you've got trust. If you've got trust, you've got them by the curlies.

There was a certain comfort in the fakery. It was part of the culture, to be as shallow and superficial as you could be, because the emotional insides of people didn't get you paid. It was all sizzle and no steak that made the money go round, so even if you were the guy writing the next Daniel Day Lewis vehicle, you still fake-smiled and fake-hugged, still drove a ridiculous car and bitched about the route you took to the meeting. You promised to call people you never had any intention of calling. For me, it was like slipping into a warm tub, to wheel and deal and take a meeting.

So we head down the Trans-Canada to our meeting with the female lead, east toward Brandon. Then, at Zac's behest, we head south on a nondescript gravel road, which soon becomes bumpy black dirt ruts with a median of tall grass. Oil wells dot the landscape like alien robot invaders, methodically pumping, pumpjacks sucking the bitumen out of the earth like thirsty birds.

I let my mind wander and it dredges up valuables of its own, little dreamlike tidbits of story I vow to remember for future scriptwriting, scenes with myself (George—I will refer to myself in this story as "George," to distinguish between the character and the real person), with Luanne (who will be "Louise"), Toon, Zac and Jill, all of whom will be named at a future date. The Zac/Jill daydream fragments remind me that I now have the leverage I need to keep Zac here until I'm ready to leave.

"So," I say above the din of dirt road. "You and Jill, huh."

"We're going on a date tonight," Zac says.

"I didn't know dating was still a thing. I thought you kids did hookups now."

"No," Zac condescends, "hookups are something different. We're going to, I don't know, eat some food and go for a walk and such."

"So you still want me to call your dad and rat you out?"

Zac turns away. Looks out at the fields, which get flatter and greener every mile. "No," he says. "You can hold off for right now."

I speed us up and smile to myself a little.

After another ten minutes or so, the land becomes completely flat and the dirt comprising the dirt road becomes so fine that it barely makes a sound beneath our tires. Oil wells disappear and a perfectly manicured wire fence runs alongside us, on our left. The field on the other side of the fence has been harvested.

"Left," Zac says, pointing to a drive-in gateway made from old telephone poles. A sign reads: Dearheart All-Organic Farms. It's all-quaint and all-cutesy and all-mildly-nauseating, with a big doe-eyed doe beneath the title, and the doe itself has two hearts—inside one heart is "Beth" and inside the other is "Misty." I can feel the saccharine pall as we drive into it. Organic farms … I wonder how much kale they grow in the arid Manitoba soil.

"Let's make this quick," I tell Zac. Misty walks out of their house to greet us.

She's wearing filthy rubber boots and that same sundress. She waves sunnily at us. "Sorry, Beth's not here right now," she says.

"We want to talk to her about the movie," Zac says. A hen-like creature marches around the corner of the farmhouse. It's quite large and more grey than white. Misty smiles and nods at Zac as she decisively shoots an index finger up. "One sec," she announces, plucking an apron from a nail on the wall. What is that brownish stain on the front of her apron? Misty then swoops down on the bird—is it a wild turkey?—and quickly stomps up the steps of her porch. She places the bird on some kind of tree stump and holds its torso down with one hand while she reaches for an axe with the other. I can barely register what's happening before me, and then I do.

"Oh my god," I exclaim. Misty stops mid-swing, the axe wavering in the air—the Axe of Damocles for this chickenesque beast. "We're right here! Do you need to do that?"

Misty comes back down the stairs, axe still in hand. The hen-like creature skitters away, twitching and blinking as Misty grants it temporary clemency. It's unaware of how close it came its end. I'm not. "This isn't a marshmallow factory. It's a farm. When you harvest a free-range chicken, this is the most humane way to do it, believe it or not."

"I choose not," Zac says.

Dainty Misty, the organic farmer, moves toward us, axe dangling from her hand. "Hey. You guys aren't here to tell Beth she's out of your movie, are you?"

No Escape from Greatness

"No, no ..." I stammer.

"Cuz that would be really disappointing for both of us," she says.

"She's the female lead," I finally spit out. "I wanted to take a meeting, that's all! Big role. Big, big role!"

"Well she's got a lot of canning to do, so not too big, I hope."

"Not too big," Zac says. He's gone white.

"Right! Not too big! A just-right role."

Misty smiles and rests on her axe as though it were a walking stick. "Hey, that's great. I'll let her know. Where can she find you?"

Zac blurts out "We're at a trailer in Luanne's drive—" before I can correct him and say "We'll be at the diner every morning until nine. Okay?" The last thing we need is Misty knowing where we sleep at night.

I slip back into the car. Zac stands frozen outside the passenger door. I call out his name, but he won't move. I poke my head out of the driver's side window and look over at him, but before I can shout at him, Misty starts to casually chat him up.

"We'll see you at the diner," she says. Zac says nothing. "I really want this to happen for Beth, okay? It's her dream. If you love somebody, you'd kill for them to have their dream, right?"

Right. Kill.

"Looking forward to it." I call out from inside the car, "Zac, dear nephew, we're running late. We should vamoose."

"Right, yeah, sorry, take care," Zac says, and finally gets back into the car. Misty turns back to do more farming and Zac slumps into the passenger seat. I put the car in reverse and nearly do a Rockford to get out of there.

"You should have been filming that," I tell him.

"Why? There's nothing funny about it," he says.

The car skids to a halt as I come out of reverse. I step on the brakes. "Why does it have to be funny?"

Zac stiffens and stutters—"No—never—I mean yeah, should have filmed it. Ha."

As I step on the gas and speed us down the sandy dirt ruts, I can feel that something's not right. Through a series of glances, I look Zac up and down. He has the look of a Cheshire cat with the canary in its mouth.

"Are you … are you *trying* to make my DVD documentary featurette funny?"

Then it washes over me like the reveal of a home makeover gone completely wrong. I see what Zac is building and I can feel the knife twisting in my back. I ask him the question though I already know the answer.

"Are you making fun of me?!"

Zac's stare out of the passenger side window confirms it. The little bastard was playing some kind of prank on me with the footage he was shooting. The car lifts slightly off the ground as we speed over a lofty part of the road. Things are getting bumpier.

Finally, after ten minutes of being tossed around in the car, he talks: "No, Uncle G, nobody's making fun of you. I just think that life is funny as much as it's sad. Things are really important and dramatic, but a real film about you has trivial stuff, too. I just wanted to keep it real, you know? Don't be all hurt."

"Keep it real," I say, more to myself than to my nephew. "I don't want real. I want me. Can you make it me, with all the gravitas and pathos and tragedy, so that we can show the audience how I rise above? That's what the DVD featurette is for, okay. I've told you before and I'll tell you again: no comedy."

"Okay, all right."

We're silent all the way back to Greatness.

11.

It's just after three o'clock and I pace inside the trailer, preparing to host Toon for our mandatory visit, which neither she nor I will be overly eager to engage in. I can't think of anything for us to do, which is hardly a surprise, since I've spent about two hours in my life as a father, I live in a talent trailer, and I'm marooned in this squalid pit of an overgrown village. The Project, which I have yet to name, weighs heavily on my mind; if I can convince Jimmy to front me production costs and a modest director's fee, I *could* put a reputable legal firm on retainer and try to get myself out of this mess. But then I need to deliver a product that looks like I've actually used Jimmy's budget for its intended purpose. I'm no thief, but I'm desperate, and overestimating one's costs is not exactly un-Hollywood …

Toon knocks on the door. She's dressed in her school uniform.

"Wearing your running-away-from-home disguise again?" I ask.

"Not this time." She plunks herself down on my loveseat and stares at the clock radio. "One hour. Aaand, begin. Sixty."

She is going to literally count the minutes. I wait to see if she's going to say anything. Time nearly freezes.

"Why don't we make the time go by a bit more quickly," I offer. "We could actually do something. Like an activity."

"Nah. Fifty-nine."

"You're going to count the minutes?"

"You don't want to do this, I don't want to do this, my mom wishes she had a time machine so neither of us could bother her. So yes, I am going to just zone out and make this time go by so I can go home and be with my devices."

"You mean go to your room?"

"Yes, but not 'going to my room' going to my room. And I really don't need to hear what your fathering instincts are telling you, okay? You don't have the right to even suggest what I should do with my life. Whoomp, there it is. Deal. Fifty-eight."

I bite my lip and open the minifridge to offer Toon a drink, and maybe have one for myself. The fridge is completely empty. Instead, I offer her this:.

"How is my day? Thanks for asking. After a sleepless night of inspired scenecraft, I dragged my subluxated skeleton off the loveseat you're currently luxuriating on and attempted to shoot an early scene, but went for breakfast instead, where I cast your town's resident thespian as the male lead. Then we went to Beth and Misty's farm, where we witnessed a scene straight out of *The Texas Chainsaw Massacre*. And now I'm afraid that if Beth doesn't get the role of a lifetime, her psychotic wife will send my headless body running around her fields with the other decapitation victims. So yes, a fine day, thanks for asking."

I manage to exude all of it in a single breath.

"Fifty-seven," Toon says, absently.

"Speaking of animal cruelty, I have an idea," I open the door. "Go get two lawn chairs and a spool of string," I tell her.

"Why?"

"We're going hunting," I announce.

"I'm not going hunting!" She doesn't move.

"It's a time-honoured Greatness tradition," I say. "Your grandfather used to pay me to do it, and now, I'm going to pay you."

"You are so not selling it."

"Just humour me, okay? I'm trying. You have to give me a chance."

"No I don't."

"Yes you do! Yes you do! It's a two-way street, Toon. We're both in this shit, so let's be in this shit together. All you need to do is give me a tiny little chink in the armour. Throw me a bone."

"Shit."

"Don't say that, you're eleven."

"Tell you what. I'll do your hunting thing, and you'll pay me for whatever I catch, but I also get to say 'shit' all I want."

"Don't tell your mother."

Toon gets up and bounds out of the trailer. Pleased with myself, I have her round up two lawn chairs from the Quonset behind her house and a giant spool of string. I try not to look inside the Quonset, not wanting to interlope, but I can't help but notice the riding lawn mower, the massive electric generator, the workbench and tools. Relics of a comfortable life I was never a part of.

Thinking on my feet, I have Toon cut the string into lengths before we go—she can only find garden shears, but it does the trick.

"Where are we going?" Toon asks me as we march down her driveway.

"There," I nod over at a patch of field just across the road. It used to be a baseball diamond, but children don't just run outside and play baseball anymore and the field looks like it hasn't been used for years.

"What are we hunting?" she asks. I look over at her with incredulity. Can she not have figured it out by now?

"Gophers, my dear. We are going to snare some gophers."

She holds up the lengths of string, trying to figure out how it's going to work. When we find a suitable place in the field, I place the lawn chairs in positions facing each other, but not too close together, and then I make nooses at the ends of the lengths of string. This is brilliant.

"Are you kidding?" she says. "I'm not strangling an animal."

"You'll just stun them," I lie. "You'll cut off their air and they'll pass out."

When we were kids, before there was any romance, Luanne was Lulu and I was Gabe and Jimmy was Mr. Welsh. Mr. Welsh offered a crisp twenty dollar bill to any kid who could help him rid his property of the hated gopher, Greatness's nuisance rodent and all around bane of existence for the townsfolk. We would grab our lawn chairs and string and sit out there for hours on a Sunday, usually in the sweltering heat—it was a thrill when a parent would visit us bearing a cold drink. We had many near misses, where we could swear that a gopher's head was just a fraction of an inch beneath the surface, ready to pop out of the hole we had our nooses around at any second. No one, in the half-dozen afternoons we spent out in the southwest Manitoba aridity, not a single child ever came close to catching one, though we all tried. When we would complain to the adults that it was impossible, they would invariably tell us to point the finger at ourselves. We were being too noisy. We had to sit in silence, perfectly still. Whoever invented this ruse was an evil genius. It must have been a Welsh.

One afternoon, Lulu and I successfully sat without movement or sound for over ninety minutes, until Daniel ruined it

No Escape from Greatness

by throwing a Frisbee at my head. We angrily marched back to the house and whined to any adult who would listen. Mr. Welsh, laughing all the while, offered each of us a crisp two dollar bill to spend at the Highway Robbery. And that was gopher hunting. I think I was about thirty-five years old when I figured out that it was an affordable, highly amusing way to keep the kids distracted so that my mother, Mr. Welsh and the other kids' parents could have a peaceful drink on a Sunday afternoon. And now, it occurs to me that they likely hunted gophers when they were children, too.

"We must sit in perfect silence," I tell Toon, convincingly, with a touch of menace, "so that we might lull the beasts into a false sense of security." I cautiously loop the bright white twine around the gopher hole, then feed the line back to Toon. I lay out my own over the neighbouring gopher hole and cautiously sit down in my lawn chair, staring at the gape in the earth as if willing the gopher out, as though I had a psychic rapport with the rodents.

"I will pay you fifty dollars per gopher," I announce in a whisper, and Toon gulps. "Curse to your heart's content."

"Shit. Shit shit shit shit," she says to herself nervously.

"Shhhh. Swear more quietly!"

"*Shit shit shit shit,*" she whispers. Then silence. Peace. Until:

"Ermmm … so they can hear us?"

"Well, we might be able to get away with some quiet talking, but I'm not sure."

"Oh, good, because this would be boring."

"I'm excited to catch one. It's been a while. Maybe we can rid this field of them and actually play some ball out here."

"I don't know. I don't have a glove. You know, no dad and stuff."

"Right." I let it slide, hoping to create a vacuum of gopher-murdering silence that she would feel obliged to fill.

She mulls for a moment or two and I move my string as though I'm cooking a marshmallow over a campfire.

"So I think I have a bully problem," she says.

"Oh," I say with surprise inflected into my voice. "You mean those two awful girls at school? Are they the reason why you so desperately want to leave town? Now I understand."

"I don't think you do."

"You'd be surprised," I tell her, leaning in a little closer. "I've been in situations where people tormented me and subjected me to their whims, humiliating me in the process."

"That's not what's happening in school."

"Oh."

"Do you ever ... you know, sometimes you get a rumble, like, in your stomach and blah? And then your eyes start to squint and it feels like you have a toque on and it's way too tight. Does that make sense?"

"Nope, not sure I follow, Toon." All the while I silently rejoice, basking in the glory of a plan well-executed. I make a mental note to ensure this scene makes it into Project G. I'm now calling it Project G.

"Like something happens around you and just, I don't know, it sets you off, like you just want to put your fist through a wall. And sometimes cute little cuddly girls with the big cute eyes and the pink ribbons in their hair, sometimes they just get in the way of your fist. You want to reach out and punch someone, you know what I mean?"

"You mean you have a bullying problem," I say.

She chews her lip, looking ashamed. "I know it's wrong."

"Yes, it's wrong. Don't hurt people. There's enough pain in the world already. You don't need to add to it."

"Maybe leaving is the best way to go. Just find some place to be somebody else."

We've completely forgotten about the fake gopher snares. The strings lay in our palms but gophers could easily climb out of these holes and lay themselves into our traps and we'd be completely oblivious. We're talking to each other. The world is just the two of us. I have to say something sage here or risk slipping away into the mundane world again. I have to keep us here.

"I feel like that sometimes," I tell Toon. "It's rage. It's just pure, acidic, uncut rage, bubbling up in you like you're full of pissed-off lava."

"Magma," she corrects me. "If it's beneath the earth's crust, it's pissed-off magma."

"Language."

"Shit. Go on."

"I know sometimes I get so enraged that everything becomes negative hyperbole that alienates people."

"Hyperba-wha?"

"When I'm full of pissed-off magma, I try not to erupt where the villagers are. I stay away from people. You know what really helps me? Ripping up boxes."

"Like cardboard boxes?"

Toon is intently listening to what I have to say, and may even be learning from it. I have never been more careful with my words in my entire life.

"Yes, cardboard boxes. Like in the back of the LC?"

"What the heck is an LC?"

It's the Liquor Commission, of course, the state-run alcohol retailer that holds a monopoly over the off-sale of all the best Manitoba liquors. And this is exactly the wrong time to explain it to Toon, or to hold it up as a shining example of places I frequent when I'm troubled.

"Not important," I ha-ha. "Really, any store will work, like the Highway Robbery. They have loads of boxes and you can rip to your heart's content."

"I bet the recycling depot has like five thousand boxes all piled up."

"Oh yes, recycling. That's a thing now."

And so we float together through some kind of gopher-trapping vortex, conversing on topics ranging from recycling and composting to a list of all the movies I was in and all the A-listers I brushed elbows with in Hollywood. She even asks me to describe the other members of Erratic Automatic, and I oblige: Shane, the holier-than-thou ringleader; JD, the Franco-Manitoban who did all the music; Gord, the red-headed yeoman who had amazing comedic range but had to do all of our fat gags; and Snorri-Stein, the Polish Icelander, the introverted freaky one who scared you six days a week and dug up comedy platinum on the seventh. You could never trust Snorri-Stein. He was too quiet. His talent was the only thing we liked about him.

There's some silence. Toon stares into the black hole where a gopher will never be. She seems to look a little further from me as she asks, "What happened with your dad?" She recoils more, as though I might take offense.

Instead, I shrug, smile at my noose a little, then tell her, "All I need to know about my father is that he wasn't here."

Neither of us are sure what to say next. I toss something out there: "He got away and I turned out fine." I hope to myself that she's not drawing those parallel lines between me and my invisible father that are suddenly so obvious to me.

"Wait, does bubble wrap work?"

"For getting away?"

"For bullying. Can I beat up bubble wrap to feel better?"

"Hm. Not really, I'd say. Bubble wrap is too dainty. You want to tear things apart, not pop them one at a time."

"Oh, man, there you are dead wrong. I'll have to show you how to strangle bubble wrap sometime. You twist it like you're twisting the water out of a cloth."

No Escape from Greatness

"You mean wringing, with a W. You wring out a cloth."

"Oh, sure. Whatever."

Silence. I corrected her and she didn't like it. Now we return to earth.

But we would have come back anyway; Luanne is walking across the road toward us.

"I was getting worried. You've been gone two hours."

"Sorry. Lost track of time."

"Seeya Dad," Toon says with a half-smile, and scampers back to her house. I grab the lawn chairs and string.

Dad.

"I can't believe you did this," Luanne says, looking slightly bemused.

"She forgot about getting paid," I say with a smile. "No white cream soda for her." White cream soda was Lulu's favourite.

INT. ROOSTER HUT - NIGHT

```
One table has been bedecked in a white
tablecloth and a tapered emergency candle
is lit inside a tall Coke tumbler. This is
what passes for a romantic dinner for two
in Greatness. The neon light bulbs overhead
have been unscrewed, so Zac and Jill can
feel even more intimate, like Lady and The
Tramp, except they're both tramps.

Jill eats her fried chicken with a fork and
knife.

                    JILL
          I had the best time today.
```

> ZAC
>
> Me too.

> JILL
>
> We're doing this tomorrow, right? I mean, this, but something different?

> ZAC
>
> Are you going to sing for me tomorrow?

Jill shakes her head, all bashful.

> JILL
>
> No, no, if you can't use me in your movie ...

> ZAC
>
> You're way better than some amateur shit-show. Don't you want to sing your operas on a real opera stage? Maybe Toronto, or New York, even, or, or Venice!

> JILL
>
> Like, California?

> ZAC
>
> No, like Italy, with the canals and the gondolas and such.

No Escape from Greatness

JILL
Right.

Jill stares into her cup of soda.

JILL (cont'd)
Actually I can't really do anything like that.

ZAC
Huh?

JILL
If I ever want to do that I'd need a passport.

ZAC
Yeah, and? We'll get you one.

JILL
I've got one. I mean, there's a passport of me out there. I just don't have it.

ZAC
Who has it?

Jill takes a way-too-big bite of chicken.

JILL
My husband.

Zac looks at Jill in disbelief.

He slides his seat back.

                JILL (cont'd)
      Wait! Don't. Let me explain.

                ZAC
      I think I get it.

Zac stands up and throws his paper napkin down as though it were a cloth one.

                JILL
      I was American!

                ZAC
      What kind of excuse is that?

                JILL
      Just sit and let me explain.
      Please.

Zac sits down, scowl still etched across his face.

                JILL (cont'd)
      I was diagnosed with
      leukemia. It would have
      cost a million dollars to
      treat it. At least. So the
      only solution I could come
      up with was to make me
      Canadian. I married into
      my health insurance, I've
      been in remission for two

> years, and now I have to make sure my husband stays close for when Citizenship and Immigration swings by so he doesn't go to jail for fraud.

Jill reaches across the table for Zac's hands.

> JILL (cont'd)
> It isn't real. This is real. I know you feel it and I feel it too.

Zac tries to keep his defences up, but it's pointless.

He melts back into the feeling.

Jill grabs her fork and knife and gets back to her chicken. Zac takes a sip of his soda.

> ZAC
> So . . . who's the husband?

END OF SCENE

12.

I sleep like a baby that night, completely oblivious to the time of night that Zac gets home from his date. When I awaken, the southwest Manitoba sun glows like a happy pumpkin in the roseate sky, not quite close enough to warm us. At some point in the past twenty-four hours, all the trees in Greatness changed colour. Autumn has arrived.

Autumn in Manitoba barely exists. Winter is in such a hurry to come that it barely gives the trees time to disrobe before it's all over them like a lecherous estate owner. Autumn could be gone tomorrow.

I sit on the steps of the trailer with my cup of pseudocoffee and watch the dawn. Today, I will write twenty script pages, take at least two meetings, and edge ever-closer to shooting Project G. I will have a pleasant visit with Toon and perhaps locate a source of funding for Project L, which is my plan to legally emancipate myself from this whole travesty.

It's going to be a good day.

I bathe in a script-concocting reverie for who knows how

long, which breaks when Luanne and Toon emerge from their house. Time to go to school. I wave at Toon. Luanne waves at me. It's all so civilized. I think that if I did escape this legal gulag, I could still come by occasionally and it wouldn't completely kill me. Maybe once or twice a year. We could go gopher hunting. I could buy us a couple of baseball gloves.

Luanne pulls her brand-new Charger out of the garage and speeds off, kicking up a rooster tail of gravel dust from the driveway.

As they leave, another car heads toward me. A 1962 all-white Cadillac Coupe de Ville with whitewall tires, white ragtop, and white leather interior. Jimmy's car.

Time to wheel and deal.

"Morning," I say to Jimmy before the gravel cloud has even passed.

"You figured out what you need yet?"

"Does anyone truly know?"

Jimmy doesn't think deeply about things. This message does not compute and he's in a hurry to tell me: "I found this online course that teaches you how to be a producer in two hours. I'm ready. What's our concept? What's the genre?"

"A drama. About a guy held captive in a small Manitoba town."

"That's not going to make us any money."

"It's not supposed to. It's a drama."

"I'm not sure I can be associated with a money-loser."

"Think of it as an Oscar vehicle."

"Whatever you do, Sunshine, as long as you're doing it here, I'm behind it a hundred percent. Whatever I can do to keep you going, that's what I'm going to do. That's what the course said: 'whatever it takes is exactly what it will take.'"

"Sage advice," I murmur.

"The online course also said you need to build your way up

No Escape from Greatness

to the A-list. Who we got from the C-list or B-list that we can throw under the bus to get ourselves an A-lister?"

"Me?"

"No offense, but are you even on a single letter, or are you on the list where the alphabet turns over and you start counting with two letters, like the AA list?"

"I'm not on the twenty-seventh list!"

"Somewhere around Q, then?"

That's probably true.

"The appeal of this story will be in its telling, not in its star power, Jimmy."

"What about your comedy friends?"

I can't lose my temper. Not with Jimmy. So behind gritted teeth, I pronounce, "We're *not* doing a comedy," and I pull my wish list out of my pocket:

- —laptop
- —proper camera equipment
- —soundboard
- —lighting
- —makeup kit
- —espresso bar with baristas (until espresso bar possible: Keurig automatic coffee maker will suffice)
- —director's folding chair
- —monitor for video village
- —$25,000

"Here," I tell him. "This is what I need for now. Can you accommodate?"

He gives the list a once-over and then looks up at me with a single squinted eye, like a jeweller appraising a cubic zirconia. "Can I write you a cheque?"

"You're the producer, Jimmy. You track down all this stuff while I create."

"Right," he says. "I'll get on it." Zac emerges from the trailer and Jimmy gestures over at him. "Can I take him?" Jimmy says to me, pointing at Zac with his thumb. Zac looks quizzical. I introduce Zac to our new executive producer and then tell him to get inside Jimmy's car, but Zac hesitates.

"But we need you," I tell him. "Jimmy doesn't have the first clue about what to buy, and most of this stuff you'll only find in Winnipeg."

"Oh. Right," Jimmy says. "I just wanted the company, tell you the truth."

"It'll have to wait 'til tomorrow," Zac says brusquely. "I have something very important I need to do today."

"Tomorrow then," Jimmy says, sliding back into his unnaturally white Caddy.

Flummoxed, I can't even close my mouth until Jimmy is gone. I just wonder at the unmitigated gall of my nephew.

"What could you have to do that is so unbelievably important that it couldn't possibly wait for a single day?"

"Actually," Zac tells me, "I need your help today, too."

"I'm sorry, I can't break my hawklike focus on the creative endeavour at hand. I must remain steadfast and forceful, like a ... like a laser beam: pure energy directed at this film."

"But I need a lookout while I break into a house."

"You want me to abet you in some kind of criminal act."

"It's criminal like Robin Hood was a criminal. I'm stealing something back for someone. The rightful owner."

"What? Explain yourself."

Zac rubs his chin, pondering. He clearly doesn't want to tell me. "Uncle G ... Gabe. If you help me with this, I will be your personal assistant, without strings or questions.

"I will never leave your side as long as you are in Greatness.

No Escape from Greatness

You can rat on me and I will still never leave. If you help me with this today, you will get me for tomorrow and a thousand tomorrows thereafter."

"No strings?"

"No strings."

"No crossed fingers?"

"My hands are in the pleading position, honestly begging you."

"How can I trust you?"

"Because if you help me, I will never lie to you about anything ever. I'll be so trustworthy, I will be like a truth-telling robot that has no sense of self-preservation or common decency."

"So like your father, then. Except the truth part."

We both laugh and head to the car.

13.

"I fell in love," Zac says, and I nearly run the car into the ditch. It was the waitress. I've completely overestimated Zac. He can't tell the difference between physical infatuation and actual romantic love. He is still an idealistic, naïve little boy.

"And you're breaking and entering for your one true love," I retort. "How noble."

"The guy has Jill's passport. I'm going to steal it back."

"But you've promised yourself to me."

"I know what I did."

"If you want to be with her, why would you enable her to leave the country while you're marooned here as my servant boy?"

"Why? Because she deserves it, Uncle G. She deserves to be free. She needs it. Turn here."

We drive down the main drag of Greatness, along 7th Avenue, where they've installed the showy traffic light, new and sparkling and constantly flashing red, enabling cars to behave like it's a four-way stop. As we pull to a stop, I think back to all the stores and how they've changed. To our immediate right was Robinson's, a small-town attempt at a department store, where each "department" was represented by half an aisle. Now there's a dollar store in its place. Up and to the left was McCloud's, the hardware store, where everyone inspected their products before walking next door and placing their orders at the Sears Catalogue Outlet. Sears made a killing in Greatness back in those days, all by mail order.

Two of the three Chinese restaurants are on 7th: Good Earth and Better Planet. Now there's a Rooster Hut where the Sears used to be and an asphalt parking lot where McCloud's used to be. I don't think Joni Mitchell would have had a big problem with any of it. It was never paradise.

That's unfair. Greatness was paradise for a child, because it was all he ever knew. Was it a liberal utopia where everyone was kind and fair and treated equally? No. But summer had a glory when it brought itself about, and clouds never stayed for long. Mother raised us alone, and Jimmy raised Lulu while caring for Joyce, and the town made sure we had presents at Christmas and a driveway that was shovelled and rides around town. My mother hated their charity but she accepted it and it was always offered.

There were games of scrub and gopher hunting and a drive-in theatre and white cream soda. And Lulu.

As we continue south on 7th, a man driving north in a gawdy black pickup truck does the Greatness wave at us: an effortless, casual raise of the hand from the top of the steering wheel and a bit of a squint and nod. The easiest hello. It's wrong for me to bristle at a simple hello.

I offer the Greatness wave back at him.

At Zac's behest, we turn right, along Queen, down a row of turn-of-the-century ramblers, beautiful limestone homes with white porches and immaculate ivy walls. The old money lives on Queen Street, just as it always did. The town fathers, who despised and resented Jimmy Welsh, all descended from remittance men who built homes here a hundred years prior.

"Stop here," Zac says in front of a house with its trim painted royal blue. I stop the car. Zac doesn't get out.

"So what happens now?" I prompt.

"I'm casing the joint."

"Expecting to find a secret entrance? Go knock on the door and make sure no one's home."

"Right," Zac says stupidly, and gets out of the car. I tap my foot and against the gas pedal as the Cavalier idles, zipping the RPMs up and down and up and down. Zac climbs the steps and walks into the front porch, stomping loudly. He rings the doorbell and waits. Nothing. After a few more moments, he raps on the door as hard as he can. Looking at me, Zac spins and kicks the door with his heel, trying to show off. It makes a huge thump, but the door doesn't budge.

I nervously scan the neighbours' places, hoping no one heard it.

No one comes out.

Zac backs away from the door and scampers back to the car. He gets back in.

"So I'm thinking I should find a basement window in the back yard and smash it. Or—or maybe I should make sure there's no motion sensor?"

I snicker to myself. "Did you try the door?"

"What do you mean?"

"I mean, this is Greatness. Good chance the door is unlocked. Did you try it?"

"Errrrr." Zac gets out of the Cavalier. He walks back up the steps, into the royal blue front porch. As though the doorknob itself can electrocute Zac and take him directly to prison, he taps the brass knob once with an index finger. When that appears to leave him unscathed, Zac clutches the knob with all his fingers, clasps it with his palm, and then, when absolutely positive that the doorknob will not transform into a police officer in mid-grasp, Zac finally turns it.

Lo and behold, it's unlocked. Some things never change. Thank goodness there's still some trust left in this town for Zac to take advantage of.

"Who lives here?" I wonder aloud, trying to figure out why some man would have the poor girl's passport. "Her parents? A forger?" It makes no sense to me, but this sure is a juicy scene. I imagine it in screenplay form—a heist! How do I make this fit in a compelling character drama … hm. Sometimes mulling aloud is quite productive, and so I reason with the steering wheel.

"What if Zac in the film has no choice but to break into this house because his one true love will die if he doesn't? What if he doesn't steal some passport? What if he steals a … magical … No! Shit! Stop it. Oscar worthy, Oscar worthy … how does it relate to the main character, Gabriel? Zac is doing something to betray Gabriel."

I gasp at my own revelation. "Yes," I reply to myself, "Zac is the Judas. He's stealing something … magical … god damn it!"

He is playing a joke on me. He is my comedic Judas. I was right the first time, back at the organic farm of horrors.

Then I spy a black car in my rear-view mirror as it turns onto Queen Street. It's a land yacht, just short of a limousine, with tinted windows. I feel like Tony Soprano is about to take a hit out on the lookout, botching this heist job and sending a message to the Pegg Cartel forever.

I grip the steering wheel, half expecting the rat-a-tat of a Tommy gun.

But the car cruises past.

A moment later, Zac struts out of the house. Zac flicks the

passport with his left hand, as though it were a stack of escort service brochures from Las Vegas. With a boastful gait, he almost prances to the Cavalier and gets in.

"Should have brought my camera," he says.

Zac is Judas. The thought nags at me and I can't contain it.

"Hello, indentured servant sworn to eternal servitude and honesty."

"Hello."

"About the camera ... about your documentary," I interject, and Zac's demeanour completely shifts. He looks down at his lap and fidgets with the passport. Zac's look tells me everything I need to know. I was right.

"You didn't volunteer to make a documentary to help me resurrect my career, did you?"

Zac looks down at the passport even harder.

"You were mocking me, every time you shot me with that little camera. You were poking fun at me, weren't you?"

"At the time, you were mockable."

"Get out."

"But it's my car."

"*Get out!*" I roar.

With steam billowing from my eye sockets, I speed through downtown Greatness, back through Gopher Trails and to the trailer. I storm into the trailer, digging around for the camera and its loathsome footage. I can't believe Zac has done this to me.

I can't find the tapes/film canisters/whatever they use in a GoPro anywhere, so I sit on the bed, fuming, my chest heaving with hot magma. My eyes want to burst out of my head and fly around the room, blasting everything with laser beams. I want to transform into a werewolf and gnaw at things, tear at things with my claws and feel the blood on my face. I want the cushions on the hide-a-bed to be Zac's throat as I wring them.

Or better yet, Daniel's, because Daniel is truly to blame for how much of a turncoat Zac is.

Instead, I find my coffee-soaked phone, the one where everything is broken except the calling part, and I call Daniel.

"Hello." There's his stupid voice.

"Your son has been scamming you."

"Who is this?"

"Very funny, Daniel. I blackmailed Zac into coming with me because I discovered he dropped out of university and blew his RESP money."

Silence on the other end of the line.

"Are you sober right now, Gabriel?"

"Am I sober?! The unmitigated gall … are you not hearing what I'm telling you? Your kid stole the college money, Daniel."

Daniel emits a defeated sigh that makes a staticky sound in the receiver. "I know," he says. "We figured it out pretty much as soon as we got rid of you."

Splendid.

"But you could use a chaperone on your little misadventure, and you got Zachary away from his … questionable social circle, so we stayed mum. Everyone wins, right Gabriel?"

That's my little brother's favourite saying: 'everyone wins.' 'Everyone wins: you, Apa Jack, me, the banks, the tax man, me …' Hearing him say it again makes me want to reach through the phone. The way he says my name, slow and enunciated like he's teaching me how to pronounce it.

"What kind of tomfuckery is this? Should I send you the bill for the care and feeding of your child? It wasn't enough for you to pilfer all of my savings on your idiotic Manitoba business deals. I mean, how is it that you still live in Tuxedo?"

"I was smart with my money."

"*I gave my money to you.*"

"You gave me the money you didn't need for your … habits.

No Escape from Greatness

Now I am genuinely concerned for your well-being, Ga-bri-el," he says it *even slower*. "It's so easy to get Prairie Caribous back home, I want to make sure the easy access doesn't cause you to backslide. Can you put Zachary on the phone?"

I am about to go supernova.

"It was a mistake to even call you, Daniel."

"Yes, it probably was."

I throw my phone at the wall like Roger Clemens in a rage: pretty hard. It hits the troutboard, ricochets forty-five degrees left, smashes into the marquee mirror and the whole mess crashes into the tiny vanity sink.

The perfect moment for Luanne to barge in.

"Not now. Not you," I say. I'm ready to go toe-to-toe with my ex-wife, but then I notice tears have been streaming from her face.

"Toon is gone."

14.

"Toon is gone," she says to me. "Something happened at morning recess and she ran off."

"It wasn't me," I tell her, but it's more of a reflex than anything, because there's nothing accusatory in her voice. Luanne is shaken, and she doesn't do shaken very often. She moves toward me, toward my chest as though she wants me to embrace her. I don't take the bait. "She can't have gone far," I say in my most reassuring tone. "It's a small town."

"Drive me around to look for her," Luanne lilts. She ostensibly goes blind when she cries, and I've known this as long as I can remember. If you know Luanne, you know she can't hold sharp objects or operate heavy machinery when she's got tears in her eyes. It's a miracle she found her way through my door.

Every fibre of my being wants it to be okay to say no to her, but it is not okay, and I want to look for Toon as well. I nod and Luanne sticks out her hand like a blind beggar sticks out the cup, except Luanne has the keys to her Charger in her palm.

Luanne tells me where to drive and I drive there. We don't

speak. I don't admire the fully loaded, all-black muscle car I'm driving. I don't look over at Luanne with any type of empathy. She doesn't look to me for any type of emotional support. We just search for Toon. We check all the stores on 7th Avenue, even the restaurants whose staff are preparing for lunch. We drive up and down the streets. We check in with Tom at the Highway Robbery, who hasn't seen Toon since the Great Audition Fire.

Luanne's crying subsides as we get busy searching for Toon. She's probably fine with driving on her own, but I don't press the issue.

We search everywhere there is to search in Greatness. It takes us an hour.

Empty-handed, we go back to the school.

What we witness at Ruml Elementary is nothing short of carnage.

Three girls: Destiny, Hope, and a girl who probably got bussed to school from Maple Lake First Nation. All three slump in chairs that have been lined up in the hallway outside the sick room. One of the girls, either Destiny or Hope, presses an ice pack up against her temple; the other, either Hope or Destiny, has gauze dangling from her blood-encrusted nose; the other girl has a black eye and fat lip.

"A fight," Luanne whispers to me as we approach. She pushes into Destiny/Hope's face and hisses "What did you do to my daughter?" before I can take her by the shoulders and pull her away. The little girl starts to cry. Then a woman emerges from the sick room; judging from her attire, she's a member of the faculty. The woman has her arm in a splint.

"You were supposed to be supervising these kids!" Luanne roars, because that's what a lioness does in this situation. The teacher is lucky Luanne isn't already picking bits of small-town public educator out of her teeth.

The teacher responds as stoically as she can. "Toon told you about her bullying problem, did she not? She said she wanted help. We sent notes home."

"I saw the notes. I told her to be more assertive and to tell you when there's a problem so she wouldn't feel afraid anymore."

The teacher recoils and a look of incredulity comes across her face. "You're kidding, right?" the teacher says. "How do you think I got this?" She tries to wave her splinted arm like a chicken attempting to fly. "Your daughter is headed for a life behind bars with behaviour like this, *Miss* Welsh." The teacher looks over at me when she pejoratively says "Miss."

"Miss Welsh, Toon *is* the bully."

I nod to myself. Makes sense.

Luanne stumbles backward and clutches her forehead. "Impossible," she murmurs to herself.

The teacher grows a sly smile, almost vengeful. "Girls," she says to the victims in the hallway, "why did Toon do this to you?"

"I don't know," Destiny sobs, or Hope, whichever. She looks at me like I know her secret—the Suckatollah secret—as she tells the teacher, "We were just talking about rainbows. Right girls?"

The other blonde sister nods as she looks up at us with a look that protests too much. The Aboriginal girl looks into her lap harder. "Right, Theresa?" There's a tinge of threat in Destiny's tone. Theresa nods, reluctantly.

"After she turned back into Dr. Banner, Toon ran off," the teacher says, her chin wrinkling and twitching with the stress of thinking back to the assault. "I think we would all appreciate it if Toon's mother could see Toon for what she is."

Luanne's fingers curl into claws and move toward the teacher's neck. I knife between them. Luanne hisses a venomous threat: "Say another word and I will cut off your water and run jackhammers outside your house every day for a month."

It dawns on me:

Bubble wrap!

"Bubble wrap!" I exclaim as I solve the mystery in my own mind. All five females look at me as though I've crossed the fine line between genius and insanity.

"Toon said she wanted to strangle bubble wrap to help her calm down," I say to Luanne. "Where is there lots of bubble wrap? Post office? Recycling depot?"

"I have a roll of bubble wrap in the Quonset," Luanne says with bewilderment.

We sprint for the car.

There used to be a visible and active RCMP detachment in Greatness. Thankfully, budgets were cut and the police rarely turn up anymore, unless it's to set up a tobacco tax sting operation on truckers smuggling cheap smokes in from Saskatchewan. Sure, there's still a cop shop, but calls would often go straight to voicemail.

If the Mounties were still patrolling town the way they used to, they would have surely nailed us for one of the two dozen gross traffic infractions we commit in the three minutes it takes us to speed from school to Luanne's house and the Quonset. Needless to say, I do not heed the four-way-stop-sign rule of the traffic light flashing red.

Sure enough, as I grind the Charger to a halt in the driveway, we can see that the giant metal doors of the Quonset are open.

Luanne explodes out of the car before I can even switch off the ignition. She races up the driveway, screaming for Toon as she runs.

Luanne disappears inside as I close the door and walk toward the Quonset. What should I do? Do I do what I imagine a father does? Do I run inside behind Luanne, embrace my daughter, and then give her hell for running away and scaring us all? Do I play bad cop to Luanne's good cop? Is it my place? Entirely unsure, I walk measuredly up the driveway. I pace in figure eights up and down the gravel driveway, staying a safe distance from the door of the Quonset. After several figure eights, Luanne pops out of the Quonset with a scowl on her face.

"She wants to talk to *you*," Luanne says.

With trepidation, I enter the Quonset.

Toon sits on a tripod stool in the middle of the gigantic shed. It looks like a bubble wrap bomb exploded in here; linear yard after linear yard of bubble wrap has been twisted, popped, maimed, defiled and strewn about the place. Toon is a bubble wrap spider and I have entered her web.

"Come sit," Toon says. Her voice clangs off the corrugated metal roof and echoes. It's fairly dark in here, so I can't quite make out her face until I take a few steps more. As I get closer, I see her clothes have been ripped from the fight and stained with grass. Toon's eye makeup has run down her face and she looks like a zombified, sleep deprived Tammy Faye Bakker. Toon wipes her nose with her arm, still clutching a length of bubble wrap. I see the bubble wrap is attached to a massive spool, which has plenty of bubble wrap left in it. Were they shipping cars from here? Why would they require so much?

"That's a whole lot of bubble wrap," I say with an uneasy chuckle.

She gestures for me to sit on a lawn chair that's across from her—the same type of lawn chair we used to snare gophers yesterday—and I sit. Toon juts out her arm. She offers me a length of bubble wrap.

"You take both hands, like this, and you twist for all you got," she says, clutching a length of the stuff and strangling it. Instead of one pop, the twisting motion makes dozens of air bubbles burst at once, like machine gun fire. She sneaks a sniffle, hoping I won't notice.

"Like this?" I mime, and lamely twist the sheet I've got in my hand. I try to lure Toon into helping me.

"Yeah, exactly," she says, foiling my plan. "Wring it like a wet cloth."

"Like a wet cloth and not your teacher's arm." I smile at her. "You're calming down."

I grab another length and do a half-assed job of popping the bubbles. Toon efficiently snares another metre length from the spool and twists, bursting two dozen bubbles at a minimum.

"Impressive," I say. "You're good at that."

"Oh. Well, there's one thing I'm good at."

"You're good at many things. I think it was Goethe who said 'talent develops in quiet places.'"

"Gerta? Who's she?"

"It's a he. Goethe. Not the point. Anyway, I believe everyone has a purpose, Toon, and it's your job to discover what yours is."

"I've been trying," she pleads.

"It's not about trying. You can't try. You can't seek out your talent or your purpose. Right. You can't do that. You just do what you do and try to be happy, and one day you'll say to yourself, 'Yes! O-ho! That's it! My garters, yes, that is my purpose.'"

"Is that how it happened for you?"

Do your kids always throw questions back at you that are increasingly difficult to answer? How *did* it happen for me?

The director in the back of my mind mimics a song-and-dance man, and the word "vamp" echoes repeatedly under the corrugations of my brain: "Vamp. Vamp. Vamp."

"Well, you know how I got together with Erratic Automatic when their train broke down here. I happened to be at the same hotel as they were holed up in. We got to talking, and we concocted the Port-O-Potty Guy sketch right there. But that was never my true purpose in life. I may have thought it was at the time, but I was wrong. and there was a part of me that knew it from the start. It came so easily that I know I am capable of more. I know I have more talent than that." *I really hope I do.*

"How? How do you know?" Toon is enthralled.

"I don't know. Maybe we're all like computers, like meat computers, and we're all programmed to perform a function that makes our world better. Only some people can sense their internal programming and some can't. Self-awareness. Somewhere along the line, I must have caught a glimpse of my own programming."

"Like dreams, you mean?"

"Yes, that's exactly what I mean."

"This is where dreams go to die," Toon says, and punctuates it with a bubble wrap strangulation.

"Not all dreams," I say, snagging a length of wrap for myself.

"Just yours."

"Not necessarily. Your grandfather, whom you should be nicer to, by the way, has got me convinced that we can do something good here. I just need to … use my talents … and evoke great performances to tell the story I want to tell. Even *my* dream could be possible here, Toon. We just have to find a dream for you."

"I know what I'm good at." Her face doesn't register a whole lot of excitement as she says this.

"You do?"

"Beating the crap out of people. They keep telling me I suck at everything, but I'm really good at punching the shit out of them." Her eyes flit over, like she's testing me to see if she can still say that word.

"Being a bully isn't your calling, my dear. There will always be cruel people and people who want to drag you down, but you can't punch them all. It would be much better to have the last laugh."

"The last laugh?"

"Right. By doing what you know to be your purpose."

"What if I don't have one?"

This possibility has never occurred to me. "I guess ... perhaps ... some people might search for that purpose and never find it."

"If I was in the city, it would help. I could look for my purpose in fancy coffee shops with the other oddballs, and we could play *Cards Against Humanity* like everybody does in fancy coffee shops. I could use my bullying skills to protect us from crime until I figured out my purpose. And when people from Greatness tried to find me I would punch them and run, and laugh the whole way. The last laugh."

She makes me smile. "Rise above all of that, Toon. You're eleven. Maybe you won't find your purpose for twenty more years. Maybe longer than that."

"Maybe never."

I shrug at this. "I guess it is possible."

Toon nods, a little disappointed in that knowledge.

"You know I can't take you from your mother. The theatre program in prison is only slightly better than dinner theatre."

We sit in a silence for a few minutes. I hear the squidge of gravel underfoot just outside the Quonset. Luanne must be pacing out there.

"I don't talk to my Grandpa because he's a drunk," she says. "My Mom told him it was the booze or us, and he chose the booze."

Something stirs, deep inside me. I think I see a curtain part just a little: Jimmy wants me here to help me reconcile things with his girls. That's why he wants me to stick around.

"He's not a mean drunk or anything, but he's embarrassing. He falls down and passes out all the time. Mom says the drinking's going to kill him. She's worried. But she'll never say she's worried. She just gets all in a huff. You know how she is."

"Your mother and I thought you ran away. You think that made her worry at all? Think it's worth an apology?"

No Escape from Greatness

Toon shrugs and we stand up. I have solved the mystery of Where Did Toon Go, talked her down from the cliff, and solved an existential mystery in the process. It's drama worthy of the screen.

There's an awkward moment where Toon and I stand across from each other, father and daughter, at the end of a crisis, and I feel like something is supposed to happen now to close off this moment. She looks up at me like I'm supposed to do something.

Toon folds her arms and averts her eyes.

My hands reach out and find … my pockets. Not what they were initially searching for.

We both look away, up at the corrugated metal. We leave this place.

"What do you think about bubble wrap?" She asks me as we make our way out of the Quonset.

"Not as violent as cardboard, but satisfying, all the same."

"I'll have to try cardboard next time," she tells me with a smile.

15.

At the front door, Toon walks past Luanne, turning sideways to avoid touching her mother.

"Sorry Mom. I had a freak-out. I'm good now." Toon just walks away.

"No," I protest, but not too harshly, "you guys should hug at least. Your mother was ill with worry."

Toon just keeps walking into the house.

"We don't do that," Luanne says. "She's not big on hugging."

I realize that I haven't actually made any physical contact with Toon. Perhaps that's why she breaks teachers' arms; it's the only way she can touch someone. My brother Daniel is like this, too. It's like something is shut off inside him, and he's afraid of what might happen if the switch flips back on. I, too, may be able to relate.

"She's gone to a bunch of big-city therapists about it and there's no evidence of any type of traumatic cause. They tried hypnosis, even. She just doesn't like human contact, with the notable exception of punching people. She doesn't seem to have an issue with that, but she won't even give me a kiss goodnight."

Toon needed therapists. Plural.

I shake off the notion blooming in my mind like a mushroom cloud that Toon seeing therapists is damage that I caused.

I have no idea what to do next. "Whatever part of that is because of me, Luanne, you have know ... I'm sorry."

Luanne looks me in the eye. Really looks into me while "sorry" reverberates between us.

"I'll be right back." She goes inside the house.

I feel awkward about standing at her front door any longer, so I pace around a little and end up resting against the hood of her car.

After a couple of awkward moments, she comes out with a thick binder beneath her arm, with a spine possibly two inches wide. She plunks it down on the hood of her car. There's masking tape on the cover of the binder.

"Petunia—Photo Album" it says. A shot of pure adrenaline sprays all over my insides and my senses ramp up to eleven.

With misty eyes, Luanne takes the binder's top cover with her fingers. She can't look up at me, whether it's out of anger or shame or some kind of emotion I don't identify with all that well.

"Here's what you missed," she says. I hold my mouth with my hand as she opens the cover. Polaroid after Polaroid encased in mylar pages, four per page, page after page. The white bottoms of each Polaroid have dates and captions scrawled on them. Luanne takes me through the life of my daughter.

It starts with her birth, at Brandon General Hospital, February 6, 2004. Luanne looks like she went through some rough labour, and did it alone. She was the one holding the camera.

"You invented the selfie," I tell her.

"I refused the epidural and thought of you," Luanne says with a wry grin. "Eighteen hours later, there she was."

No Escape from Greatness

Toon was a beautiful, pudgy little baby with the roundest cheeks you have ever seen. She doubled in weight before she was three months old. She learned to walk at eleven months. Her first word was "mama." Luanne held her all the time.

Toon had several ridiculous onesies with Yorkshire Terriers on them. Thankfully, Luanne was never one to trifle with princesses from magic kingdoms, so there weren't a lot of those cartoon characters in the photos. As Toon became a toddler, there was a brief Hannah Montana phase, apparently. And then a lot of skulls and zombies. Suddenly the photos don't include Luanne anymore. Just Toon, riding a tricycle, playing Timbits soccer, opening Christmas presents that were never from me, dressed up in a Dalmatian costume crafted from white long underwear and black fabric circles. Toon's nose was adorned with black makeup.

The caption reads: "Grade 1 Musical."

"I missed a lot of recitals," I tell Luanne.

"I didn't exactly send you an invite," she says as she turns the page.

"There was never another man?" I ask her.

She can't speak. Her face curdles a little. "There's only ever been you," she says, and the dam breaks. She melts into a cry that hits bumps and descends like a boulder rolling down a granite mountain. And I wish I was at the bottom of that mountain. Perhaps a part of me is down there, beneath Luanne's torment, getting crushed by the boulders.

"Uh, please don't do that," I tell Luanne. "It's okay now."

The cry becomes a softer blubber.

"There ... there ..." I stammer, and awkwardly place my palm on her shoulder, robotically patting it, wishing she could apply an oil can to my heart so I could truly be there for her.

Luanne touches my hand and smiles through her tears. She looks down at me with a wet sniff, her ice-blue eyes shimmering with the glaze of warm teardrops. I find myself smiling back.

"Thank you," she whispers.

I realize that my eyes have been locked on hers for too long, and I force them to search for something else to look at, and they find her lips, and her eyes find my lips, and before I can stop it, or scream out, or hide my lips inside my own mouth, we kiss. It is a warm, gentle brushing of middle-aged lips, tender but weathered, knowledgeable and unwise, not too sweet and not too bitter, familiar and novel, gorgeous and treacherous. I am awash in tingles. Her fingers reach up and slide through my hair, as they did all those years ago, before life happened and I knew what I wanted. Suddenly we aren't terrible to each other anymore.

Then Luanne breaks from the kiss and covers her mouth. Shock registers on her face and her eyes beam at me.

"That was you!" I bellow.

She snatches up the photo album and stumbles backward to her house, shaking her head. Then she turns around and sprints for the door in a panic. The moment is over and we're back to the war.

"It wasn't *that* bad," I tell the door after she slams it.

I turn toward the trailer, knowing we have to put the swords and shields back on again. There's a light on in the trailer. I presume the traitorous Zac has dared to return. I rub my lips and realize Luanne's lipstick has reddened them; if Zac sees it I will have a lot of explaining to do.

I pull my shirt up to my mouth and scrub. Out, out, damned spot.

When I try the door to the trailer, it's locked. I call for Zac—no answer.

I know I didn't leave lights on. The sun was so overbearing there would have been no need. I fish around for keys. Damn it.

I have no choice but to knock on Luanne's door again.

"I locked my keys in the trailer and Zac is either not home or sound asleep." Luanne is less than impressed.

No Escape from Greatness

"I don't have a key," she says.

But what neither of us realize is that Zac isn't home at all. What lurks in the trailer is a complete disaster. Here is a dramatic recollection of the events leading up to said disaster:

INT. FOUR WINDS TRUCK STOP DINER - MORNING

MISTY pushes the door of the diner so hard that the bells ring wrong. SHOELACE looks up from his copy of <u>The Christian Science Monitor.</u> BETH scurries in behind Misty.

          MISTY
What the hell. He's not here.

          BETH
Oh, that's okay.

          MISTY
No, it's not okay, he said he was here every morning and this was where we should meet him. Pegg stood us up. Son of a <u>bitch!</u>

          BETH
I'm sure it was a misunderstanding ...

          MISTY
Aw, honey. Don't be hurt.

> BETH
> I'm fine. Really.

> MISTY
> Sure it's devastating and you feel heartbroken, but this won't stop us. His word is his bond and my fist will be his gag!

JILL approaches with a tray of pancakes on her shoulder.

> MISTY
> Hi, Jill. Was Mr. Pegg here this morning?

> JILL
> Haven't seen him, Misty. Sorry.

> BETH
> Oh, that's ok.

> MISTY
> Let's wait here until that bastard does show his face.

> BETH
> Let's go home. He knows how to reach us if he needs to.

No Escape from Greatness

> MISTY
> Oh, he is going to pay for this.

Misty takes Beth by the hand and they exit.

EXT. FOUR WINDS TRUCK STOP DINER - DAY

ZAC strolls up to the diner door, proudly examining a U.S. PASSPORT. When he sees Beth and Misty, he punches the air and snaps his fingers.

> ZAC
> Oh! We didn't show up this morning. Right.

> MISTY
> Leaving the country? You'll need to leave this dimension to get away from me.

> BETH
> Misty, please.

> ZAC
> Whoa, whoa, we just got distracted and forgot about what we said. Nothing has changed, I promise.

Misty's eyes bulge out of her head.

MISTY
Oh, something's changed all right. Big time.

BETH
Sorry, Zac. Let's just go, Misty.

ZAC
Wait, why don't you go see Gabe right now? I'm sure he's at home.

MISTY
(snarling)
Where's home?

INT. TRAILER - DAY

MISTY sits on the loveseat, watching television with the sound turned up. BETH stands in the middle of the trailer and fidgets, unsure of what to do with herself.

MISTY
I can't believe they live in this dump.

BETH
Should we clean it?

MISTY
Are you kidding?

No Escape from Greatness

There's a knock at the door. Beth turns with a start. They both look over at the door.

>   BETH
>   Did you hear that? I told
>   you I heard a knock before.
>
>   MISTY
>   I'm sure it was nothing.

SFX: BOOM!

GABRIEL and LUANNE fall through the door, knocking Gabriel flat on his back. Luanne falls rights on top of Gabriel and something in his back cracks, causing Gabriel an immense amount of pain.

Beth and Misty are gobsmacked.

>   LUANNE
>   This isn't what it looks
>   like.
>
>   GABRIEL
>   (still prone)
>   Oh, hello.
>
>   MISTY
>   You stood us up.

Beth helps Luanne over and up.

GABRIEL
The diner! Right. Oops.

MISTY
Oops? What kind of junk production are you running, Pegg? You think I would allow Beth to get caught up in this circus?

GABRIEL
I think I broke my back.

MISTY
Do you remember what I said I would do to you if you hurt my wife, the person who I love most in this world?

GABRIEL
She's still L—

Luanne shoots a suspicious look to Gabriel from the loveseat.

GABRIEL (cont'd)
—the female lead. Nothing's changed.

MISTY
Beth quits.

BETH/GABRIEL
What?!

No Escape from Greatness

>MISTY
>She's out. She's not doing it. We're taking all this—

Misty showcases Beth with her hands, like Vanna White showcases a vowel.

>MISTY (cont'd)
>And we're getting the hell off your set. Come on, Babe.

They step over Gabriel, who lies on his back like a piteous paraplegic platypus, legs still slooped over the steps.

>LUANNE
>Did I hear what I think I heard?

>GABRIEL
>Does no one believe my spine may actually be severed?

>LUANNE
>You're not writing me into your little skits, are you? Gabriel can't speak.

>LUANNE
>That's it. Now you're done.

Luanne steps over him and toward the door. She turns for a parting shot:

> LUANNE
> I can't believe you tried to kiss me.
>
> GABRIEL
> Me?! Try?! There was no try.
>
> LUANNE
> You're black magic. You're like a Rasputin of sexiness.
>
> GABRIEL
> Thank you?
>
> LUANNE
> I'm getting rid of you before you can poison me completely.

She storms out, leaving Gabriel alone. Gabriel stares up at the ceiling for a beat.

> GABRIEL
> Hello? Can someone fetch me an ambulance? Or at least a chiropractor?

END OF SCENE

I drag myself inside like a slug, finally rolling onto my back and propping myself up against the loveseat that has served as my combination bed-slash-iron maiden for the past few days. The industrial carpet is abrasive and hard; it still smells of cigarette smoke from the days when people smoked inside talent trailers. It reminds me of when Luanne and I shared a smoke inside one of these trailers, on the set of *Shinny Shih Tzus,* after the time we spawned the creature that would become Toon.

What if this isn't just a trailer *like* the trailer my future-ex-wife seduced me inside? What if this is *the* trailer?

I need a stiff drink. I fall back into the memory of Luanne rapping on the door—maybe this very door right here that we have just fallen through—barging in on me in my drunken fog. I remember I slid a cup of Prairie Caribou over to her as she walked in, acting as though I wasn't surprised to see her in Hollywood, on my movie set, in my trailer.

She asked me where I got the blood. I lied, told her I was a star and it was a rider in my contract. The truth is that it was beef blood from the butcher, and I needed to ask ten butchers before I found one who would stoop low enough to sell it to me.

Luanne took a pull from the cup, quivered like it was Buckley's Mixture, and asked me how I was feeling.

I told her.

It's not like I was cheating on anyone. We were already married. After we did the deed on the hide-a-bed, which was exactly the same type of hide-a-bed that Zac has been sleeping on these past few nights, Luanne pulled out a pack of du Mauriers and lit one up. She took a quick pull and passed it to me, and I took it for three long drags, letting the Canadian tobacco smoke burn in my lungs and throb my temples. For a moment, we were a husband and wife sharing a post-coital cigarette and I could see all the lines in Luanne's face melt away. Her eyes closed a little.

This was forever. It hit me square in the forehead like an Apa Jack cyst.

Luanne was re-attaching herself, like a barnacle on my hull, like an eco-warrior trying to board me from her rainbow zodiac and force me to drop anchor before I could kill all the dolphins I was destined to kill. I couldn't allow that to happen.

"I can never see you again, Luanne," I told her calmly as I handed back the cigarette, which we had nearly smoked to the stub. "Please get your things, leave here, and never try to contact me again."

The lines in her face instantly came back. Her eyes widened and her face reddened. She flicked the cigarette, still lit, across the room and it landed ... beneath the fold-out table.

I get to my feet, clutching my aching lumbar spine, and search the carpet beneath the fold-out table. Sure enough, there's a cigarette burn in the industrial carpet, black and flat and oval and proclaiming Luanne's cringeworthy love for me.

This is the trailer.

16.

Zac arrives home a few minutes after my discovery. Vibrating with this new knowledge of the depths to which Luanne's love for me runs, I am busily writing scenes for Project G in longhand.

"For what it's worth, I'm sorry I lied to you about the documentary," he says, but I don't stop working. It's only partially because of Zac and how much I am enraged by him; it's also because if I don't keep hammering away at this, I may end up at a bar, and there's a bar not far from here that once served my favourite cocktail.

"You don't want to sleep on the hide-a-bed anymore," I utter, ready to disgust him with tales of what has taken place on there.

But Zac agrees before I can explain. "No problem. It was wrong of me to call dibs in the first place."

I look up suspiciously. He's being too nice.

"Look, Uncle Gabe. Maybe I started off not taking this whole trip to Greatness all that seriously. But I changed my mind. I want to help you, for real."

"For real. As real as the documentary you were recording?"

"I'm serious. I want to be the director of photography, and help you make the best movie ever, just like you planned."

I continue to squint for a few seconds. "Is this about the passport? Whose house did we break into, anyway?"

Zac strikes a sheepish pose. He opens the minifridge, looking for a drink, but there's nothing. He looks in the fridge anyway. "This is about Jill. And this is about you not calling my Dad, okay? Please? I mean, when he finds out about my voluntary withdrawal, well, he's probably gonna make me sweep the floors in his office until I'm your age."

Zac looks me dead in the eye, with those damn puppy dog nephew eyes.

"Okay," I tell him. "You seem contrite enough."

"If contrite means I feel bad, I do. I know they're gonna find out eventually, but let's not make any rash decisions just because of a dumb prank. I'll tell them myself, all right? Maybe after Christmas."

"You know, just because you're a dropout doesn't mean you can't pick up a book and add to your vocabulary. If it worked for me, it can work for you. So yes, contrite means you honestly feel like crap, and feeling honestly crappy makes me less furious, so you can stop worrying."

"You're not going to tell?"

"I will not say a word to Daniel," I lie.

Zac smiles, almost in disbelief. "You know, Uncle G, you're a decent guy, deep down."

"It has been an eventful day, and my back is nearly broken. I am going pull out the hide-a-bed and I am going to sleep."

I hobble my way to my new sleeping quarters, clutching my poor subluxated discs. Zac stands there, gawking. "Can you find something to do that's quiet, or something?"

"Sure. I'll destroy all the video."

No Escape from Greatness

I lie down on the hide-a-bed and try not to think of the unspeakable acts that have taken place on it. One of the bedsprings presses into my back like an angry masseur's fingers, deep and direct in precisely the wrong spot. I stare up at the fibrous ceiling and try to calm my mind.

Zac sucks his teeth. He clicks buttons on his equipment. Clicks and clacks. In the act of attempting to be quiet, Zac seems louder than ever. Finally, he decides to lumber across the tiny trailer and sit on the creaky loveseat. Zac may as well be a hippopotamus on a rusty trampoline.

"Do you mind?" I hiss after a moment.

"Sorry," he says, and tries even harder to be silent, which makes him sound even more obnoxious, if that is possible.

"Zac, you have taken the principle of slowly unwrapping your candy in the movie theatre to a whole new level."

"I don't know what to do with myself."

With a pained sigh, I accept defeat and tell him, "Let's go scout locations." We hop in the car, and since I'm feeling magnanimous and also dog tired, I suggest to Zac that he drive. He nearly mauls me with appreciation.

We sit down and I catch a glimpse of myself in the passenger side mirror. I look happy. Tired, but happy. Some of Zac's mindless canine glee must have sunk in.

"Where to, Unc?"

"Let's start at Roscoe Apartments," I tell him. He puts the car in drive and I'm reminded of why I insist on driving in the first place; Zac is the worst driver I have ever encountered in all my years on this earth. Jerky on the brakes, timid on the gas, nervous and indecisive. This is what happens when you forego drivers' ed and hang out in your buddies' garage after school.

After twenty minutes, we finish the two-minute drive to Roscoe Apartments, a motel-style complex just north and west of 7th Avenue, across from Centennial Park. The four playground implements in the park look like they celebrated the centennial the park was named after—back in 1974—and no one uses the greenspace.

There's a vacancy sign in the window of the Patricks' old apartment.

I'm not entirely sure what drew me here, but the Patricks were a family who lived by the park. They happened to be little people. Sometimes I would sit on the swing set and swing alone for hours, lost in thought, and there was nothing else to look at but the Patricks. I didn't look at them because of their stature. They were an oddity to me because they were so happy. They gardened together. They played lawn darts. They smiled and laughed and hugged a lot.

I wished, on more than one occasion, to be them.

I haven't written everything yet, but I know several of the locations that will absolutely have to be in Project G. I direct Zac to Jimmy's house.

Jimmy is there, already drunk. He stumbles out to welcome us. His house is the nicest house in Greatness (at least until Gopher Trails is complete), a fieldstone house that sprawls like an old boarding school. Rumour has it that Irish masons built it as a temple, but the Welsh Clan somehow grafted the deed to the house from the Templars themselves. If the rumour was true, it would surprise no one who had ever met a Welsh of Greatness.

"Sunshine," Jimmy says as he stumbles from the wraparound porch, "come have a drink with your ollld old man."

"I don't drink anymore, Jimmy," I remind him, and remind myself. I open the white cast iron gate that has been set into a fieldstone fence, which borders the two-acre property.

Jimmy looks over at Zac and points at him, the shaking finger almost accusatory in its drunken pointedness. "How about you, kid. Let's have a drink and figure out if we're related." Jimmy puts an arm around Zac, who huddles fearfully. "I figure it'll take us three to find out. I call it the 'under-the-table' test."

"We're just scouting locations, Jimmy."

"You need to make the movie here? Why?" He's dragging Zac into the house to drink. I need to act fast or we're stuck here for a while.

"Why? Because I met Luanne here, that's why."

Jimmy stops cold. Zac slides out from under the old man's arm.

"I mean, this will be the place where the two main characters, the protagonist and antagonist, will have met for the first time. It's a crucial battleground, dramatically speaking."

The wheels turn in Jimmy's mind. I expect an outburst of some kind from him.

"Sure!" he blurts out. "Come over and shoot your movie. Have a drink."

"I don't drink."

"Drink? Don't mind if I do." And with that, Jimmy limps back into the house.

Zac passes me on the way back to the car. "Did you want interiors here? Because I'm not interested in scouting that right now."

"Well, yes, there's a bedroom I wanted. You're not missing a lot, I suppose. Four walls painted white with some Shaun Cassidy posters on it."

"We don't just want a bunch of white rooms, Uncle G. Give me something interesting here. Otherwise we could just dress a set with white walls and shoot everything there. Snore-a-palooza."

Zac is goading me for an interesting location. It is as though the Fates themselves are guiding me toward an inevitable rendezvous with the den of iniquity that began my descent into damnation. Damnation, what W.H. Auden called "the terminal point of addiction." It's becoming harder to fight. It's a part of the story ... circumstance pulls me there like gravity pulls water through an eavestrough, over the sidewalk and onto the road, through the grate and into the sewer. I am the water, circumstance is the gravity, and The Clayton Marvin is my sewer.

"Okay," I say in surrender to Zac. "Okay. I'll give you interesting."

17.

We drive up to the Highway Robbery and turn into a small parking area, the other end of which empties into a dirt driveway. Of course, Zac runs over the curb and nearly spins us right into the grocery store itself, because the dirt road is so hard to see. Originally, it was a utility road that got you to a radio tower, but over the years it had simply become Clayton Marvin Road. The radio tower used to run a massive air raid siren at noon every day, and the proprietor of The Clayton Marvin, Czech Willie, would open his doors immediately after the deafening siren. I'd be deaf when I walked in. I always wondered if he was trying to hurt me by waiting to unlock the doors.

"Here is good, park here," I tell Zac as we approach the chocolate brown box. It's a hundred metres from the Trans-Canada Highway, but hidden behind other buildings and nearly impossible for non-Greatnessites to spot. That made The Clayton Marvin a local hidden gem where tourists passing through on the highway would rarely stop in, despite the restaurant and lounge being so close. Czech Willie, all five feet of him, made for one of the better drinking companions in town; he was a little less boisterous and a little more humorous than Jimmy Welsh. He sure could mix a cocktail, and then he'd pour himself one, too. I'm sure that didn't go over too well with Czech Willie's wife, who raised five kids at home. We all felt for her, but we didn't send Czech Willie home a single time, not even Christmas Eve.

"What is this place?" Zac says.

"The Clayton Marvin Restaurant and Lounge."

Gravel dust coats the building and years of neglect have faded the brown paint, but here it is, the same as ever. I wonder if Czech Willie is still inside, pickled in some kind of sarcophagus or haunting the place like a ghost. A rabble of butterflies rushes up into my stomach, and then a colony of carnivorous bats rushes out of its cave and gobbles the rabble up, making everything inside me black.

"Aaand why are we here?" Zac says.

"This is where George drinks his first Prairie Caribou."

"His first what?"

"It was a local specialty. My poison of choice."

Zac leans back into his seat and he considers what that means. It finally dawns on him that we're at the scene of my earliest fall from grace.

"So are we going in?" Zac's eyes bulge with excitement.

The carnivorous bats bounce against my chest, looking for meat. My head begins to autonomously move to the left and right, and I am shaking my head "no" before I can even form a word.

Zac studies me for a moment, then studies the building.

"Is it even open?" he says to himself as he gets out of the car.

I watch him make his way to the back door, but I can't even motion for him to go around to the front entrance. He raps on the wooden door that's been painted chocolate brown. A woman

No Escape from Greatness

in kitchen whites, who looks like she has recently attempted to bread herself like a schnitzel, swings the door open and tells Zac to head around front for the lounge.

I wonder if the lounge is still black with a reddish tint. I wonder if all the dollar bills with greetings to Czech Willie are still stapled to the ceiling and walls in the lounge. I wonder if they put in VLTs. I wonder if they still have a jar of blood in the fridge beneath the wet bar. Then I realize that Czech Willie would have to be a hundred years old by now, and a life poorly lived surely would have done him in decades ago.

Zac rounds the building and comes back into the car.

"It's dingy in there," he says, and I know it's still The Clayton Marvin, birthplace of my addiction.

"Going to be tough to light, but I like the feel of it. It's seedy," Zac says as he backs up the Cavalier onto the dirt road. "It'll offset the white rooms we're inevitably going to have. I'd like to take another look at the Welsh Community Theatre, too," Zac tells me as he makes his way toward the Trans-Canada.

"Don't bother," I tell him. "Luanne won't let us shoot there."

Zac stops the car right where it is on Clayton Marvin Road. We wait for a moment, both thinking of where to go.

"You know what we should do? We should figure out who is going to be our female lead," I say.

"So you caught up with Beth and Misty, then."

"Yes, I met Beth and Misty, then," I sneer, "and I suppose you must have sent them to me so they could break into our home and lay in wait for me like a couple of crazed stalkers."

"I didn't know about that part, but yeah, I told them where to find you."

"Well you'll be happy to know that we don't have a Louise anymore."

"At least you escaped with your head intact," Zac says, to which I reply, "True dat, as they say. True dat."

"No one says that," Zac says dismissively. "So who's going to be not-Luanne?"

"How about your little girlfriend, there?"

"Jill doesn't act. She has different talents."

"That's disgusting."

"Not like that. I mean she's a singer."

"What, like pop music? Chantal Kreviazuk?"

"Nope. Opera."

"Opera? Ironical."

I say ironical because Greatness, this small town with big, big dreams that had long been dashed, once had an opera house that could seat five hundred people. Impressive for a town with a population of eight hundred, as it was in 1912. Of course, it was unsustainable, and so it became a movie theatre, which now plays second-run features and cartoon matinees on Saturdays, according to the marquee we passed on our travels through town.

Now Zac's girlfriend wants to sing opera, in Greatness of all places, and there was at one time an actual venue for that type of frivolity. Too bad for her that Greatness is the place where dreams go to die, and the Opera House dream was quickly and efficiently dashed before she was even germinated.

Zac reaches into his pocket and pulls out his wallet. He takes a debit card out and hands it to me.

"I've got ninety-five dollars left on this," he tells me. "The PIN is 0000. Let's buy some groceries, okay?"

We head to the Highway Robbery and get some essentials: corn chips, Pizza Pops (the one Manitoba business that would have been a great investment), two litres of white cream soda, and four green bananas to cover our fruit and vegetable needs for the week. I decide at the last moment that four bananas is woefully inefficient, and so I pick up a bottle of V8.

The aisles at the Highway Robbery are so narrow they can't

even allow carts to run through the store. Zac and I agree to save the rest of the money on the card for gas. Having missed the baskets at the front door, we carry all of our items in our arms, dumping them down on the old wooden counter before any cashier arrives.

"What happens when we run out of this stuff?" Zac asks me.

I have no idea what happens. We'll probably need to walk the streets of Greatness, begging for handouts like a couple of hobos.

"We'll make do," I tell him. "Don't worry."

No cashier has bothered to come greet us. Even as we straighten our groceries out so that they are as close together and baggable as possible, no one comes. I smile to myself as it occurs to me that perhaps Tom is not so excited to see me in his store, what with him setting the theatre on fire during his attempt to sabotage the auditions.

"Hallo?" I call out pleasantly. "Tom, I'm not angry, if that's what you're thinking."

"Down here," a voice says. It's not Tom's voice. Zac and I simultaneously peer over the counter. It's Tom's sidekick, Karl. He lies on his back, looking up at the ceiling. He doesn't look distressed or anything. He's just there.

"We're ready to check out," I tell him, but he shows no signs of moving. "Can we pay for our food please?"

Karl just blinks.

"What's the trouble?" Zac says.

"Well, I was standing at cash, like I do every Tuesday, Thursday, and Saturday from noon until eight, and every Friday from eleven to seven, except for the times when I'm not standing at cash because I'm dealing with inventory in the back, and it occurred to me that the fire we caused with our juggling act was quite traumatic and brought a number of issues to the forefront of my consciousness; most notably, I began to realize that

I had suffered from selective mutism for eleven years and how debilitating that has been for me. I want relationships. I want to be happy. Who doesn't want to be happy? But how could I create a meaningful bond with another living soul if I had this humungous psychological barrier to overcome? It was in that moment, about half an hour ago, that I realized how much I needed to change, and change for the better, and try to become the human being I always wanted to be—not like a movie version of a person, but like the best version of me that I could possibly be—and I was running out of time. I'm almost forty, for fuck sake! Oh goodness, I'm sorry, I shouldn't curse; that is completely unprofessional. I was thinking about my boss, Tom, and his wife, Carol, and how they are so in love and how they care for me despite my pathology, and then I realized they had never heard me talk and it hit me: what if they hated the talking version of me? Because they don't know me like this. They just know silent Karl, kind enough, but clumsy and idiotic. My whole world was going to change, and I need stability in my life. I have problems trusting as it is, so if the world isn't the world that I trust to be there every day, what is going to happen to me? And then the atmosphere felt really super heavy and I decided to lie down for a spell. Now I feel like I can't get up."

Zac and I can't find anything to do except look at each other, as though the mutism has somehow spread to us.

"Do you want us to call you a doctor?" Zac says.

"I have a doctor in Brandon. Holy sh—, holy smackers," he corrects himself, "she is going to be pretty happy that I'm talking. Call Brandon General and ask for Dr. Ross. She'll drive here to come see me, I'm sure of it."

Zac pulls out his phone. "I'll figure out how to reach her," Zac says to me as he heads for the exit. "You keep talking. It's a breakthrough, Gabe." Zac smiles slyly at me. Jerk.

"It is a breakthrough, Port-O-Potty Guy," Karl says, which

instantly makes me convulse, "and I have you to thank. If we hadn't done our terrible juggling act and nearly killed everyone in the Welsh Community Theatre, none of this would have been possible, because the stress was like the extra two degrees that got me to the boiling point. And now, here I am, talking away, and I have so much to say, but I can't seem to get up to my feet and walk the earth anymore. Everything is too heavy, so I can't get up. You ever feel like you have too much to say for one lifetime, Port-O-Potty Guy?"

Realizing he's going to prattle on for as long as I let him, I interrupt. "Karl, is it? Karl, it's great that you've had this breakthrough, but I have a dilemma. You see, I'm quite famished and I need a cashier to ring us through so I can eat these groceries and gain the food energy I require to continue writing the film we're going to shoot here in Greatness. You know, maybe you could have a speaking role ... anyway, is Tom here? I need to go."

Zac comes back inside. "She's on her way."

"Wonderful news, isn't it, Karl? Can you get Tom?"

"Tom's not here," Karl says from the floor behind the cash counter. "I'd love it if you could stay with me until Dr. Ross arrives. Interacting with people using verbal communication seems to be making the atmosphere feel a whole lot more manageable. And a lot less heavy. I can breathe. I can't really get up, but I can breathe, enough to keep talking, and the talking feels wonderful and frightening at the same time, like flying a crop duster. You ever fly a crop duster? It's just like this. Anyway can you stay?"

"Yeah, we can stay," Zac says. My forehead begins to pulse and I rub my temples in frustration.

"But I am famished, Zac, and Brandon is an hour away."

"Actually, her receptionist said she was in the middle of appointments, so she's going to be a couple of hours. Maybe three."

"Why don't I show you how to scan your own stuff, then you can pay for it, and then it's okay to eat," says the floor.

"No," I say.

Karl is silent for a split second. "Well, leave the wrapper and we'll figure something out."

Zac unpeels a banana. We're in it for the long haul.

18.

For the next three hours, as the don't-give-a-shit sun abandons Greatness, we stand there listening to the ramblings of a man who hasn't spoken in over a decade. I stare at the door of the Highway Robbery, trying to will another soul to enter the store and rescue us. Instead, I hear about Karl's thoughts on the last eleven seasons of the Winnipeg Blue Bombers and the elite performance of the Winnipeg Goldeyes (is that lacrosse? Sportfishing?). I'm treated to Karl's hour-long prostrate treatise on the last eleven seasons of *Coronation Street*. Finally, in the third hour, Karl seems to run low on energy. There's more space between his words. He blinks more slowly. There's a pause, then a massive yawn, and Karl utters one phrase and lets it float into the ether like a black balloon:

"I'm so scared of spending the rest of my life all alone."

It floats there, daring us to reach for it. I take a step back from the counter I was slouched against. Zac looks to me for a response.

"Say something," Zac says.

"I'm rubber and you're glue, whatever you say bounces off me and sticks to you," I whisper to Zac, "you say something."

"I can hear you guys," Karl says.

"We're all scared of being alone," Zac says, polishing the cash counter with the palm of his hand. "Hopefully when we go, we get to say we loved and we were loved. Right Uncle G?"

I don't think of life in these saccharine, clichéd terms. Life is pain and then you die. That's why we enjoy watching the drama play out on the screen or on stage; we want to feel what they're feeling, the fictitious characters designed to go through hell. We want to escape what we are mired in. It's a kind of schadenfreude, a joy of watching other people suffer. Romantic love is only interesting because those who desire it are crushed by its absence. Audiences eat that up.

"Yes, Zac," I say. "What meaning has life if it is not shared?"

"Who said that?" Karl asks.

"I did," I say. And I guess that is true.

Finally, a middle-aged woman wearing a blue blazer walks through the door. She scans around, looking for someone—obviously she's the shrink. We're free.

"He's behind the counter and he's talking. All the best," I tell her.

"Hey, you're—"

"Gabriel Pegg," I interject, before she can call me what I know she's about to call me.

"I read about you in the paper," she says.

I had no idea I had made the headlines up here. Maybe I'm bigger in Canada than I thought.

And then Dr. Ross, Karl's psychologist from Brandon, Manitoba, hands me her business card. I don't believe it to be a flirtatious passing of the card. It's not a solicitous one; Dr. Ross seems … charitable.

No Escape from Greatness

"We can set up something if you feel you need to talk. We're all big fans and we can help."

Exactly what was in the newspaper about me?

As we slip out of the store and finally make our way back home, I badger Zac with that very question until he finally tells me: a few weeks ago, in the *Winnipeg Free Press,* which everyone in this province apparently reads from cover to cover, a half-page column ran in the entertainment section that read something like this:

"PORT-O-POTTY GUY"
FREE FROM CONFINEMENT
Manitoba-born Pegg flushes life away
with booze; free from celebrity alimony

WINNIPEG – Lawyers for former Manitoban Gabriel Pegg had his temporary injunction removed today, enabling him to enter Canada without fear of arrest for unpaid child support and alimony payments.

"Gabriel is pleased with this decision and is excited to move on with his life," said his media spokesperson, entertainment lawyer Erin Ziprick.

"This ruling is fair to all parties involved, and we hope to welcome Gabriel back to showbiz very soon, as soon as he deals with his mental health issues," Ziprick said.

The oddball Erratic Automatic comedy troupe member, best known for the recurring character who lives his life confined inside a blue portable commode, is cited as the driving creative force behind the Canadian comedy troupe, who struck it big on American cable TV in the mid-'90s.

Pegg has reportedly fallen on hard times in recent

years, having been arrested twice for drunk and disorderly conduct in Orange County, California—the first arrest for allegedly urinating a very long distance from a public urinal; the second for appearing at his hearing intoxicated.

Pegg declared bankruptcy in 2010 and a warrant was issued for his arrest after his failure to keep up with a staggering $30,000 in monthly divorce-related bills.

Tuesday's Manitoba Court of Queen's Bench ruling cited Pegg's infirm mental state, substance abuse issues and remote likelihood of future financial solvency as reason enough to allow Pegg to cross the border.

Shane Wilson, the most well-known member of Erratic Automatic, said the court ruling could herald a long-awaited reunion tour for the troupe.

"It's possible," Wilson said. "I haven't talked to the guys about it, but last time I checked they all still needed to eat. All the old hatchets have been buried for so long they're probably oil by now. So I think it would be fun."

"Mental health issues?" Thanks, Erin. That would explain Dr. Ross's offer.

Zac puts the groceries we haven't already eaten in the fridge (Karl gave them to us for free as a thank you), and I slip out of my clothes and sprawl out on the hide-a-bed mattress, with its uneven coils and dubious history.

What a day. I let the air slide out of my lungs. Yes, I smile to myself a little. I accomplished a lot. Tomorrow, Jimmy and Zac will get me the equipment I need to shoot a movie. I will pick up Toon from school and we'll visit, which fills me with an exciting warmth. I will chat with Luanne, who quite obviously still cares about me, with whom I shared a kiss today. I touch my lips, remembering what happened.

"Hey, Uncle G?" Zac says, leaning against the doorway to the sitting-area-cum-bedroom. "Did you mean what you said to Karl?"

"What did I say to him?"

"He said he was scared to die alone and you said life was meaningless if it isn't shared. So who are you sharing your life with?"

"Oh, right," I say and roll over in bed, glorious bed. "No, I didn't mean it at all. It's okay to not have someone. Especially when they're trying to sleep."

Zac pauses for a moment. I can feel his disappointment in my answer. "You know," he says, "I think it's pretty cool that you're changing peoples' lives around here already."

"This hide-a-bed is going to change my life, Zac," I tell him. "See you in the morning."

"Good night," he says. I smile to myself as Zac finds a way to sleep in the god-awful loveseat. I smile in my sleep, and my cheeks hurt in the morning from sleep-smiling.

19.

I rub my face and try to smooth out the muscles, then strap on a pair of boxers and trudge to the kitchenette. Zac is long gone, but the sun is here, an autumnal sun that shines without scalding. Perfect natural light for filming.

I microwave a breakfast biscuit sandwich and eat it with a cup of coffee, which I make into a French press by jerry-rigging three paper coffee filters, a soup ladle and a jar. It works almost perfectly and my coffee is slightly better than drinkable, which is about one thousand percent better than any cup of sludge I've had in Greatness to date. The breakfast biscuit sandwich is loaded with sodium and grease and the meat could be from any animal at all, but it's delectable all the same.

I pore over my draft of the screenplay. The night fertilized my mind and I'm loaded like an automatic rifle, ready to strafe ideas indiscriminately and kill this script in time for the filming. Ordinarily, a production problem like having your female lead quit just prior to shooting would block me completely. But today I am on a roll. Today nothing can stop the words from falling out. I erect scene after scene like a downtown skyline, and soon, the cityscape is complete. I have a first draft. A first draft! It's not even noon! Here's how the first draft ends:

EXT. GRAVEYARD — DAY

GEORGE stands at his mother's gravestone, flower still in his lapel.

> GEORGE
> I did it, Mother. They love what I created. Louise has lost. I'll never be back here.

George touches the gravestone gently.

A black LIMOUSINE pulls up on the road in the BG. The driver gets out – it's ZANE. Zane wears a black driver's hat.

He circles the car and opens the door for George.

> GEORGE
> Goodbye, Greatness. Hello, magnificence.

George bounds for the limousine.

FADE TO BLACK.

No Escape from Greatness

Fade to black! It's a first draft, and subject to rewrite after rewrite, but the first draft is complete.

Jimmy and Zac rumble up the driveway at noon on the dot. I greet them outside as soon as I hear the gravel crackle beneath Jimmy's whitewall tires.

"That was quick," I say as Zac stumbles out of the passenger side. Jimmy rolls down his Cadillac power window and leans his head out.

"Jimmy woke me up at five in the morning," Zac says, traumatized. Jimmy just smiles when he hears it.

"Kids these days are giant pussies," Jimmy says, then barks "Get the stuff" to Zac and Zac obeys, wheeling around to the trunk of the Caddy and lifting it up. I scuffle back to see what's there.

It's all there.

Brand-new MacBook. Proper camera equipment in unscuffed canvas bags. An 8-track sound recorder. Scaffolding and lights. A tackle box that contains makeup. A small video monitor. A director's folding chair, with a green canvas back that says Director. Jimmy even got me a bullhorn. No baristas, though. Just a Keurig with boxes serving coffee and espresso.

"Holy shitsauce, right?" Zac whispers to me behind the trunk.

"This will suffice," I say. We lay everything out on the gravel and Zac begins to walk the equipment into our trailer.

Jimmy grunts as he swings his legs out of the car and stands up straight.

"I said I would do what it takes for you stay," Jimmy says. "Here."

Jimmy sticks his hand into his pocket and pulls out a cheque. He hands it to me with his shaky hand. I'm so flabbergasted by this gesture that I robotically stick my hand out to accept the piece of paper, not realizing what it is.

It's a cheque for forty thousand dollars.

I asked for twenty-five; he's giving me forty so that I will stay.

"You can keep the change," he says to me with a smile, like we're sharing a secret. He knows I don't need a third of this money. And I can't rightly put lawyers on retainer to escape. Not right now. Not if I want to live.

I hand the cheque back to him. "Jimmy," I say, but he blocks my move and shoves my hand back into my gut.

"Nope," he says. "This is an investment. I'm not just producing a movie here, Sunshine."

"No?"

"No. I'm investing in all of us. You, me, that kid. Our girls. A family that's together. This here is one of the last big plays I got."

"That's setting the bar quite high. Movie shoots tend to tear families apart, Jimmy, not bring them closer."

Jimmy's eyes get glassy and the corners turn red.

"I don't have a plan B. If I'm gonna get those girls to love me, this is all I got. And before you say it, asking me to quit drinking is like asking a snake to stop having scales. I'm too old to turn that leaf. So this is it."

I look at the cheque and the number that's scrawled on it, and I know that I could spend four hundred thousand dollars in Hollywood and produce something that I could produce for forty thousand here. I won't have a crew, or union actors, or post-production giving me dailies to screen. But I also won't have a studio telling me to make dreck, or unions forcing me to pay triple-overtime or hire their preferred contractors.

"Well," Jimmy says, looking at his watch, "it's rye thirty." And with that, he hobbles back into his white Cadillac Coupe de Ville.

"Thanks, Jimmy," I say. All he does is raise his hand like he's letting the air wash over it, and he drives home to go get hammered.

No Escape from Greatness

Maybe, just maybe, this is all going to work out.

I run inside, where Zac is already setting up the equipment. I assist in the best way I can, which is to pull out the Keurig and make us two cups of Americano. One sip of espresso and Greatness becomes Strawberry Fields; I am in the sky with diamonds. I am laughing with Zac and having actual fun and beginning to salivate at the cinematic prospects before us. We look at the equipment with bulbous eyes, like kings watching the silver platters arrive at our table, wetting our chops as the vassals lift the lids.

"We are really going to do this," Zac says.

"I know."

We sip our Americanos in unison and survey our feast.

"Jimmy gave me a cheque for forty thousand dollars," I say softly to Zac. He looks over at me, slowly, and I sip my coffee again, trying not to notice.

"What are you gonna do with it?"

"I could get us out of here."

"Seems wrong."

"We could rent a house."

"Why? This is free."

"You want to pay back your father?"

Zac laughs. I join in. After we reach a point in time where any further laughter would be unfair to hapless Daniel (which is quite a length of time), we stop, and Zac says, "We could get some pros to come in from Winnipeg. Maybe a sound guy and lighting guy. Maybe a real actor."

"No," I say. "No union people, because the price will be too high. Let's go with all locals, cast and crew."

He nods in agreement. "All these new toys—let's go play."

"That sounds like a fabulous idea. Time to make the magic happen."

"Wait—who's gonna be Louise?"

I had forgotten about that conundrum.

"I have two scenes with George and people who aren't Louise, which we could shoot right away. There's one in the diner and one at The Clayton Marvin. Can we get a twenty on our George?"

"No problem." Zac pulls out a brand-new smartphone, courtesy of our executive producer, and dials a number.

Someone answers the phone and Zac starts to speak in very hushed tones. He turns away from me as he speaks, then slides the phone back into his pocket with a big shit-eating grin on his face.

"That was Jill, wasn't it?"

"She says hello. Apparently, Shoelace works for some kind of online ecommerce thing and doesn't have an office or shop. He could be anywhere."

"Why don't we check his house?"

A nervous look comes over Zac.

"Jill says he likes to work at the log cabin. Does that make sense?"

"Yes, it does."

The log cabin is just outside of town. A labour of love for the farmer who built it over thirty years, the log cabin was completed in 1986, and the farmer died exactly one month to the day of its completion, as though his purpose had been fulfilled. The farmer had bequeathed the shack to the Town of Greatness, who decided to do absolutely nothing with it. They didn't even put up a no-trespassing sign. No surprise that Shoelace would like to spend time there.

Might not be a bad location to shoot some scenes. We pack up the car and head out.

Sure enough, Shoelace is there. His tiny hybrid is parked outside. Shoelace opens the door for us before we get there. He doesn't look happy to see us. For whatever reason, his massive face appears to be covered in a brownish-green mud. His hair is slicked back, too. He looks like Martin Sheen rising out of the water in *Apocalypse Now*.

"Do you have a script for me?" he says. His low voice reverberates at a frequency that buzzes my hipbones.

I show him the script, hand-written in the spiral-bound scribbler, with pages coming loose and threads of former pages jutting and dangling out like a scarecrow's wrist.

"You don't have Final Draft? That's industry standard."

"We're working on it."

After a scowl at us, he reverberates a "come in" as he turns his back to us, all the time squinting at the handwritten words. "Your penmanship is deplorable," he says.

The inside of the log cabin smells like someone has been smoking something sweet in it. There's a bit of a haze in the air, too. I notice little bundles of dried green vegetation hanging everywhere, set in a boundary where the ceiling meets the wall. Is this some kind of grow op?

"Nice medicines," Zac says to Shoelace.

Shoelace looks up at him. "Thanks, but they aren't mine. I'm just a visitor. Some elders from Maple Lake set this place up as a kind of lodge. A healing lodge. A teaching lodge, too."

"But doesn't this belong to the Town of Greatness?"

Shoelace smiles wryly at me. "Are you suggesting that the town fathers should be angry with the First Nations for stealing their land and using their property?"

Fair enough. Shoelace flips the page and keeps reading my script. I begin to get nervous, as though he could derail the entire project with a single word of critique. Then I realize that I don't need his approval—if he doesn't want to do it, I'll just be George myself. All the same, I yearn for his approval.

We sit there in silence for a few minutes. I feel a cough percolating in my chest from the piquant, sweet smoke whisping through our respiratory systems. Zac and I look around at this log cabin teaching lodge, and then look at each other.

Out of nowhere, Shoelace slaps the manuscript shut and it startles us both. Shoelace says, "Tell me about George's need and want."

"George needs to escape from Oilton to be with his one true love."

"That's his want."

"That's his need, too."

"I disagree," Shoelace says. "I think his need should be to appreciate what's in front of him and stop pining for fantasies. In this draft, he behaves like a patsy to his own delusions of grandeur."

The nerve of this behemoth. "Well," I say as politely as I can, "that sounds like a fantastic thing to give a character in the screenplay that you write someday."

"I don't need to write screenplays," Shoelace says. "I don't need therapeutic make-believe to deal with some deep-seated longing for acceptance."

Zac can see my face turning red and my temples bulging as my jaw clenches, and he tries to raise his hands at me to signal "calm down."

Too late.

"Why do you hate me so much, Shoelace? Did I do something to offend you?"

He smiles at me. "Of course not," he says. "I just don't waste my time pandering to anyone, or euphemizing my thoughts and beliefs. You can't offend me, Pegg, because offending me would infer that I expect something from your behaviour."

"So that's why they call you Shoelace," I tell him. "Because you make people want to strangle themselves with a shoelace."

"No," Shoelace says, "my parents called me Shoelace because it was the first thing I ate."

No Escape from Greatness

"So what's your birth name?" Zac asks.

"Shoelace. My parents were lost people. Not very kind, but they were also in a lot of pain."

"How old were you?" I ask him.

"I don't know. Three? I don't know what they called me before that. My birth records only say Baby Boy Doe."

"They sound like terrible people," I offer. "Horrible."

"I don't see it that way," Shoelace says. He looks right into me, through me. "They went down a crooked path ... substances ... they had no business raising a child. Sadly, those are often the kind of people who are likely to have one."

"Jesus," Zac says. "Puts things in perspective."

"It's history. I got placed with a foster family when I was thirteen, and they adopted me, educated me and loved me, renamed me Henry and moved me all around the eastern seaboard."

"Henry," I say to him, happy I don't need to call him something so belittling. "A fine name."

"But when I became a man, I retook ownership of my given name. I am proud to be Shoelace, because that is who I am."

"Oh."

He looks right through me still. "I don't let history colour my future, Gabriel. Now why don't you give me time to read through the remainder of your ... attempt at drama."

Shoelace sits cross-legged in the middle of the lodge and reads the rest of Project G. I stare at him and wonder how this man came from where he came from and still ended up so ... actualized.

20.

"Not bad," Shoelace says as he closes the manuscript, and I feel like the pediatric surgeon has just informed me that the baby is going to survive.

"There's something here," he continues, "if we polish some things up."

"We were thinking of shooting a scene today," Zac says. "You know, get it up on its feet."

Shoelace ponders it for a moment. "I can do it in an hour," Shoelace says as he rises. "I need to wash all this off, then go to the cop shop and see if I can track down a cop to file a report."

"Okay," Zac says, "so let's meet at Centennial Park in an hour?"

"Wait," I interrupt, "what happened in Greatness that requires police interv—" But I figure it out before I finish.

"Break and enter," Shoelace confirms.

I quickly say "Oh, that's too bad, kids these days, see you later," and corral Zac to get out of here before Shoelace realizes

Zac is the felon and Shoelace's wife plans to cheat on him with my nephew.

We get outside and I box Zac's ear. "Holy shit, Zac," I whisper-shout. "Holy shit holy shit holy shit."

"Ow! Just be cool," he says to me and slips into the car.

I slam the door and continue to berate him, now in full throat. "Shoelace is her husband? Are you kidding me? If he finds out you broke into his house—"

"You're guilty too. You were my lookout."

"He's going to crush us in his bare hands like we are teeny tiny little teensy wee crushable things that crush easily in his angry meat fists! On top of that, he's going to quit *Descent into Greatness*."

"*Descent into Greatness?* Is that what we're calling it now?" Zac says with disapproval in his voice.

"Don't change the subject." I put the pedal to the metal and we speed back to town. "What are we going to do?"

"We're not going to do anything," Zac says. "Just calm yourself down and everything will be splendid."

"Everything *was* splendid, Zac. For a second I fooled myself into thinking life was lifting me up and the Fates were smiling. Turns out the Fates were just gassy. Everything is back to terrible."

To explain what happens next, I need to provide some background. When we first got together, Luanne was tough as nails and that was exactly what I needed. She pushed back at my mother in my defence; she spun Daniel in circles when he attempted to tell me what to do. Luanne made it very clear that she was in control, once we were together, and I gladly allowed that to happen, because I needed muscle.

When I had problems and couldn't handle them, she roared at them so loudly, the problems would often simply run away.

And I suppose that is why I knock on her door as soon as we get home.

No Escape from Greatness

She opens the door and says, "Nope."

"I need you to help me with the police," I say in my most earnest tone.

"Police? Where's Toon? Is she all right?"

Toon.

I forgot to pick up Toon.

It was part of my to-do list before bed last night, and I still forgot.

I am exactly as self-centred as people think I am.

"She's fine," I lie. "It's just that—"

Then Toon appears on the road, covered in brown road dirt, her backpack making her slouch. Clearly she has walked here from school, and Luanne's eyes flicker with rage. "You forgot. You forgot and then you lied."

"I got side-tracked. Come on, Luanne. Please. I helped you find Toon, and then when we found her, I got her to feel better. We're bonding, she and I. I'm doing some good here, I can feel it. If you help me, you can even blame me for what happened with the photo albums, because, you see, I've run into a small legal issue ..."

Luanne is abrupt and stern.

"Let me tell you what happens now with you and your legal issues. You're going to visit Toon, six days out of seven, one hour per day, precisely sixty minutes and not a second more. Good luck getting her to even say a word to you after pulling this today. And since you can't be trusted with transportation, I will drop her off at your new home, because as of tomorrow, you are out of the trailer. You will not talk to me. You will have Zac or your lawyer communicate with me, or else you will give Toon a written, signed note. You will not include me or my likeness in anything you do, ever, and until my lawyer approves a copy of your script, you will not have a permit to shoot anything, anywhere in town. If you don't comply to the letter, I'm going to make sure the police help themselves."

"Please. Please, Luanne."

"One last question: am I in your stupid movie?"

"No. I changed all the names."

"I am shutting you down."

Toon gets to the driveway and so I attempt to hush myself as I plead: "Luanne, I'm begging you, don't do this. If you have any feelings for me at all …"

"I don't have a single feeling for you except disgust, Gabriel." The way she says my name makes my throat feel like her fingers are wrapped around it. "I didn't kiss you. That was a scared little girl who did that."

"Funny. It felt like your lips."

And then we both realize that Toon has heard us. She knows we have kissed, her mother and me. Luanne and I watch as Toon's face begins to quiver and twitch and her eyes widen; then she stuffs any feelings she may have back into a jar. Toon's countenance becomes one of a Roman statue. I reach for Toon with an open hand, murmur, "I'm sorry, Toon," but she says "Don't touch me" robotically and slinks between us, into the house, and slams a door loud enough for us to hear it. Something metal crashes to the floor.

Luanne roars at me, like a lioness roars at a pack of zebras so she can have a good run before breakfast. It's not a metaphorical roar. It is an actual roar, full of bloodthirsty rage and murderous hatred. Birds flee in neighbouring municipalities. It echoes across the road and into the earth's core, vibrating the mantle enough to scare the gophers, who are always watching from inside their gopher holes.

"You could win ten Oscars, save the whales and find the cure for cancer, but there's nothing in you that anyone could ever love." Luanne slams the door.

Then she opens it again.

"The next time you see my face, you will go to jail. I want you out by morning."

She re-slams the door. I look down at my stomach, like I need to examine a knife wound.

Luanne opens the door again.

"I wish I had never even been to a single Firefighters Rodeo!" she exclaims, which hits me below the belt, more than anything else she could say or do.

EXT. GRANDSTANDS – DAY

GEORGE (19) and LOUISE (18) sit in the crowd, eating popcorn, waiting for the show to begin.

                LOUISE
        I hope this year is as good
        as last year.

                GEORGE
        How could it even compare?

They look into each others' eyes sweetly. Louise smiles at George. George smiles back.

They SMOOCH.

Something makes George startle.

                    GEORGE
          Hey!

George's index finger is now inside a CHINESE FINGER PRISON.

Louise's index finger is lodged inside the other end of the constricting paper cylinder.

                    LOUISE
          Got you.

George playfully tugs with his hand, trying to free himself, but Louise knows he can't get out.

                    LOUISE
          You're trapped.

More tugging. George really plays it up, as though he actually wants to be free of it. The popcorn spills all over the place.

                    GEORGE
          Yeargh!

                    LOUISE
          This is us, George. We move
          together now. Not just our
          index fingers.

George stops fighting.

No Escape from Greatness

> LOUISE
> Don't fight it.

> GEORGE
> I'm not.

> LOUISE
> Good.

She YANKS her arm back and they jostle even more now. The popcorn tub topples over. George and Louise clasp their other hands as they pull and push.

> GEORGE
> (struggling)
> I was wrong. This year is way better.

> LOUISE
> I hope we never find our way out of this thing.

> GEORGE
> But then how could you show the other firefighters your prowess with a hose?

Louise lovingly PUNCHES George.

END OF SCENE

I break the news to Zac that we have been evicted, but I can't even deliver the lines with false pathos. I feel numb inside, like

I'm floating above myself in some kind of near-death experience, a ghost watching its corporeal host for a few final moments.

Zac has some kind of reaction to the news, but it doesn't register with me. I'm far, far away, a thousand million miles from Greatness right now, barely even on this planet. I watch Zac leave the trailer, and then he turns to me and waves his arms around, and I follow him out of the trailer to the car.

Greatness passes through the window like a scrolling parallax movie background; not quite real, but enough to make my eyes believe that we're moving. After a second or an hour we reach Jimmy's house and he comes out to greet us. Jimmy stares at me through the window for a moment before I realize I have the ability to open the car door and get to my feet.

Jimmy and Zac say words to each other. Zac uses open, explaining hands. Jimmy finishes his glass of whiskey and tosses the glass onto his lawn in disgust. Jimmy folds his arms and shakes his head. He looks over at me with some kind of facial expression—is it disappointment? Defeat? Does Jimmy love me still?

"The truth is I'm old," Jimmy says and the words rattle around in my head. "Luanne calls the shots around here, it's true. If she wants to shut us down …"

And then Jimmy gets about ten years older in the blink of an eye, and he really begins to tremble and hunch over like a weakling.

My mouth fills with fire, like a dragon that can no longer suppress its fury.

"Whatever it takes!" I scream at him, and Zac gets between me and Jimmy. "That's what you said to me! Not just one little shopping trip where you hand out your walking-around money. All that talk about keeping us around was bullshit." My fury scorches him.

No Escape from Greatness

"Whatever it takes is what it will take, that's what I said, Sunshine, but …"

"No! I'm not your Sunshine, or your son, and I never was. You only gave a shit about yourself and now you're too weak to even keep the peace with your own daughter, let alone make amends for being a useless lush."

Zac pushes me up against the car and tries to calm me but my eyes are trained on Jimmy.

"You can stay with me," Jimmy offers.

Zac stops restraining me and turns to Jimmy.

"That would be great," Zac says, but in my mind, a deafening air raid siren sounds, reaching that awful high note. The siren doesn't even exist anymore, but the sound fills me up all the same. Open for business.

"Not a snowball's chance in Hades," I spit at Jimmy, and I march down the street, down 7th, past that blinking traffic light.

I pass by Roscoe Centennial Park as I continue my march. The air raid siren inside of me continues to bluster. At the park, not far from the farmhouse, Toon swings on the swing set by herself. She sees me walking down the street and our eyes meet. I smile at her and raise my hand a little, in a subtle, apologetic wave.

Toon drags her feet into the leaves and dirt to stop her pendulous motion, then hops off the swing. Her scowl never leaves her lips. She looks at me like I'm the cause of all her problems. Toon turns her back to me and faces the Roscoe Apartments. She walks away.

The air raid siren gets louder and won't abate. I have to snuff it. I march for another ten minutes and arrive at the front doors to my own personal sewer:

The Clayton Marvin.

21.

It's dark and dingy in The Clayton Marvin Restaurant and Lounge. The smell of roast beef and mirepoix is still soaked into the walls, along with a peppery hint of tobacco smoke that still hasn't released its grip on the royal burgundy carpets.

No one stands at the hostess podium, because it's mid-day and the only activity is in the lounge, off to the left. As I pass through the dining room, I glance over at the smorg table, which is very likely the same apparatus that fed me prime rib thirty years ago. Now there's a Chinese food buffet in steam trays.

The tables in the dining room used to have white tablecloths on them, but now they lay bare. The deep red glass candle jars have been replaced by fake LED candle devices. Chopsticks have replaced the silverware.

The white fluorescent lights from the kitchen spill into the dining room through oval windows in the swinging doors. It spoils any attempt at ambience anyone has ever made, ever.

I look into the lounge, as though looking into the maw of the great beast that had swallowed me all those years before.

The dollar bills are gone, no longer stapled and taped to the ceiling with signed messages to Czech Willie. There is a bank of three VLTs in the far corner where the cigarette machine and jukebox used to be. Otherwise, everything is exactly the same, from the smell of urinal puck to mask the vomit, all the way to the upholstered wet bar one might find in an eighties heavy metal band's rec room: black with diamond-shaped metal studs sewn into the centre of every leathery square.

I sit on one of the barstools and wait for the bartender to arrive. Part of me wishes for Czech Willie, despite the impossibility it. Sure enough, a small Asian man dressed like one of the Reservoir Dogs emerges from the men's room and walks behind the bar.

Part of me is sad that the Prairie Caribou is gone. Another part of me is quite relieved.

"What's your pleasure?" he says to me.

"A drink."

He gives me a quizzical look, perhaps checking to see if I'm being facetious.

"Narrow it down for me a little."

I order three fingers of his cheapest scotch and slap Zac's debit card on the table, which I hadn't had an opportunity to return since our debacle at the Highway Robbery.

"Tab," I tell him.

He takes the card, pours me a generous tumbler full of scotch, and pulls out an iPad to check his blasted email or some such.

"What happened to Czech Willie?" I say to him. He looks up from his tablet and chuckles at me.

"Dead. They call me China Joe because of that guy," China Joe says. "My family is from Laos and I was born in Elkhorn. Dicks."

No Escape from Greatness

I stare into the glass of scotch and ponder whether to sip or chug. Once it touches my lips, I am officially off the wagon. I will be like King Kong, free from his shackles, ready to lay waste to everything built around me.

"To Czech Willie," I say as I raise my glass.

I decide to sip, then change my mind and prepare to tilt the glass straight back. But in that moment of pause before the poison can reach my lips, Joe says, "Because you cared about him? Or because he made you Prairie Carries?"

I slam the scotch on the bar and slide the glass away from me.

"What the hell am I doing? I don't even like scotch."

Joe shakes his head a little and turns around, reaching for a minifridge—the same minifridge where Czech Willie kept the blood—and he opens the little door.

He turns back to me with a mason jar of elk blood, just like Czech Willie used to keep. The part of me that cried for restraint flees in terror as a tsunami roils inside my gut. We're going to drink of the Prairie Caribou, and we're going to remind ourselves what Hell really feels like. And a part of me could not be more excited.

The evil part.

Joe unscrews the lid on the jar and sniffs its crimson contents. He nods, approving of its freshness, and readies a pour into a shot glass. The deep red fills the two-ounce glass and Joe puts it into a highball tumbler.

He doesn't pour any for himself.

"I have work to do today," he says, then proceeds to mix one Prairie Caribou and one virgin Prairie Carrie. Joe includes everything the ages-old recipe calls for: a wine of a certain type, a tree-based gin of a certain type, a third alcohol of a completely different type, certain salts, seasonings and seeds. He tops it off with a dash of chokecherry juice. It fizzes a little and smells of brimstone, or what I imagine brimstone to smell like.

There's no trepidation. No compunctions or qualms. I don't hesitate. I don't offer a cheers. I pound it back with an open throat and it wages chemical warfare on my insides, just as I hoped it would. It burns, but tastes thick and primal, familiar and evil and like freshly bottled water from the River Styx. Then it finishes with a spicy piquant kick, like a burro hoofing you in the breadbasket.

It tastes like Greatness.

But it goes further. Further than any drink should go. Something is wrong. I am falling down some kind of rabbit hole. A Prairie Caribou is just a drink. I think I am losing my mind.

I'm not in the lounge at The Clayton Marvin anymore. Trees surround me and it's dark and dank. Something inside me knows that this is both a dream and also the true essence of the land. The spirit of Manitoba itself—I'm having some kind of vision. There's a gigantic elk standing in front of me.

The elk stands on its hind legs, eight feet up, its snout shooting steam as the lightning spasmodically backlights it, the giant animal's majestic belly exposed to me. A word, ancient and tribal, finds its way into my mind: *Manitou-Bah*. Breath of the Creator. That is the name of this fearsome beast.

"Pay attention, Gibbers," *Manitou-Bah* bellows. Its voice thunders through the trees and birds flee their perches.

"Sorry," I manage. *Gibbers*? No one has called me that since I was a boy—my friend Bruce from Maple Lake called me that.

The creature remains on its hind legs, gently swimming the air with her forepaws to maintain her balance. Her eye never unlocks from mine. I'm stultified.

"This is your day of reckoning, Gibbers. You have partaken of the Caribou for the last time, and now the spirits call you home."

In the pit of my stomach, right down to my deepest recesses, I know I am about to die. Plus the spirit just told me so. The

No Escape from Greatness

spirits call me home. It never occurred to me before why hard liquor is called spirits. Perhaps it is the essence of death in there. "I have so much to do," I plead with the spirit. "It's not the right time."

It takes a couple of steps away from me, then the spirit—a prairie caribou?—turns and snorts at me.

"What is there for you to do?"

"I need to get back to greatness. I mean, Greatness, with a capital G, because I haven't done anything meaningful with my life yet."

Steam spews from its snout. It remains on its hind legs, staring at me.

"Give others their wings so they can help you fly." Then it walks away, into the dark folds of the moonlit woods. I know Manitoba itself has just communed with me. I sit down on the dank, leafy ground, made uneven and uncomfortable by the web of tree roots crisscrossing everywhere, and I contemplate what *Manitou-Bah* has told me. The spirits are calling me home. *Home?*

I just sit there and wait for the Prairie Caribou to wear off so I can be clear-headed before dawn.

22.

It doesn't happen.
    Dawn arrives and I am still in this impossible vision quest forest. I can see frosty sun but I can't feel it at all as it glows red through the endless forest around me.
    I stumble through the forest, wobbly and feeble, trying to find a way out or a water source or someone to help me. I don't know how long I search for, but it feels like the better part of the day, and the sun manages to whisper behind my ear before descending again. The twilight sucks the colour out of everything. I search and stumble until I can no longer move, at which point I simply fall backwards and stare up at the canopy of oak and elm that imprisons me.
    I decide, almost casually, to let the spirits come and find me. Gabriel Pegg will die.
    I can't put all the puzzle pieces together. My irresponsible choices have finally caught up to me. How do I give people wings when those closest to me are filled with hard feelings, regrets, embarrassment, shame? Feelings I gave them. All because of some ego-driven sense of purpose.

My legacy is Port-O-Potty Guy and I will never escape it. They will say I didn't amount to much—just a guy who we laughed at back in the nineties. Left behind a family who's better off without him. A daughter he never knew. Never held her hand and showed her the world.

In the end, you can never escape Manitoba, Port-O-Potty Guy.

Take me home, spirits. I'm ready.

Then I feel a tickling sensation on the underside of my belly. At first I believe it to be my spleen twitching, but I catch the slightest movement in my peripheral vision and look down, over my nose. I see a gopher standing on my belly, looking back at me, doing its annoying little twitch-sniff that gophers do.

Then another gopher scampers up my right thigh and stands beside the first, staring up at me. Two more gophers appear to my right. Three to the left. I am surrounded by dozens of gophers, unafraid, twitch-sniffing and staring at me. A gopher's stare is twice as stultifying as any elk spirit.

Like thunder, a voice booms into my mind that sounds a bit like Shoelace's voice, or maybe a chorus of Shoelace voices in some kind of bass-heavy harmony, rumbling my eardrums and shaking the earth I'm sprawled out on in mortal surrender.

"We are the Ubermind," the voices say. Are these voices … the gophers? They sound like that deep fake voice reporters use to protect the identity of the victim they're interviewing. Except many voices. It doesn't sound very gopherish. "Yes, we are the Ubermind!" the voices say telepathically, it seems. "The Ubermind comes to deliver you home."

"I should have known," I cackle. "God damned gophers. You're the spirits come to take me away. Fine, show me the light and I'll head for it."

The gophers on my belly look at each other, as though

communicating silently. Can a gopher look incredulous? The one on the left does.

"No, idiot," the Ubermind says. "Like to your house? That home."

"You must dig to where the world needs you to dig and then, to be happy, you must learn to stop digging." Gopher Deepak Chopra. Splendid.

A thought strikes me and I ask the gophers: "But what if you want to hit oil? You can't just stop digging?"

"We're making a home, not digging for oil," the Ubermind says to me.

I nod, knowingly. Of course you are, collective consciousness. Of course you are.

I close my eyes for a split second as I nod, and when I reopen them, I'm blinded by neon kitchen lights.

I am in the kitchen of The Clayton Marvin Restaurant and Lounge. There's a man working some dough on a stainless steel prep counter, and he's got a big bulging cyst on his bald forehead.

"*Jak się masz*, Funny Guy," he says to me.

He's Apa Jack. I am hallucinating Apa Jack.

He's making perogies at The Clayton Marvin.

"It's kind of funny," he says cheerfully in his accent. "I'm really good at making perogies, so I don't need my greatest invention."

"Are you the devil?" I ask him.

He continues, unabated. "All of us, we all got some skill or other, Funny Guy. Sometimes what we make isn't for us, you know?

"I don't need the Apa Jack PerogyMatic, but I need all the things that the Apa Jack PerogyMatic has brought me. People … a little bit of money …"

"Money?! I invested in you."

"Don't know nothing bout that," he says, and his accent

seems to get a bit thicker. "I'm a hallucination, stupid. A vision. Anyway, maybe you don't need your PerogyMatic, but you need what it brings you. Think about that. *Dziękuje.*"

And then my hallucinations end, and cold reality snaps back into view, and Luanne's voice echoes in the kitchen behind me. I turn around and she is there, with Zac, and the cook who actually works in this kitchen whom I have terrified, and Joe from Elkhorn who looks sad for me.

I see Luanne's face again and remember her promise. I'm going to jail.

But Luanne says, "Thank God." There's something different in her eyes, but I'm too blasted to know what it is and too far gone to care. Returning home from these nightmares, I shudder as though emerging from beneath the frozen winter ice of Maple Lake.

I look back to see if Apa Jack is still there, and there's not even so much as a crumb of dough on the countertop. Suddenly I am aware of myself again, but parts of me have died forever, and I realize that I have no idea whether two hours or two weeks have passed. Did I miss my second straight mandatory visit? Am I about to go to jail?

Guilt and shame well up inside me. Everything feels different, tinged with a sad electricity, drained of colour and sour to the taste.

Luanne touches her own face and moves in toward me.

"Jimmy died," Luanne tells me, and then she melts into my chest and cries.

23.

"He just went to sleep and never woke up," she says. All I can think of is how he promised me to do whatever it takes to make me stay, and how this would greatly reduce his odds of keeping this vow. A final letdown. The fact that I had bailed on him first seems less important than his abandoning me before I could help him bring his family together.

I push, far into an untended annex of my mind, any thought of how Jimmy Welsh was like a father to me. Everyone fucking leaves. I'm not the only one who does it.

"I heard him talking in his sleep, that night—the night he ..." Zac says, red-eyed and tired-looking himself. "He kept on calling your name, Uncle G. I know he was sorry for Wednesday. We're all sorry for Wednesday." *Wednesday? What day is today?*

"He had some kind of infection but he never went to see a doctor," Luanne blubbers. "Some kind of cut on his foot."

The garter snake bite!

I lean to my left and manage to vomit into a garbage can. Mostly.

As Luanne and Zac drape me over their shoulders and drag me to the car, which is parked in a haphazard angle at the back of The Clayton Marvin, we come upon Karl, who leans against the car.

Karl marches up to me and lands a haymaker, straight onto the bridge of my nose. I'm launched into the black dirt of Clayton Marvin Road, my nose surely broken.

Zac tries to insinuate himself into the situation and Karl raises his fist to Zac. Zac backs off. "What the hell's the matter with you?" Zac says to him, and in four hundred words, Karl says he was fired from the Highway Robbery for being an accessory to shoplifting, for allowing us to walk out of the store without paying, and then Karl marches toward the Trans-Canada before I can muster the energy to apologize to him.

"You have a black tie?" Luanne says to me as I bury myself into the plush leather passenger seat of the Charger. I shake my head a little.

"What about you?" she says through the rear-view mirror to Zac.

"Nope."

"The stores don't open 'til eleven," she says. "You'll have to borrow a couple from Jimmy." Luanne sniffs.

"Eleven? Jesus Christ. It's Sunday?" I murmur. *SUNDAY?!*

"Yes, Gabriel, it is Sunday. And the funeral is in ninety minutes."

I twitch my nose and then wipe it. Still no blood.

In an hour, I am showered and shaved, with bread in my uncertain belly, coffeed up and coherent enough to put a Windsor knot into a couple of Jimmy's black ties, which are as old as we are. Zac and I stand at the front porch of Jimmy's house, waiting for our ride. We don't speak. I'm not thinking about the eleven times I needed to walk down the hallway past Jimmy's bedroom, where the sheets were still ruffled and the bed

No Escape from Greatness

unmade. Who would sleep in the bed? Who would wash the linens? Who would dare erase Jimmy's smell from the his home?

Finally, the black Charger pulls up. I can see Toon's face in the rear window, staring blankly at the sky. Luanne gets out of the car before we can get down the steps. She doesn't entirely turn to face her childhood house; instead, she leaves the car running and slips into the back seat, her head slightly turned so she doesn't have to look over here.

"So you're drinking now," Zac says to me as he opens the half-sized iron gate.

"No," I tell him, but I can't find any words to support my assertion. We both walk around the front of the car, both of us stopping by the driver's side headlight. Zac looks incredulously at me, and I know I'm still too soused to drive, so I slink backward, all the way to the passenger seat, and Zac takes us to the Welsh Community Theatre.

I dip my head down and look into the mirror, back at Toon. She continues to stare at the sky. She's still upset because I forgot to pick her up from school on Wednesday. All I can feel is a longing, for a quiet morning of sitting on lawn chairs, with our cute nooses draped around gopher holes.

I cover my mouth to stifle anything I might emit from it and accidentally touch my nose, the cartilage of which must surely have been twisted by Karl's violent attack. Pain shoots back from my proboscis into the roots from my upper front teeth and I lurch backward, bouncing my head off the headrest, which stops my lurch violently enough to force trauma into my neck. I let out a nasal "shit sakes," but no one even looks in my direction.

The median ditch in the middle of the highway is overrun with four-by-fours and cars; everyone in Greatness has come to the funeral. When we reach the doors of the Welsh Community Theatre, I can still smell a slight charring in the air. Jill greets Zac at the door and they embrace; I search for Shoelace's figure along the rows and rows of filled seats and I find him—thankfully, Shoelace hasn't seen the embrace. Before I can hiss at Zac to keep his youthful concupiscence to himself, he has taken the seat Jill saved for him. An old man—one of the former town fathers—hands us a program.

"I thought you all hated Jimmy," I tell him.

"We made our peace with each other," he says to me as he hands me a program, "before it was too late." Ouch. The usher opens his arm to direct us to the front row of theatre seats, which now serve as makeshift pews, which they were supposed to replace. As soon as he does, all of Greatness stands up and looks back at us.

Luanne, Toon, and me.

The family.

We are seated, front row centre, and the service begins with a bagpiper from some infantry unit that Jimmy served in called the Picklies. I never did catch the full name, though I notice the PPCLI on the bagpiper's shoulder and infer the acronym to be where "Pickly" came from. Regardless of the background of this bagpiper, he ought to be shot and dragged through the streets of Greatness for what he was doing to the contraption in his mouth, or, more accurately, for what he was doing to all of us.

Finally it ends, and Luanne offers me a look that says "Thank God that's over." A procession of geriatric rednecks take turns telling Greatness how they used to run the town, and even though they hated Welsh, they hated him like a brother, and he had earned their respect, and Greatness was better for having had Jimmy Welsh in it.

None of the former town fathers mentions Luanne, but their resentment for her is there, between every word, in their disrespectful glances toward us. One or two offer condolences to "the family." I wish Luanne would get up and spit in their faces, the hypocrites.

No Escape from Greatness

Toon stares at her boots, bored and not overly concerned about who notices. She won't look at me.

As the seventh or eighth person from the olden days gets up to the podium, Luanne looks over at me and whispers, "I'm glad you're here."

"I thought you were shutting me down," I seethe. "Does this count as visitation time?"

Toon looks up at me after that comment, a little bit of fire in her eye.

"Maybe I overreacted," Luanne whispers to me. "Jimmy wanted to help you."

"He wanted to win your love back," I say to her. "You must know what that feels like," I refrain from saying.

"I have decided that I'm going to respect his wishes."

"Well you can't respect his wishes, because I don't have a movie to make."

"That's what I'm saying," Luanne whispers a bit louder. "Whatever you need. The theatre ... other locations ... permits ..."

"Oh, so you're saying I can write Louise into the film and you won't explode? That's just great, Luanne, much appreciated, except I don't have anyone to play Louise anyhow, so what's the point." My voice barely maintains a whisper. I can feel eyes on the back of my neck.

Luanne grimaces a little. "Fine," she says. "I will be your Louise, okay? Does that make up for it?"

Toon and I both look at Luanne in disbelief. I immediately picture her locked in a Chinese finger prison with Shoelace, and then kissing him at a bush party ... yes. Yes, this will work.

"I think I can work with that," I say to her. And perhaps, somewhere just above or below us, Jimmy Welsh is smiling. Whatever it takes, Jimmy. Whatever it takes, indeed.

Jimmy is dead.

My eyes glass over with tears that sting like drops of vinegar. Old ducts toil and swell with a product that feels unnatural when not produced on command.

I won't cry. Not even for Jimmy. But a weepy gasp comes out of me, like a hiccup, straight from my twitching diaphragm, and I make a sound.

The sound cracks through the Welsh Community Theatre like the sound of an emu yodeling: foreign and unexpected, heard by all and appreciated by none. I don't emit the sound; rather, it is like a sound implosion, created in the vacuum my gasp makes, like how a bathtub drain makes noise.

"YEWP."

The dusty fart standing at the podium stops bleating. All eyes press against my skin. I hold two fingers up to my mouth like I'm about to vomit once more. I can feel my diaphragm twitch again and I have to gasp.

"YEWP." A second yewp, louder than before, reverberates and refracts off the ex-church walls and into every eardrum. But it is *not* a cry. It is *not*.

Luanne attempts to put an arm around my shoulder and I brush it away. I shuffle in front of her, trying to make my way out of here, while everyone looks on. And then the old man up at the podium, with the fez on his head, says, "It appears Mr. Pegg would like to say a few words about our James."

Just like that, we are all in a moment of complete silent stillness. I am in the bush again, and I am a fawn who just heard a twig snap some yards away. Everyone in this audience looks at me like the wolf who heard the twig snap beneath its own paw. Nothing moves. Not a single eyeball.

"Mr. Pegg," the Shriner cackles, like a November wind shuffling through the dead leaves. Some people begin to purse their lips sympathetically at me. One or two of them nod at me. As though moved by their group telekinesis, I step backward, past

No Escape from Greatness

the Shriner, and find myself grasping the edges of the podium, searching for just the right words.

"Jimmy," I begin, noticing that Luanne has buried her face into her hands. Toon nibbles at her cuticles, trying to look bored, but her eyes are glassy, too. That burning sensation in my tear ducts comes back and I force my eyes to the back of the room. "Jimmy Welsh was," I say, and then I'm stifled again. I see my brother Daniel leaning against the back wall of the theatre. He nods at me in a gentle "Hey there," and my eyes try to project a "What the hell are you doing here?" back at him, and then I realize that he knew Jimmy like some kind of relative too. And now that Daniel can see me in this condition, he's going to take Zac away. I look at Zac, who is holding hands with Jill, just four rows behind Shoelace, whose house I have abetted in the breaking and entering of. I am losing it. I know this because I am now ending my thoughts with prepositions. Even more to be ashamed of. Take me home, gophers and hallucination elk.

Tom from the grocery store looks up at me with that wide-eyed half-smile, as though I'm too overcome by emotion to conjure up the right words for a eulogy and I need his encouraging face. I rub the contusion on the bridge of my nose, which he inadvertently caused by firing Karl, and I squint at him.

"Say something, Dad," Toon says. Everyone can hear it, even though she made her voice into a whisper. I look back at her encouraging half-smile, then she says, "Use your words," says it like I'm a toddler, and I hear a couple of snickers.

"Do your business, Port-O-Potty Guy, so the next person can go," someone heckles. No one laughs. Toon smiles wryly at me, her arms crossed. Luanne elbows Toon in the side.

"I don't know what it means to be a father," I tell the audience. "I didn't have one and I'm not a very good one. Would you agree, Toon?"

Toon nods enthusiastically.

"Jimmy wasn't my father. He was my ex-wife's father. But he tried his best with me, because we had matching problems and neither of us could go up against Luanne alone."

The citizens of Greatness chuckle knowingly, to my surprise. I'm emboldened. Luanne looks at her knees even harder.

"I'm not really sure what Jimmy's purpose in life was, but I have a theory. If you are a subscriber to the Cartesian notion of existence being merely a dream narrative—" I am met with two hundred puzzled faces and I begin again: "If I'm the main character in my own movie, then maybe Jimmy Welsh's purpose was to be a father to me, and there's nothing deeper to dig for than that."

These next words fall out of me, just filling the uncomfortable silence I've made. "Sometimes you just need to know when to stop digging, according to the gophers."

In the hubbub of confusion, I step down. Organ music hurriedly begins to play: all rise, the family is exiting.

I rush down the aisle, surfing the wave of rising funeral-goers, passing Daniel before he can approach me. I burst through the doors like I'm popping the lid off the pill bottle and the sunlight blinds me, scalding the backs of my corneas.

I hear an "oof" on the other side of the doors.

As my eyes adjust, fading from white into colour and detail, I realize that I have bowled over Dr. Ross, alleged psychological therapist of the formerly mute pugilist Karl, who got fired and punched me this morning. I have crushed her against the door as I made it fly open.

It's not poetic justice, but perhaps it's within the realm of poetry. Maybe lyrical justice.

"Sorry," I blurt, and I make my way for Luanne's car. It's open, of course, because no one locks their doors around here, but I don't have keys for the Charger's ignition. I just sit in the passenger seat and watch the Welsh Community Theatre slowly secrete its contents all over the highway ditch.

No Escape from Greatness

I replay what I just said to the funeral-goers about what the gophers told me. Images of dirty leaves and the mighty elk spirit *Manitou-Bah* flash through my mind. Suddenly I realize I may have gone insane.

I get back out of the car and paddle through mourners, each trying to sad-smile at me and softly touch my shoulder, and I make my way to Dr. Ross, who sits against the wall where she took her tumble. She rubs her head. Daniel tends to her. They both look up at me in bewilderment.

"Are ... are you hurt?" I manage.

"She'll be fine, Gabriel," Daniel says to me. "And what about you?"

"Leave it alone, Daniel. I'm in no condition to refrain from giving you every gram of my vitriol."

And then Zac walks out of the theatre with Jill, hand in hand, and sees his father. He puts his head down and starts tugging Jill like a trailer.

Daniel clocks them and gives chase, leaving me alone with Dr. Ross.

"Have you seen Karl?" she says as she brushes grass from her hair. "I missed his call this morning and I suspect he is distressed."

"Actually, I wanted to talk to you, Doctor," I tell her. "You gave me your card, and I never imagined I would admit to this, but ..."

Her eyes brighten. "Yes," she interjects, "perhaps we could spend some time together? I mean, not now, of course. I'm sorry for your loss, but perhaps tomorrow after my appointments? Say, seven o'clock?"

"Oh," I say. "Right. It's just that I have a lot on my mind right now ..."

Dr. Ross stands up. "I need to find Karl."

"He wasn't here. Perhaps try The Clayton Marvin."

"I'll do that. See you tomorrow night?"

"Fine."

"It's a date," she says to me with a small smile, and stalks off like she hasn't just crossed a massive line.

Luanne walks up to me with Toon not far behind, and I am escorted to the burial site at Lions War Memorial Cemetery. We watch Jimmy's coffin get lowered into the ground.

Luanne melts into my chest again and sobs. I wrap my arm around her back. Toon is exactly one half-pace too far from us to make it look as though the three of us are together. But we are almost together.

I scan about, determined to look anywhere but at the coffin as it sinks into the earth, closer to the oil, and I notice Daniel and Zac standing together. It occurs to me that Daniel will take Zac away now. I'm not sure that I care, anymore. I can see their lips moving as they stand solemnly. They're whispering to each other.

Jill sidles up to Zac. Zac's face curdles a bit and I can tell he's confronting his father. Then Jill says something to Daniel and clutches Zac's arm, bringing herself in close to him.

Jill reaches for Daniel—reaches to touch him gently.

Daniel storms off before she can.

We stand at the edge of the grave and stare at the coffin in the ground. I glance to the left and realize that Toon is not there. No one else is there but Luanne and me. Everyone else has made their way to a reception. I move a little, pulling on Luanne to suggest that we go.

She pays no heed to it. Instead, without breaking her gaze on the grave, Luanne says, "Everybody's got their different, stupid-headed ways of coping. I'm no different. You're no different. Tomorrow, we'll go back to being … what we are. Today, I'm glad you're giving me your arm."

No Escape from Greatness

What kind of a person would not give her an arm in this moment? I use my other arm to bring her in a bit closer.

"He wanted to fix everything, Lulu. He wanted to make amends."

Luanne nods. "I know. But to do that, he needed to stop drinking for once in his life. He needed to tell me straight, to my face, how he was going to change. Plus I was busy." Luanne snickers to herself. "I got so busy building my little empire, just like he did. I became him, Gabriel. Only now can I see that. Now that he's gone."

My hangover reminds me that it's there, throbbing behind my eyes like gentle waves lapping against the shore.

"I need a minute," Luanne says to me. "Alone. I have a lot to let go of."

I turn from Jimmy's coffin and leave her there, despite my impulse to hold her, to hang on to this moment, even if it is merely a truce. Even if being kind to me is her stupid-headed way of coping.

Daniel marches up to me as soon as I turn from Luanne. Jill and Zac trail behind him like scolded children.

"We're headed back to the city, Gabriel. Would you like a ride?"

"You know I can't leave, Daniel."

"Just putting it out there."

"Tell him we can't go, Uncle G," Zac says.

"Yeah," Jill interjects. "Tell him we can't go, Uncle G," she says. She recoils on my eyebrow-cock.

"He's not a child anymore, Daniel. He wants to stay." A tidal bore roils into my frontal lobe and runs it through like a sabre, reminding me it is still Thursday for most of my body. I am suddenly very, very hung over. My fingers find my temples.

"I'm not going to let my boy partake in your debauched flights of fancy, Gabriel. Luanne told me what's going on and … I didn't know it was possible to make things any worse, but in that department you are a wild success. You're proof positive that comedy is no laughing matter."

I'm not going to lie. I am slightly rankled by this comment.

"It's. Not. A. Comedy." My fingers curl, preparing to find Daniel's throat.

"Zachary won't be following your piss-poor example, not if I can help it. My way may not be the most … thrilling way, but at least I can keep myself sane and sober enough to function."

"Functional," I mock, "now there's a rainbow to shoot for."

There's something in Daniel's voice that I've never heard before. A sadness. Zac looks at him curiously, too, and I know it isn't just my imagination. Despite having the forever marriage and all the money he needs for annual all-inclusive vacations and a son who is not without some future potential, Daniel isn't happy with his life.

What a pleasant surprise.

Zac looks to me to say something.

"Do you have a purpose in life, Daniel? Zac believes he is finding his own life's purpose. Maybe he is, and maybe he is completely wrong and this is nothing remotely close to his life's true meaning. Perhaps this blunder is so great that he will become just like you, with the investments and the double-breasted blazers and the suburban Winnipeg ennui. Someday Zac may choose to be as unfulfilled as you. And maybe Jill will break his heart. Maybe he will break hers. But it doesn't matter to us, Daniel. Because those are Zac's mistakes to make. And him and me, we're not just going to switch ourselves off. Right, Zac?"

Daniel reaches deeper into his pocket. His eyes partially close as he seethes.

I look over to Zac for his testimony, eloquent and impassioned, in his own defence.

"Yeah," Zac says, eloquently and impassioned, and pulls Jill in a little closer.

No Escape from Greatness

"Everyone in your world has to serve your purpose," Daniel says. "And what is your purpose, exactly? To manipulate and abandon and use people up? I don't want to see Zac become one of the speed bumps under your bus."

"Daniel, it's time you treated Zac like a man. Real men fuck things up royally, and all the time, and without fear of making the same mistakes over and over and over, in the remote chance that one day, history may decide not to repeat itself. Your problem, Daniel, is that you're too pigeon-hearted to have ever attempted to be a real man. Icarus, Daniel. Icarus. Even if we fuck up, we'll have far better tans than you."

Luanne walks past us like a ghost, slowly floating her way back to the car. We all watch her float by. Daniel has nothing to say to me. I have bested him.

"Now," I tell Daniel, "if you'll excuse us, Zac and I have a film to make." And with that, we all head back to the car, leaving Daniel in our wake.

"Neither of you will amount to anything here," he calls at us. "This town is where dreams go to die."

"Have some class, Daniel. We're at a funeral."

Daniel knows it's customary not to shout about things dying when you're around the bereaved.

Toon sits in the car when we arrive, and Zac granny-drives the five of us to the reception, at the Legion, where they've printed a big picture of Jimmy and adorned it with flowers. Zac keeps looking into his rear-view mirror to catch glimpses of Jill, and their eyes smile at each other.

"Can I go home?" Toon asks Luanne while looking at the picture. "I never even liked him."

"You should have given Jimmy a chance," I say.

"Why? He never gave me one," Toon replies, and Luanne gives her permission to go home, a twenty-minute walk. I look at Jimmy's face and straighten my tie. I imagine him calling me

Sunshine. I wonder if he died so Luanne would help me make my film.

The reception is awful. The white bread finger sandwiches are the most palatable thing about it. My stomach decides to accept four of them. Luanne never lets go of my arm as she makes the rounds, thanking people and painting on a smile to mask her unending anger at Jimmy. Jill and Zac stay at the reception for five minutes before disappearing. Dr. Ross keeps her distance with Luanne on my arm, and for that, I am thankful. I tell Tom that Karl didn't steal from him. I pay him forty dollars for groceries (I know, highway robbery) and urge him to forgive Karl, which is quite magnanimous of me given the soreness I feel in my nose.

Finally, Luanne takes me back to Jimmy's house. She stops outside and looks away from the house, as though seeing it could make her burst into tears all over again.

"Why don't you come in?" I ask her.

She shakes her head. Without looking at me, she says, "Thank you for today. I hope … I hope you figure out some other way to cope."

"I'm never having a drink again, Luanne. Manitoba won't let me. Thanks for respecting Jimmy's wishes—"

"Get some sleep," Luanne says, and urges me out of her car. I get a twinge in the base of my spine as I get to the wrought iron gate—the truce is over. I look back to nod at her, but it's no use. She's already gone.

Zac doesn't speak, either, when I get in the house. He steals little glances at me like he doesn't know who I am. Without speaking, he opens the fridge, pulls out some of Jimmy's bacon and eggs, and turns on the stove. I pass out at the breakfast nook, but the ceramic clang of plate hitting melamine awakens me with a start. I eat a homemade breakfast, in silence, then crawl up to Jimmy's bed and fall asleep until Tuesday, without a single dream that I care to recall.

24.

My brain feels as though it is inside out and backwards when I awaken. I lift my neck up and cry out in pain, then look around me and realize that I am sleeping in Jimmy Welsh's bed, and Jimmy Welsh is dead, and I'm horrified to be lying here where he ought to be.

So I know I have regained my full faculties.

I shuffle downstairs and notice the sun is up. The clock says it's two in the afternoon. I desperately need to eat. I call out for Zac, but he's not home. I fix myself a pod of Americano and crack open the fridge. I elect to take the one-pound brick of cheese and eat it like it was an apple, gnawing off a corner and washing it down with robo-espresso. The walls still feel like Jimmy is inside of them. I miss the talent trailer. It occurs to me that I have a rehearsal for *Descent into Greatness* tonight. Then it occurs to me that I have an appointment with Dr. Ross. Perhaps even a date. Perhaps she saw what I couldn't see at the time: despite my low feelings, I don't need help. In fact, I'm attractive to someone such as Dr. Ross, who must have insights into such things. Of course I'm fine.

The watery Americano dulls the throb in my brain and the vivid memories of my Caribou-induced hallucinations finally begin to weaken. I feel as though the deck has been shuffled, like every day is a new card, and I am about to hit blackjacks over and over again. Tropical Storm Luanne has been downgraded to a Category 1; I don't even know if I still need to see Toon every day. I'm sure Toon would be all right with it if I didn't.

Waking up alone with a killer headache, unsure of where I am, is something I am not entirely unfamiliar with. It happened after I was fired from my most recent job in Hollywood.

The Toby Project was an awful sitcom pilot by some silver-spoon son of a Hollywood blue-blood. After our first day of shooting, the producers pulled me aside. They were both men my age, but they dressed like they were Zac's age, with Justin Bieber high-tops and ridiculous popped collars. They had flowing blond hair, so similar to one another that they could have been brothers. They were most certainly not Chip and Pepper.

"So listen, Bruh," one of them said to me. I have come to understand that "Bruh" is an evolutionary expression of the word "Brother." These men earned seven figures per year.

"We were hoping it would work out, but it looks like Karma's not in your favour, right?"

"I'm not sure what you mean," I said limply, because I knew where this was headed.

"Homeslice," the other said, "the recognition of Port-O-Potty Guy is just too much to overcome for us, because the creator of the show wants to steer clear of, like, goofball whack-a-doodle, so he can hit that couch potato demo, get me?"

The other executive clone jumped back in: "Gotta take the edge off our comedy, Bruh, and make it wholesome like Corn Pops. No poop humour."

No Escape from Greatness

"But I had two lines today. And I played them completely straight," I uttered in a lame defence.

"Naw, it's not what you say that we have a problem with, Chimichanga," one said to me. And the other completed the sentence: "It's who you are, Mang."

I stormed out of the studio, off the lot, and straight into a Prairie Caribou bender. It had taken me years to find the southwest Manitoba ex-pats who knew the recipe, but by the end of my time in Los Angeles, I could get the hook-up and be drinking the stuff within an hour, at least a version with beef blood.

That night, the night I went from the Hollywood G-list to the Q-list, I did something to make my foot bleed, ate a raw T-bone steak, bleached the carpet in my condominium, doused my Erratic Automatic scripts in some kind of chemical, then tried to set them alight but couldn't get the chemical to ignite.

When I awoke from my post-Caribou slumber, I had no idea where I was. I had vague, shaky memories of the things I had done, and some sort of shame lingered in me like an errant cloud. After a coffee and an hour-long shower, I was hit by a horrid revelation: I hadn't bleached the carpet in my condominium. I no longer owned a condominium. I had just trashed Shane's place.

I had eaten his steak. I had bleached his carpet. I had melted black holes into his cork floor and, at some point in the evening, I had thrown a script into his seventy-five-gallon aquarium, which teemed with all sorts of iridescent tropical fish, and the chemicals imbued in the paper had turned the waters into toxic broth. By morning, the fish were croutons. Even the coral had found a way to dislodge itself from the artificial sea bottom and join its aquatic brethren in the Aquapocalypse.

That ended my stay at Shane's.

Those same errant clouds of shame drift inside me now, like poisoned tropical fish floating in the murk of my inner

Aquapocalypse. Sipping my Americano on the porch does nothing to dispel it.

Zac comes home some time later with a large smile on his face. "This is really happening," he says to me. "Just like Jimmy wanted. Everything is set up—as soon as everybody's done their work stuff for the day, we're having a rehearsal. A full-blown rehearsal! This movie is really happening. I am stoked, Uncle G."

I take a sip of my coffee. Deep down, I feel the excitement, too. I wonder how it's all going to explode in my face this time.

At five o'clock, Zac takes me to the Welsh Community Theatre, where Shoelace and Luanne quietly throw lines at each other from rolled-up scripts. Toon sits in the theatre seats, beside Jill. Dr. Ross is here, too. She nods at me and smiles. Is it a therapist smile or date smile?

Zac claps his hands. "Let's get organized, people. George and Louise, I've marked your spots in gender-appropriate colours. Toon, you're okay with the sound rig?"

Toon shoots me a devilish look. "Under control," she says to Zac, and she picks up a boom mic, which looks like a massive push broom. She slides on her massive headphones and takes the stage as well.

I'm mystified. As I walk absently toward the stage, Zac smiles at me and picks up a camera: not a tiny GoPro, but one of the RED cameras Jimmy bought for us. It looks magnificent.

I feel a hand on mine and it confuses me. Luanne is up on stage ... then I realize the hand belongs to Dr. Ross and I withdraw it.

"It's all right if I watch?" she says to me. "I thought maybe we could have our get-together afterwards."

"It's fine," I say absently, moving forward to the front row of seats, where Zac has created a small video village, the command centre for a movie shoot. He's written with Sharpie on a piece of paper and taped it to the back of the "Director" chair so that it reads: "Gabriel Pegg, Director."

"You like?" Zac says to me.

"I like." I take my seat.

"I assume you plan to make those changes we discussed still?" Shoelace bellows.

"Yes, George," Zac says before I can respond. "Our director has been somewhat occupied, as you can appreciate, what with the passing of our executive producer."

Shoelace, a.k.a. George, nods. Okay.

Jill snaps pictures with her phone. All the pictures have Zac in them.

Zac speaks at the top of his voice. "I'm going to call ready, and then the director will call action, and then we will run the scene. Roll with your mistakes. Don't play to the camera. Just be George and Louise, authentically George and Louise, and don't try to feel it."

Impressive, Zac.

Luanne and Shoelace nod and look at each other.

"Roll sound," Zac says to Toon. She presses a button on the small box that sits on her hip.

"Sound ready," Toon says, like an old pro. It makes me smile to myself.

"Rolling," Zac calls out. Then he thrusts his chin at Jill.

"Oh," Jill says, and jogs in front of the camera with two pieces of wood. "What do I say again?" Jill asks Zac.

"Descent into Greatness, Scene 4, Take 1," Zac replies in a whisper, and she says it with authority: "Descent into Greatness, Scene 4, Take 1." She claps her two pieces of wood together to simulate a clapboard.

Toon, Jill and Zac turn their gazes to me. I get a chill that tingles my skin from bottom to top, right into my spine, as though I had just sprouted wings. This is happening. I fill my lungs with breath. My throat tightens. One word will begin my film. I'm one word away from putting my life's purpose on this stage. I'm one word from turning my dream into reality.

"Action."

25.

We're going full-bore on a scene where Louise gives George the divorce papers and they end up getting blotto and conceiving a child (whom I have yet to write in the screenplay).

The chemistry between George and Louise is excellent, but Shoelace disrupts any magic when he looks over at me with his gigantic arms extended plaintively. "This line has to come out," he says.

He points to a line in the script that happened in real life, to me, when Luanne asked me why I never came back, and I told her that I had broken my own heart to gain my freedom, and that freedom lets me be as free to be miserable as I want to be. I love this line because it's true.

"No, here," he says, and points at Luanne's line, where she says: "That's a little on-the-nose, don't you think?"

Shoelace bellows, "No one says 'on-the-nose' who isn't a writer."

"Were you there, George?" I ask him.

"No."

"Did you break in like a cat burglar and witness what was said?"

Zac starts slashing his hand across his throat to tell me to cut it out, but Shoelace cocks his head and offers me a quizzical look.

He mouths a phrase, silently, to himself: "Break in?"

Oh shit. I nod and shake my head, shrug and snigger. "Could be anything that I mean," I stammer. "Why, did someone break into your place?" Now I have done it. Zac's shoulders slump and he smacks his own forehead. A lightbulb goes off in Shoelace's head, then the lightbulb explodes.

"It was you," Shoelace says to me.

While I don't verbally implicate Zac, my expression does enough to damn him. My eyes dart over to Zac, over and over, and Shoelace gets a little puzzled, but not puzzled enough, so I mouth silently "it was him" with eye gesture accompaniment, and finally Shoelace understands.

Shoelace seethes like a bear that has been fitted with a horseshoe. He looks at Zac with blazing murderous eyes, and Zac takes a step back.

He looks over my shoulder and behind me, at Jill, and hollers, "You got these buffoons to steal it, didn't you?!"

I prepare to flee from the Welsh Community Theatre as though it has been set ablaze once again.

Jill reluctantly nods at Shoelace, and the jig, as they say, is up.

We stand in the theatre, each of us in stunned silence, waiting to see what Shoelace will do next.

Including Shoelace. He takes a step back as though we may all attack him simultaneously. His eyes become as big as golf balls. He looks ready to smash us all.

"Calm down, Shoelace," Jill says. "My passport is mine. You know it was wrong for you to keep it."

"I can't believe you did this to me."

"She didn't," Zac says, resting the camera at his side. "It was me and no one else. Jill didn't ask me to do it."

How very valiant of Zac. And idiotic.

"Zac!" I exclaim. "I can't believe this!" And then I turn to Shoelace and mewl, "Surely, this won't affect your ability to turn in a stellar performance as George?"

Luanne hisses something at me, trying to shut me up, but I don't hear it.

"That depends," Shoelace says. He takes a step toward me, like Godzilla treading through a banking district in Tokyo, and I press harder into the back of my director's chair. "I'm not working with him. So it's him or me."

To some, this may seem like a slam-dunk decision not even worthy of debate. Zac is my blood, my second-in-command, the executioner of my ideas. He just gave Shoelace an alibi that exonerates me. But I can get another camera guy. Plus it would render Zac's alibi moot if I fired Shoelace. There is no one in Greatness who can play the role of George. No one.

I guess I pause long enough to make Zac uneasy.

"Thanks for your support, Unc," Zac says.

"Gabriel!" Luanne barks.

"I'm thinking! Everyone just be patient."

"I'm sorry, Jill," Shoelace utters. "I know it was wrong, but I wanted to protect myself in case of investigation. And I suppose a part of me wanted our marriage to be real."

"You guys are married?" Toon says, and Luanne shushes her.

Shoelace hops off the stage and gets about ten feet from me so he can address Jill.

"I knew I would never possess you, Jill. I guess your legal identity documentation, proving your citizenship, and offering you the comfort and protection of our nation's sovereignty was the next best thing to having you. But I'm not ashamed."

Something changes in Shoelace's demeanor, as though he's just discovered something within himself.

"Actually, this is good," Shoelace says. "Now I will do what I should have done. I will fight for your hand and heart, rather than trying to capture a piece of it through immigration law. Yes, I will fight for you."

"No, please don't do that," Jill says.

"Because you are worth fighting for. I've known you were worth fighting for since that day you sang at Juillard and I got to hear you. I've known it since then."

INT. JUILLARD HALLWAY - DAY

Young SHOELACE lumbers past a rehearsal room when he hears a MAGICAL ANGEL VOICE. It sings opera.

Shoelace presses his ear against the door and hears pure enchantment.

Two students walk past him, eyeing him suspiciously. Shoelace glares at them — the students quicken their pace to escape his glare.

Shoelace presses his ear even more tightly to the door.

But suddenly, the song stops—

The singer falters—

No Escape from Greatness

And, after a violent cough, Shoelace hears a girl's gentle cries.

Unsure of what to do, Shoelace grasps the door handle, then lets go ... the girl continues to sob.

Shoelace steels himself, fills his lungs and opens the door.

INSIDE THE REHEARSAL ROOM

JILL sits on the floor, her head in her hands, crying.

>   SHOELACE
>   What's wrong?

Jill looks up at Shoelace. She's a little heavier because she hasn't done any chemo yet.

>   JILL
>   It was my dream to go here.
>   But I get so tired.

>   SHOELACE
>   You sing beautifully.

Jill looks away, bashful.

>   JILL
> I can't even do it for more than eight bars.
>
>   SHOELACE
> Eight bars was enough for me.

Jill looks into Shoelace's eyes

>   SHOELACE
> It makes me want to give you anything you ever wanted and make your tears go away.
>
>   JILL
> Eight bars.
>
>   SHOELACE
> Yes.

END OF SCENE

"I'm an old fashioned man who believes in romance, Jill," Shoelace pronounces.

I can see the strain on his face. He means every word he is saying.

Shoelace turns on a heel, his spine rigid, and pronounces: "Zachary Pegg—"

"No Shoelace, I'm begging you," Jill says, then she looks over to where her boyfriend Zac was standing only a second earlier, at the exact same time as everyone else, and realizes that Zac has made a break for it.

"Where is he?" Shoelace bellows.

No Escape from Greatness

"Excuse me?" says a mousy voice from the back of the seats: Dr. Ross. "Can I say something here? Obviously there are a lot of issues that need talking about in this room ... many unmet needs and such. But violence isn't the answer, is it? Breaking and entering? Identity theft? Does this not seem inappropriate to anyone?"

We all look at Dr. Ross, from Brandon, and we all silently frown at her interloping.

Toon raises her hand as though in a classroom.

"He's up there," Toon says to Shoelace, and she points at the top of the charred curtain that adorns the back of the old chapel.

"I don't see anything," Shoelace says, and then, from behind the curtain, Zac skitters a little to stage right. Zac has slunk behind the curtains, found nowhere to go but up, and presently hangs there like an Adam's apple, hoping his romantic rival will simply assume that he has evaporated into thin air or found a back door that everyone in Greatness knows doesn't exist.

"Ah." Shoelace walks up to the curtain.

Dr. Ross stands up and pleads: "I am a trained, licensed psychological professional. Sir, in my professional opinion, you are huge. Pounding that boy into oblivion won't solve your problems. This young lady won't love you, will she? Will you, young lady?"

Jill shakes her head. "Please, Shoelace."

Shoelace looks up at the top of the curtain as it rustles about, as if a lost gorilla is behind it looking for escape. Shoelace turns and gives Jill a look of betrayal that pulls hot tears from her eyes. I silently wish that we could have been rolling when Shoelace gives her that look, because that look is supersaturated with so much raw emotion that I could wring it out like a cloth and it could have been a clip worthy of a "for your consideration" submission. But alas, it isn't filmed, and Shoelace lumbers up to me solemnly, takes the rolled-up script he has been holding in his right paw, and stuffs the sweat-soaked paper down the neck of my shirt, scratching my chest with dozens of paper cuts.

"Goodbye," Shoelace says, and I'm pretty sure he is saying it to everyone. He strides up to the doors and leaves the Welsh Community Theatre, slamming the door behind him.

The slam of the door is the only sound in the place. The soundwaves reverberate through the rafters and into the walls with such ferocity, it jars Zac loose from his place of suspension and he plummets to the hardwood stage, rolling like a tumbleweed down from his perch, a twenty-foot fall that Zac punctuates with an understated "ow."

We all rush to his rescue, but Jill gets there first, moving tapestry away to reveal Zac sitting in an involuntary Crumpled Lotus position, his ankles twisted around each other tightly enough that Jill must manually untangle them.

With Toon's help, Jill slides her arm beneath Zac's back and helps prop him up to a standing position, which is when the groans and grimaces commence in earnest. Everyone gathers around Zac to dote on him as the grim realization strikes me: I have lost the services of both my lead actor and my camera operator for *Descent into Greatness*.

"He's not gonna call the police, is he?" Zac says through gritted teeth.

"Doubtful," Luanne tells him. "I've never seen Shoelace that upset, but sometimes he'll get broody about stuff and just disappear for a while. I'd be more worried about your tibia, Evel Knievel." And then she turns to me with a dulcet face, with those pretty blue eyes blinking sympathetically at me, the way that always makes me relax like when your head touches the pillow, and she says, "I tried. Sorry, Gabriel."

And just like that, *Descent into Greatness* is kaput once more.

"Toon is signed up for some intramural class thing after school tomorrow. Can you bring her home after that? Five-thirty?"

No Escape from Greatness

I nod. "I won't forget."

"I believe you."

Toon doesn't smile when she sees the devastation on my face, nor does she register any anger toward me. She just stalks away.

"See you tomorrow," Luanne says as she and Toon follow Jill and Zac to the parking lot.

I'm left with Dr. Ross.

"Well I guess we can get started a bit early," she says, smiling at me as though I might see a silver lining in having my entire production obliterated once again.

Perhaps it is fortunate to have a therapist here, after all. I move my head up and down, yes, yes, let's talk about things and help me deal with this mess. "Should we sit down?" I ask.

"Is there a place to eat around here? How about that spot just off the highway? Clayton somesuch?"

I move my head side to side: no, no, please don't let me go there.

"Dr. Ross," I say.

"Karen," she says with a wink. "Call me Karen."

"Karen, I need some help." I tell it to her like I'm Frankenstein's monster, mechanical and deep, a flesh automaton incapable of feeling, else lightning may strike.

"Oh, is this one of your characters from the show?" she says, thrilled at the prospect. "I don't remember that one. Do another one, maybe I'll get it."

"Let's do Chinese, Karen. There's a place on 7th Avenue, just kitty-corner to the traffic light. We can talk there, okay?"

Karen bites her lower lip and wriggles her nose at me. "Shall we?" she says, and she offers her arm for me to interlock with, as though she were Dorothy and I was the Tin Man, and suddenly I'm off to eat some General Tao's Chicken.

I'm not sure if it's the smell of fryer grease or Karen's ebullience that makes me quake with nausea. The Chinese restaurant,

Better Planet, was a bourgeois café some time ago, with hardwood floors and unfinished maple accents, and the décor still has that coffee shop feel. But instead of the aroma of espresso, the porous wood has now absorbed the aroma of old wonton.

The consommé arrives, but Karen doesn't touch it. She is mooney-eyed, her face propped up by her closed hands, she looks up into my eyes and I can just feel her anticipation that I'm going to break into some kind of Erratic Automatic character, or do something to make her laugh. But I can't stop thinking about *Descent into Greatness*. The failure is crushing me, and I don't know what to do next. Every effort just explodes in my face like a prank cigar, cheap and idiotic, and my drive to serve my life's true purpose just becomes Destiny's parlour trick once again; *Descent into Greatness* is just a wind-up tchotchke that makes farting noises and can be found in a little plastic box on the back shelf of a dollar store.

I can't medicate the pain away. I need to deal with it and I need to deal with it right now.

"Sometimes, Karen, I wonder if I am equipped to deal with all the difficult things life throws at me."

"Oh," she says, and the mooney eyes go away. She tastes her consommé.

"The truth is, I am stuck here in this town for the next seven years while I am forced to spend time with my daughter, who doesn't even like me. What do I do?"

I can tell Karen is trying not to give me advice. She's biting her tongue. I know that look because it's the same look I have when asked to do Port-O-Potty Guy for the twentieth time in a day.

"I mean, using your expertise, Karen, what are your thoughts? Part of me wants to just drink my situation away, but I can't do that anymore. I saw these ... dream animals ... not sure what I was seeing. At any rate, they told me I would die soon. They were coming for me to take me home. It makes me feel uncomfortable."

Karen looks at me like I'm crazy.

I can see her mouth holding back words, like a dam repressing the flood. I'm trying to offer her a case study so juicy, she has no choice but to bite.

I bat my eyelashes innocently. "Dr. Ross. Karen. I'm in a pickle here. It's all I can think about. It's all I'm going to be able to talk about. My relapse."

Finally, the dam bursts, and Karen scowls as she bleats out her therapeutic advice. "It's not uncommon for a narcissist—sorry, a person with narcissistic traits—to run to substances as a crutch when they are shown a flaw in themselves. They believe they have the outside world fooled into seeing them as perfect, so when the illusion bursts, it's glug glug glug." Karen pantomimes the cannonballing of some kind of drink. "Or snifffffff," she says, with the prolonged fs, and she snorts an imaginary line of something right along the table as the waiter arrives with our Egg Foo Yong. To his credit, the server plunks our food down, turns on a heel without reaction, and escapes this scene. I was looking for free professional advice but not much of that was professional.

Karen whispers this next part: "It's called dependency for a reason, Gabriel. You need something that you can count on and sometimes the most dependable thing … is a thing. Sometimes whatever that thing does to you, good or bad or negligible, isn't as important as the consistency. Because the consistency is what makes it reliable, and then you can trust it, and you won't have to worry about feeling betrayed. Until it betrays you. Then you have a bigger crisis on your hands than you ever dreamed possible, because you threw away everything that was ever truly important to you. What I tell my patients is that they need to get over themselves. Trust others and trust yourself to be imperfect.

Don't beat yourself up about relapses, but don't trigger them, either. Sometimes, the best thing to do is focus on what you can do for other people."

Karen reaches over for my hand. I get the sense she is referring to herself.

I taste the Egg Foo Yong. It's surprisingly delicious.

Karen's ebullience drains from her face. "Listen to me, talking shop. Can we change the subject?"

"So I can't trust the thing I was dependent on any longer, my narcissistic attempt at creating my masterpiece has utterly failed, once and for all, and I remain legally bound to stay in Greatness for seven more years. How do I cope with this reality, doctor? Think about someone else instead of my own problems?"

I don't let the subject change and Karen spoons up her cold consommé without a trace of pleasantry on her face. I have her in full-on psychologist mode, and she hates me for it. She slurps the broth from her spoon. Then, without raising her eyes up to me she says, "One small change. Just start with one thing. Can't change it all. That's what I tell my patients, but usually I mean to try getting out of bed in the morning before noon, or to try stepping on a phone book before you try climbing a ladder, or to try communicating by blinking your eyelids before speaking in full sentences. Where do I send my bill?"

As I'm about to offer to buy dinner, a chain reaction of thoughts leads to a lightning strike: I think of Karen's shrink bill; then, I think of who will pay for dinner and how offering to pay would be much more affordable than whatever Karen charges; immediately after, I think of how I can afford either, or even both, because Jimmy gave me forty thousand dollars for a film production that appears to have been sunk forever.

Then I have my lightning strike: Project L. My plan to engage a team of *good* lawyers to emancipate myself from Greatness, Luanne, and Toon forever. And in return, they will be free of me forever. I will spend the remaining money to free them from all of this, as I should have done in the first place. It's one small thing. Karen was right.

"A small thing, you say? Excuse me while I make a phone call."

26.

"Erin, it's Gabriel Pegg, and your dreams have at long last come true."

Silence on the other end of the line. I can hear breath but it's probably not the exhalation of disappointment I've become so accustomed to hearing from Erin.

"I have a little over thirty-nine thousand dollars here, Erin, and I would like to buy my final, immediate and unending emancipation with it. Put a real lawyer on retainer this time, my dear. Put two on retainer. Two of them, with grey, receding hairlines and moral compasses to match: grey and receding. And then I will be free to work in Stratford, or Toronto, or wherever you care to put me."

Erin may have fleeced me, and she may never have loved me, but she did look up to me once, because I was the spark that ignited her career as an agent for top Canadian screen talent. As Erratic Automatic became what it was, Erin was the only one in the business who knew me as a man and not Port-O-Potty Guy, that excremental caricature who ruined my life. I trusted her because she was the only one in the business who knew the real Gabriel Pegg, if knowing the real Gabriel Pegg was possible. And, of course, the real Gabriel Pegg ruined any chance Erin had of being happy with me.

"You're serious," is all I hear on the other side of the line.

"I can wire you the funds tonight. And then I can be at your doorstep tomorrow, or I can disappear, Erin. You'll never have to hear from me again. How would you like that?"

After some thought: "I would like that."

"Okay. What shall I do?"

"Wire me all of it. Every penny. I'll put it in a trust for you, so you can't touch it and neither can the lawyers until they get the job done. But you have to do it now, Gabriel. No mistakes. No second thoughts. I want thirty-nine thousand dollars, Western Union. Okay?"

I hesitate, probably because I will miss having all this money at my disposal. There may be other reasons for me to hesitate but I'm not admitting to them. "Okay."

"Let me be clear. You are turning the key to a nuclear missile launch, Gabriel. You are going to nuke your family, nuke your career, and everyone who has known you in all your life will want nothing to do with you. Not even me."

"I know there will be damage," I tell her.

"You're disgusting. Knowingly hurting people."

"I'm not hurting them, Erin. I'm freeing them, too. My therapist says to focus on them."

"I can't do this." Erin's voice gets a little shaky and hesitant as she continues: "I don't want to hear your voice ever again, you get me? Never again. You gross me out. You're the worst thing that ever happened to me."

I can hear pain. Old scars. I know what old scars sound like.

"I understand, Erin." I put some softness into my candor. I have broken Erin to the point where she will no longer help me. "Very well. Thank you."

No Escape from Greatness

"Goodbye."

Karen comes out of the restaurant and points at my phone as I stuff it into my pocket.

"I was trying to do one small thing, as you suggested. I don't think it worked."

"I thought you were having a secret smoke," she says, and she pulls out a cigarette. "I'm sure if you put positivity into the world, positivity will come back to you, Gabriel." She lights up her cigarette.

"That's a disgusting habit, Karen," I hiss at her, and I walk away.

"Are you serious?" Karen yells at my back. "You can't just walk away because I smoke."

"Don't tell me what I can't do, Karen."

"No, you can't walk away. You need to pay for dinner."

And then a voice echoes out behind me. A male voice. Deep and familiar, like a recurring childhood nightmare.

"Good on you," echoes the voice, "making him buy you dinner first."

I turn and there he is, tall and square and handsome as ever, with that stupid cocky smile that could have never come from Manitoba. Manitoba is too hard a place to make a smile like Shane's.

Shane lights up a smoke, too, and approaches Karen.

"Shane Wilson," he says to her.

"I know you," she grins. "From the show, right? What are you doing in Greatness? Oh what a stupid question," she says with a flustered giggle.

"A perfectly valid question, Shane. What are you doing in Greatness?"

"I'm here to get you back, Gabriel. We need to get the guys back together before we're all too old."

"Too late for that," I tell him. "Don't you hate me because I destroyed your home?"

He smiles. "Took me a while to get over my anger, I'm not going to fib. But you had fallen on hard times and I understood you were in a tough place when I offered you to crash. You didn't have to leave, you know. You can't run from your problems forever, man."

"Shane, this is my therapist, Dr. Ross. Karen, this is Shane."

Befuddled, Karen doesn't correct me. She just accepts my invitation to come over and shake Shane's hand.

"I've got places to be, Gabe. What say you? Come back with us."

"Shane, do you ever wonder what would have happened if your train didn't stop here? If I wasn't in the same lounge as you that night? Or what if I had kept my mouth shut?"

"It happened, Gabe. Usually people have unrealistic fantasies about the future, not the past they can't change."

Shane and his smug handsomeness. His Torontoness. He's still smiling at me, despite my hostility. He even tosses a little smile at Karen as they smoke together in the cold night. Karen stands closer to Shane than to me. Perhaps it's because of Shane's magnetism.

"I want us to be friends again, Gabe. Not just Erratic Automatic. Us. Friends."

"We're friends, Shane. I'm just not going to be Port-O-Potty Guy ever again."

"Even Gord wants you back."

The last time I saw Gord, both of his hands were clenched into fists and he vowed to knock my teeth out if he ever saw me again. "No … no. I need to stay here."

"Maybe it would be good for you, Gabriel. To understand how much joy you bring to everybody."

"It would be healthy," Dr. Karen affirms gently.

"Oh shut up, Karen. You have no idea what you're talking about. I bring joy to people the same way a banana peel does.

No Escape from Greatness

But it doesn't matter, because I am quite busy here in Greatness, anyhow. I have a film to produce. A film that I wrote and I'm directing ... and starring in."

"Oh," Shane says, surprised. "Sounds like a big project."

"It is. Perhaps you could make a cameo appearance," I say.

Shane agrees to make a cameo appearance.

Now I've done it.

27.

I go inside to pay for the food. When I return, Karen and Shane are gone, which doesn't surprise me tremendously. No doubt they have gone somewhere for a nightcap, and my erstwhile therapist has now aligned herself with the enemy.

I trudge home.

Zac waits for me on the porch when I get there. His leg is in a white cast up to the knee. He props it up on the railing, sitting on one of Jimmy's old rockers, a beer in his hand.

"You can really see stars out here," he says. "You see 'em?"

"I'm not in the mood, Zac," I drone as I try to make my way inside.

"Toon's in there," Zac says to me.

"What? Why?"

"Said she needed to talk with you, and then she found a *Less than Kind* marathon on Movie Central and she's been zoned out in front of the TV ever since."

"Isn't it past her bedtime?" I look at my phone. It's eight

o'clock, so I guess it isn't. "And is that an age-appropriate program for an eleven-year-old?"

"Yeah," Zac says absently as he stares out at the late October sky. It's crisp outside, to the point where we can see our breath. Frost is coming.

"It's beautiful," he says to me, then swigs the beer while staring up and out. "Everything about this place is beautiful."

"Can you shoot tomorrow with that thing on your leg?"

Zac looks down at his cast, and I notice he has a signature on it already: Toon's. "Sure, I can still shoot," he tells me. "All I need is an eye and a finger, but we don't have a George—"

"—Good. Shane Wilson from the troupe is in town. I'm going to play me, opposite Luanne playing herself, and we're going to do some scenes for Shane."

"Serious? Why?"

"Why? So he will get off my back."

I leave Zac to contemplate how pretty the stars look from way, way down here. If Zac were aboard the *S.S. Titanic*, he would be Captain of Deckchair Appreciation.

Toon reclines on our couch, watching TV. She pauses it when I come in.

"Hey," she says.

"Hey yourself. Good job on sound today."

Toon's face looks sallow. The corners of her eye sockets are inflamed and pink, like she's been rubbing them a lot. She sucks in her cheeks like she's got a bad lozenge in her mouth. Toon holds up a book: *Dependency Dos and Don'ts* is the title.

"I've been reading this," she says to me soberly.

"Toon, I made a scheduling error, which led to me being extremely late, so late that I wasn't able to pick you up from school, but it will never, ever happen again."

Toon tilts her head and glares at me like I'm speaking Swahili.

No Escape from Greatness

"This isn't about that. This isn't even about you. It is, but it isn't. Come sit."

"Oh." Toon scooches over and I sit beside her—not too close beside her, though. She leaves a full couch cushion of space between us, takes a deep breath, and clutches the dependency book with both hands, like she has been rehearsing what she's going to say.

"Okay," she begins, "I've been wondering what's going to happen to me. Like, in my life. Am I going to end up like mom and be the Grand Poobah of Greatness, all sad and alone and blah? Or am I gonna end up like you and screw up everything I touch, to the point where I push everyone away and live my life all sad and alone and blah? Either way I'm stuck here."

Ouch. I need a moment to recoil from that jab, but Toon doesn't give me one. She continues: "I tried breaking cardboard."

"You did?" I smile, but she continues unabated.

"Not as good as bubble wrap for when you're really upset and lonely. Maybe it's because bubble wrap protects better, I don't know. More satisfying to destroy bubble wrap. Thankfully, Mom's last attempt at a relationship, Barry, was an internet pharmacist from Moosomin, and he had left all his shipping supplies with us when he got sent to jail. I figure I have enough bubble wrap for another year or so, maybe six month if things keep going like they have been this week."

"Oh."

"Plus sometimes you find stuff in cardboard boxes." She looks down at the book. "Like this. This book ... this book says you're not good for me, Dad."

I can't say anything. Certainly I can't argue. She studies my face, waiting for some kind of plea that never reaches my lips.

"I wanted something from you that you can't give me, and that's okay. You're nothing to me, really. Nothing that's going to last, if you think about it. If I create a dependent relationship with you, I will just be let down because you didn't earn it and you can't return the favour because of your own damage as a human being. It says in here to keep your hands free so you can carry your own baggage."

I nod. We both get something in our eye at the same time.

I have to fill the air with some kind of noise—a grunt, a squeal, a soliloquy—something.

"So ..." I quiver, "so where does that leave us?"

Toon smiles in one corner of her mouth. "I guess I'm breaking up with you. As my dad."

Part of me thinks "Everyone needs a father" would be the right thing to say here, but I grew up with no father, and I turned out fine, didn't I? Instead, I say "Okay," as though there was a single molecule in my body that wants to agree with her, and I acknowledge her through a nod.

She throws a facial expression at me that might be a look of betrayal, or maybe it's of relief, but it's hard to discern from the bluish light of the paused television.

"So you're free," Toon tells me. "We're not father-daughter anymore. Okay?"

It takes me a second to get my head to move up and down, but it does.

Toon claps her hands, exclaims, "Whew!" and smiles at me. It's like an entirely different child is smiling at me. I don't know this girl.

"I thought you were going to make that a lot tougher," she says, and I can see there's real happiness in her eyes. She really doesn't want me. My vision starts to blur.

Toon goes on: "This is great. Now I can find out who I am."

Once in a while, you put a lot of effort into composing the tone of a single word. I craft the first word from my lips with the precision of a model boat builder, inserting the word into this room as though it were the prow, and Jimmy's living room

No Escape from Greatness

the glass bottle. I insert the word with tweezers, trying to relax as I insert.

"Well."

It's a pleasant "well," but not too pleasant. Businesslike, yet amicable, hardly any tension in its insertion. I place my hands on my knees as I say it and manage to compose my embouchure in such a way as to create a perfect horizontal line, neither smiling nor frowning. I leave a pause that would be a near-equivalent to the boat modeller's examination of his glass bottle, admiring his new prow, ensuring it wasn't crooked and wouldn't tumble right off. And then I complete the sentence.

"I wish you all the best in your future endeavours." I extend my right hand and offer a handshake. I have raised the glass boat bottle over my head and smashed it on the floor, roller skated on the shards, then set the floor on fire with a blue angel. "It was nice to know you."

Toon doesn't take my hand, because that would mean something to us both. Instead she stands up. "It's late. I should go."

My stomach turns upside down as Toon takes a step away from me.

"So five-thirty tomorrow?" She says.

"For what?"

"Pick me up from boxing after school. Wait, did you—?" Toon points, then rolls her index fingers backwards, replaying our conversation in her mind. A rush of cool air floods into my heart, like when someone opens a window on the first spring day. Toon snickers to herself. Of course we'll still see each other. Of course.

"Gabriel," she says to me, "you still have your legal obligations and nothing I say can get you out of those. That's up to my mom and the Court of Queen's Bench. It's just that we're not going to build a fake co-dependent relationship overtop of your obligations anymore."

Gabriel, she calls me.

Toon leaves me there in the Manitoba autumn night, alone in a blue room, with Nancy Sorel's face frozen on the flat screen. I feel like I am on pause, too, unable to change my face and unable to skip to the ending, where all is whole and the tempest passed.

After a few minutes, Zac hobbles into the house and spies me from the kitchen. He peg-legs his way into the living room and I wipe my face, composing it as though it were made of stiff clay.

"You all right?" he offers.

"No. Today has been a nightmare."

"Hey, there's always tomorrow. Just start over," he says. Then he turns and heads to the stairs, upstairs to his bedroom. "Rebuild," Zac says over his shoulder. "Make tomorrow Day One." I stare at the ceiling, on the living room couch, all of it still tinted blue from the frozen face of Clara Fine As Played By Nancy Sorel. Tears come and tears go, like how the first snow melts before the full winter freeze rests inside of you.

Once things are sufficiently frozen, I make a plan.

28

Zac hops on one foot down the stairs, booming each step like a timpanist. It's not even eight o'clock in the morning. The sound prods me awake. I find the energy to turn the television off as I unpeel myself from the leather couch.

I want coffee.

I shall accept the ability to want something as a promising sign.

"Jill's coming over," Zac says to me as he sets up a K-Cup.

"I've got to go tell Luanne the news. About me playing me. And then we should probably rehearse before Shane shows up."

Zac passes me an Americano. He's learned to prepare them in such a way that I can imagine him as a barista in some urban minimalist café, part of the gentrifying vanguard in a depressed Winnipeg streetscape, twisting and tugging the stainless steel appendages, mispronouncing people's names to keep irony alive in a post-ironic netherworld.

"So what would bring Shane Wilson from Erratic Automatic

to Greatness, I wonder?" Zac says to me with a suspicious squint in his eyes.

I shrug it away.

"Maybe he just misses the smell, I guess," Zac says.

"He's getting the troupe back together for one last milking of the cow," I murmur over the lip of my mug.

Zac slams down his coffee and leans in from across the kitchen table, agog. "That's great! That's totally what you need."

"What I need? Oh, please do tell me what I need, university-drop-out-cum-ironic-documentarian-cum-philanderer-with-a-limp."

Zac swallows a comeback and then smiles gently, before saying: "You need the money, man. Get your career a kick in the pants and then steer it once it's flying again."

"I can't. You and I both know why."

"No, you won't," Zac says. "And it's because you look down your nose at your own reflection. Right, Uncle G?"

"No, I can't. C-A-N-T can't."

"Nobody tells Gabriel Pegg what he can't do. Nobody except Gabriel Pegg."

Zac takes a victory sip of his robo-coffee. If you asked her nicely and acted reasonably, I'm sure you and Luanne could figure it out.

"I'd best be off then," I say to him, brushing my hair with the palm of my hand.

"What are you going to do?" Zac asks. "For Shane Wilson. What scene?"

I refuse to tell him.

INT. ALEXANDRA HOTEL — NIGHT

GEORGE sits at the dark, past-its-prime bar, nursing a Manhattan. He swizzles it with a toothpick.

No Escape from Greatness

The BARTENDER (stupidly handsome, winning smile) polishes his way up the counter to George.

>BARTENDER
>I thought you liked deer blood in your drinks.

>GEORGE
>Getting ready for a life without it.

>BARTENDER
>Oh?

>GEORGE
>They don't have it at The Big Time, and that's where I'm headed. The Big Time. On the 8:30 Via. Tonight.

>BARTENDER
>Oh. You sing or some such?

>GEORGE
>Isn't it obvious? I'm a comedian.

The door slams.

LOUISE is here. Mascara streams down her face, making patches like a raccoon's mask. Her hair is mussed. At some point she had been sad, but it has given way to abject rage.

The Bartender clocks that George is the object of her anger and he slinks away.

George finishes his drink in a single gulp. Louise marches up to him.

          LOUISE
Now you listen to me. If you get on that train, it will be the biggest mistake of your life. All you need is right here in this town. Whatever rainbow you think you need to chase, it doesn't start here, George. It ends here.

          GEORGE
I have to do this, Louise.

          LOUISE
No you don't. I know who you are, George. You think you can degrade yourself, night after night and not go crazy? Those boys, they don't know you. I know you, George. I know you.

No Escape from Greatness

> GEORGE
> You saw how funny we were together.

> LOUISE
> That outhouse skit was just stupid.

> GEORGE
> We changed outhouse to Port-O-Potty and now it's hilarious.

George slurps up an ice cube.

> LOUISE
> I gave you my heart, George, and you just crunched down on it like it was an ice cube in one of your fucking drinks.

Louise snatches the glass from George's hand and smashes it on the floor.

They stare silently for a moment. Louise's tears begin to bubble up again. George finally breaks.

> GEORGE
> There has to be more than this.

> LOUISE
> What does that say about me?

> GEORGE
> It means you're better than me. You know how to be happy.

> LOUISE
> I thought I did. I thought I was.

> GEORGE
> I can't make this be enough.

Louise rushes out.

George watches the door close.

The bartender mixes a Manhattan.

> BARTENDER
> Woo. A lot of drama for a Wednesday night.

The bartender pounds back the drink.

> BARTENDER (cont'd)
> You want something?

END OF SCENE

No Escape from Greatness

When I arrive at the farmhouse, Luanne's car is out of the driveway—she's dropping Toon off at school, no doubt. I breathe a sigh of relief and recline in the driver's seat of Jimmy's Cadillac. I stare up at its luxuriously upholstered ceiling, yellowed by twenty years of dusty Greatness air, and the occasional cigar.

My phone rings. It's Erin. *Erin!* My body immediately dives into a system-wide shock response as—from the bottom of the ocean of memory—something I told Erin jars itself loose from the ocean floor and gains buoyancy. Trembling, my finger finds the Answer Call button. The phone flounders as I raise it to my cheek, but, always the professional, I am able to offer my expected wit:

"I thought you never wanted to hear my voice again."

"I don't. Be perfectly silent or I will hang up this phone."

A tiny voice in my head whispers something, but I can't quite hear it. The memory of what I told Erin nears the surface.

"Listen carefully, Gabriel, because I will not be taking any questions or providing any additional information. I meant what I said, but … the truth is that I did care for you once. And my personal feelings got all mixed up with my professional gratitude and … you weren't completely wrong, is all."

The thing I told Erin surfaces and splashes around in my head: "Project L."

"So my boyfriend is the best family litigator in Toronto, and I asked him to do this favour for me so you will never bother me again, and he has filed the motion for you. The hearing is set for tomorrow."

My brain swims. I can't believe what I'm hearing.

"Boyfriend?! Why didn't I hear about this sooner?"

"I told you to be silent, Gabriel. I'm going to need you to wire thirty-five thousand dollars to his firm today. I don't want to hear your voice. Press one if you'll do it and two for no."

"I—"

"No! One for yes and two for no."

I have a movie to make. But Toon doesn't want me here anyway. It's what I wanted in the first place ... wasn't it? Suddenly an image of gophers pops into my head, and an elk ... and the apparition of a perogy-making entrepreneur.

If I press one, I get what I wanted.

If I press two, there will never be more than this.

I press one and put the phone back up to my ear.

Erin pauses for a moment before a flummoxed sigh. "Was that a one or a two?"

Luanne pulls into the driveway.

"One."

"Goodbye forever, Gabriel. I hope you find light from somewhere."

Erin hangs up as Luanne gets out of her car.

"Big things are happening, Luanne," I say before she can get a word in. "Shane Wilson is in town and he wants to be in the film and I will play myself opposite you for him—I mean George and Louise, of course, these characters aren't us—in just one scene, tonight, at the theatre, eight o'clock. Okay?"

Luanne leans against her car and leers at me.

"I know," she says. "You forget I run this town. I know Shane is here. I know Zac broke his ankle. I know you went on a *date* with that shrink from Brandon last night."

She says *date* with a heave of revulsion. I'm surprised, but I'm not going to acknowledge it.

"So will you? Play Louise opposite my George?"

I half expect her to slap me across the face and kick gravel onto my pant leg, but she doesn't. She scowls a bit and flashes me a disapproving look.

"I'm not doing Port-O-Potty Guy again. I *can't* do it again. This way, if you'll help me, I can show Shane that I'm more than just a scatological caricature."

No Escape from Greatness

"I said I'd do it, so I'll do it," she says, tersely. "Anything else?"

Anything else ... well I suppose I could have mentioned that this one scene would be my final one in Greatness; that I had nuked any chance of having a family here; that my next errand was to go over to the Highway Robbery and wire all of Jimmy's money to Toronto, and that I was soon to follow the dollars to the Big Smoke and emancipation. I suppose I could have mentioned it. But I'm not a big fan of lacerations.

Instead, like slipping into a pair of slippers at the end of the day, I fall into the comfort of throwing a below-the-belt counterpunch.

"Just one last thing, Luanne. Why are you so obsessed with my romantic life?"

She doesn't take the bait. She seems to swallow her tongue a bit, sucking in her cheeks and pursing her lips, the way only Luanne can. "So will you bring Toon directly to the theatre, then?"

29.

The Greatness Curling Club is a dilapidated barn, kitty-corner to Ruml Elementary, featuring the only sheet of indoor ice in fifty miles. To the immediate left of the Curling Club is a gravel road that slithers between buildings and leads to the Firefighters' Rodeo grounds. The Curling Club has a banquet room with a patch of parquet flooring—a dance floor that does double duty as an activity centre.

I watch Toon from the opposite wall as she boxercises. This isn't boxing at all. Some kind of techno music blares through the ancient PA system as Toon hops side to side and flails spasmodically at the air, alongside four women in their sixties and the instructor, a young man I've never seen before. They box like they've got bricks in their gloves.

"One last grapevine," the instructor shouts, and they all line-dance across the floor, air-punching all the while. It's an atrocity to watch.

Finally, the thumping ceases and the boxercisers double over, out of breath. The instructor claps his hands and pats a couple of the ladies on the back, then saunters right past me, out of the room. The ladies converse with one another on their way out, but no one even throws Toon an acknowledging nod. The seniors nod and smile at me, knowing who I am, but I don't give them the satisfaction of a returning smile.

Toon sits on the parquet floor, cross-legged, waiting for me to come to her, but why would I do that if I'm not her father anymore? Once I'm sure Toon has sensed the deliberateness of my delayed reaction, I approach. We've got places to be, so I can't have a stand-off over who's going to walk up to whom. That's why I do it. Efficiency.

Toon looks up at me and then clambers to her feet. "Hard work," she says.

"Not boxing," I say to her.

"Funny thing about this class," she says, trying to scratch her nose with her boxing glove, "it really, really, makes you wish you could punch something."

"So you asked me to come here so you could punch me?"

"What? No! I was hoping maybe, since I have the gloves on and everything ... maybe you could teach me some boxing. Just so I can shadow-box without looking like an idiot. I swear I won't touch anybody. And no sappy wannabe-Dad moments."

"I'm not going to hit you."

"Just tell me what you know, Gabriel. Please?"

There's my name again. It makes me seethe.

"We have places to go, *Petunia*." I hope that grates on her. "I have a very important scene rehearsal today."

"Come on, I know you know the punches. Tell me the punches. Please please pretty please with brown sugar and gumdrops on top? I'll never ask for anything ever again ever." Toon even bats her eyelashes at me. I feel the manipulation, but allow it anyway.

With a harrumph, I assume the pugilists' stance and Toon

No Escape from Greatness

does a good job of mirroring me. "Good," I say, "now first, jab." I jab with the right, darting my first and even getting a little bounce into my stance. Toon catches on easily. It's hard not to smile.

"Okay, now the occasional cross—jab, jab, cross—jab, jab, cross." I'm getting winded. I've never boxed before. I've just watched it on Wide World of Sports. It is incredibly difficult. I need to wrap it up before my heart explodes.

"Uppercut!" I bellow, and swing upward at my invisible opponent's chin. Toon swings upward as well, not all that strong, but good enough, and I stop. I hunch over, trying to regain my breath.

I hear Toon say "Jab, jab, cross—uppercut!" and then I feel the wake of her boxing glove brush against my left ear.

Staggering back, I yell, "Hey!" I clutch my ear as though she had hit me. And then I realize—"Hey, you almost touched me there."

"But I didn't," she says.

"But you almost did." I widen my eyes in mocking incredulity. "What would happen if you actually touched me? Oh my." I smile.

Toon smiles back and I get a flash of how she will look when she starts flirting with boys. "It wouldn't count anyway, because I'm not touching you, the boxing glove is touching you." She gives me a Cheshire grin.

I walk up to her and she gets that look—the look I imagine a little kid gets when she knows she is about to be tickled, or chased when they want to be caught. I imagine that is what is happening here, because I have never seen it before in my own daughter. She doesn't know what I'm about to do, and she likes it.

Like a scorpion, I snap my arms out and strike at her boxing glove, grabbing her right hand with my two hands. She gasps and the smile disappears from her face entirely. In fact, Toon goes white as I raise her hand up in my own.

"But you've got your pugilistic prophylactic on," I tell her.

"Say that ten times fast," she says, forcing herself to relax. I can see in her hazel eyes that she is anxious.

"That that that that that, that that that that that."

We look into each other's eyes for a moment. And then we burst out laughing. Toon withdraws her glove, but that's okay; the damage has been done and I have touched her hand, boxing glove or no. It's okay right now. Everything is okay right now.

As our laughter subsides, I ask, "Why don't you like touching?"

"Do you like nails on a chalkboard? Do you like forks scraping on plates? Same thing for me and having somebody's germy skin smear its guck all over me."

"But not even a hug? A kiss?"

"Yuck and ew."

"Toon, you can't go through life without ever touching a person. If you don't allow yourself to touch ... to be touched ... you'll never know how great those things can be."

"I am aware of this."

"Germs don't work the way you think they work. You won't get sick from touching me. Or from letting me hold your hand, say."

"It's not my thinking brain that needs to understand this, Gabriel. It's like an instinct. It's something way bigger than my thinking brain."

She takes a step closer to me. I wonder if maybe she's leaving herself open to possibility of allowing me to rest the palm of my hand on her t-shirt shoulder—would that be so frightening? I rub my fingers against my palm in preparation.

"I think I need to see a doctor," she says meekly.

No Escape from Greatness

"I think so too," I say, and begin to raise my hand.

"But I'm gonna have to get in line."

Toon delivers a cinder-block right jab into my breadbasket, a complete sucker-punch that makes my lungs leap into my throat. I expel every air molecule in my body and the resulting vacuum makes me croak. I fall to the floor.

Through my squinting eyes, I peer up at Toon. She stands above me with her hands on her hips.

"What did I say about sappy Dad moments?"

I feel a vibration in my leg and realize that I am having a heart attack.

Another vibration pulsates through my femoral artery. This is the big one. Toon has killed me with a single punch.

"Phone," Toon says as she pulls at the laces on her boxing glove with her teeth. The pulsating happens a third time, in rhythm, and I realize that Toon is right: it's no heart attack. Just the phone. I roll to my other side and fish out the infernal device. It's Erin.

"Done," she says. "Motion granted. You're free in seven days."

I hang up.

"Who was it?" Toon asks.

"Airline scam," I tell her, and my chest tightens for real.

I'm free. The feeling isn't as joyful as I expected it to be.

I must use my liberation well, now that I have it back. I have to if I'm going to make it worthwhile. I'm going to send Shane packing and prove to him that I have what it takes to do what I was meant to do.

I can't look at Toon, or smile, or register any emotion at all, the entire way down to the Welsh Community Theatre. It doesn't take Toon very long to pick up on it.

"Hey, I'm sorry I punched you in the gut. I didn't think it would hurt so bad."

"It's fine."

"You're really soft there. What's in there, marshmallows and kitty cats?"

I manage a scowl, which makes her grin mischievously.

Suddenly I feel the cost of my freedom more deeply than I ever have before.

I pull into the Welsh Community Theatre's dirt parking area, in the middle ditch between the two stretches of the Trans-Canada Highway. Everyone is already here it seems, by the number of vehicles outside. My legs feel like they weigh an extra fifty pounds each as we walk toward the church doors; it's as though my body can't go through with the labour of walking, of remaining earth-bound, any longer, now that I'm free but remaining silent. Suddenly the air feels like it's pushing down on me. I look over and down at my daughter, who has disowned me and is now closer to me than ever, and I wonder what my news will make her become, twenty years from now. If my absence contributed to her aversion to touching, I wonder what this will do.

Shane sits where I sat just a few days ago, when I auditioned the local oddballs to try and "make lemonade," as Zac suggested. I should have known it was all a plot to make fun of me. Of course it was. I'm not sure what I was thinking in the first place: *Descent into Greatness* needs to be made in Toronto, or the West End, or on Broadway, and so it's for the best that the production won't go forward.

Zac, my former protégé, fiddles with the settings on a brand-new RED camera, while moony-eyed Jill looks up at him like he put the bop in the bop shebop shebop. He darts over to look at a monitor, then moves behind the camera and pulls focus on Luanne's face. Luanne has covered herself in makeup; she looks almost as young as she did the day she pleaded with me to stay in Greatness all those years ago. She doesn't ever wear makeup anymore, as far as I know. But she did back then.

No Escape from Greatness

Luanne leans against a six-foot-wide solid oak bar, which has somehow transported itself from a basement rec room into this theatre. I see Tom and Carol leaning against a far wall, and I presume this bar must belong to them. I've just seen Tom this morning, when I learned the true meaning of highway robbery: wiring thirty-five thousand dollars at Tom's store cost me nearly three hundred in usurious fees. Tom smiles at me, that nauseating "have a nice day" smile that might be genuine or might be a complete lie, and I pretend that I've never seen Tom before.

I breeze by Shane and inspect the marks in front of and behind the bar, pretending Luanne isn't even there. "Looks good. Zac, can we reduce the light in here by about a thousand percent?"

"Sure," Zac says and makes his way to an unseen bank of light switches, behind the charred curtains.

"Got the script?" I say to Shane, and he nods. "Any questions?"

"Umm ... can we talk for a second?" Begrudgingly, I make my way over to our guest star. He nods over at Luanne, who memorizes her lines at the bar, and whispers to me: "Isn't that—Luanne? Like, your ex, Luanne?"

"Pitchfork and all," I tell him. I immediately feel bad for saying it.

"We don't get along, Gabe. She blames me for taking you away. Don't you remember that?"

"Perish the thought, Shane." I call out to Luanne: "Luanne, do you harbour a deep-seated resentment of poor Shane, here, because he asked me to join the troupe? I tried to tell him that's ridiculous, but ..." I stop talking. Luanne's face drains of blood. She does. Luanne shrugs a little and tries to shake her head, but it's such a weak denial.

"That's ridiculous," she says with a forced snicker. "Ancient history."

And suddenly, like a dysenteric seagull, twenty years of

Luanne's heartbreaking pain falls from the sky, onto my head, and splashes all over me. I get it. For the first time in my life, I can admit to myself that I feel it. Her pain must be terrible.

"Good enough for me," Shane pronounces. "Are we ready to shoot yet?"

I clap twice and shout for places. Luanne can't even look Shane in the eye.

She shrouds herself in a curtain, ready to enter from stage right. She examines her shoes. Shane grabs a bar towel and starts wiping.

"Sound, Uncle G," Zac hisses at me, and I cue sound. Toon lifts the boom mic. In this light, I look at Toon's face and see my own. How many times did Luanne see my face in Toon's in eleven years? How many times did the very sight of her make a little incision into Luanne's soul?

Everyone stares at me, the director and creator of all of this, and I am finally, for the first time in my life, able to see the damage I have created. In many ways, the damage is my life's horrible purpose.

"G—your mark." Zac says, and I realize that I am out of place. I move to my mark at the side of the bar and give a half-hearted "Action." This twisted-up fakery is my way to weasel out of my destiny, at the expense of everyone I see around me: Zac, Toon, Luanne, Shane … even the locals, like Zac's married girlfriend and the Highway Robbery owners. This scene isn't going to benefit anyone except me. And how is it going to benefit me, exactly?

"I thought you liked deer blood in your drinks," Shane says to me, handing me what appears to be a glass of flat cola.

"Getting ready for life without it," I reply. "They don't have it at The Big Time, and …" I choke on the words. "That's where I'm going," I say emptily. I've never been there. "On the 8:30 Via, tonight."

Shane polishes his bar. "You sing or some such?"

No Escape from Greatness

"A comedian," I say.

Mascara streams down Luanne's face. She's no actress. These tears are real.

"Slam," Toon yells, and Luanne stomps up to me. Shane slinks away.

I look down the bottom of the prop cola.

Luanne is ready to deliver her lines, and suddenly I am not ready to hear them.

"Now you listen to me," she says. "If you get on that train, it will be the biggest mistake of your life."

"It will be," I say to her.

Everyone stands in silence. Toon lowers the boom on my head, perhaps the most literal demonstration of lowering the boom in human history. The boom flattens me, pushing the stool out from under me. My prop cocktail smashes on the floor, covering my face with flat cola, ice cubes and shards of glass. My cheek burns.

"I can't make this be enough," I bellow from the floor.

"What are you saying, Gabriel?" Luanne wipes her face with her forearm. "What are you telling me?"

"I'm telling you that you've wasted enough of your life on me, Luanne. I'm getting back together with Erratic Automatic."

"You can't," Toon blurts. "Mom, he can't …"

"That's what the money was for," Luanne says. "The money you wired this morning."

I sit up and pluck a triangle of glass from my face. "Way to keep that to yourself for a whole hour, Tom."

"You son of a bitch," Luanne murmurs.

"That's right, everyone. Big announcement: I am a son of a bitch. I used the movie money to hire good lawyers, and the good lawyers got me my well-deserved freedom this morning, and now we are ready to inflict our comedy on the world once more."

"That's good news," Shane says. Isn't it?

30.

I'm not overly shocked by Luanne's seething anger, or Shane's avaricious glee, or even Toon's dejected look. But Jill says something to Zac, something hurtful but not angry, and he stumbles backward and falls into a theatre seat like a prizefighter who just stumbled back to his corner.

I don't understand, but I can't dwell. Shane is in my face now.

"We need to get the buzz going right away—start promoting," he says. "If we rush rehearsals, we can do SketchFest in San Francisco in three weeks."

"Three weeks? No, that's too soon."

"Come on, Gabe. Are you doing this or not?"

This is really happening.

Something inside me that stood at the precipice of a very deep pit just slipped, and is falling, falling down into the pit, and the pit feels as though it may be bottomless. I'm doing it. I'm falling.

"I can't leave town for another seven days, is all."

"Oh." Shane looks up at the sky. Out of the corner of my eye,

I can see Luanne and Toon storm out of the theatre. "I've got it," Shane says. "Let's have our big presser where it all began: right here in Greatness!"

"That is preposterous. How in the blazes are you going to get the media to turn up here?"

"We'll stream it!"

I assume that a 'stream' is something internet-related.

"Yeah, this'll work," Shane says. "Greatness, the place where the dream was born. We'll get the guys to come down and we'll stream our announcement, then maybe we could do a quick sketch, maybe. Just a quick one." With a smirk, he says, "You know, that gives me time to seal the deal with your shrink."

"Dr. Ross is not my therapist," I pronounce. "We were on a bad date."

"Oh, jeez. Sorry for mowing your grass, there," Shane says with his dentist-arousing smile. As though pulled by magnets, my gaze returns to Zac and his girlfriend. He's slouched over like marionette without strings. Jill consoles him, rubbing his back.

"It's fine. I actually got what I needed, I think, which ended up being some therapy," I tell Shane absently. Jill whispers something to Zac, and Zac shoots up from his seat and limps with determination for the door.

"Excuse me, I need to talk to my nephew."

I have to call after Zac to get him to slow down. When he turns, I see his eyes are laced with tears and pink.

"After everything, you do this without telling me?" He runs his hands through his hair.

"Why don't you just stay, then? Better yet, why don't the two of you just shack up in Winnipeg?"

"She's married, Gabe. She won't leave Shoelace, because Shoelace saved her life. And she won't share her talent, either."

"Talent?"

"Yeah … have you not heard about her singing? She sings the

way angels wish they could sing," Zac says to me. "She makes music more musical. It brings tears to the eyes of the notes themselves, man. You've heard nothing like it. Her singing … *does* something to me. She should be singing in velvety amphitheatres in front of royalty, and, and Burton Cummings."

Clearly, something quite deleterious has happened to my nephew's heart.

"She told me there's nothing to keep me here, anymore, and I shouldn't waste my life chasing a feeling, because she's trapped here."

"Nobody likes to be trapped, Zac," I say with my most earnestly conjured sympathy.

"She's choosing the trap over me. Because she's that good of a person. It's just her kindness that's keeping her here. The thing I love the most about her is the thing that made the trap."

Zac looks like he's about to bawl. This is all so … sanguine. Saturated with it. It makes me shift in my stance and clench my fists. I can't undo what I've done. I can't let up now.

"She chose wrong," I tell Zac. "She shoud have chosen you if it meant getting out of here."

"I hope you're a big deal in the big time like you want so bad. I hope it's all worth it." Zac mimics a two-handed tossing away of me and everything I'm about, then stumbles away, crying.

I've never felt smaller. I've done things that were reprehensible, horrible and hurtful and heinous before, but that was when I didn't *feel* anything or at least anything I could admit to myself. Losing Jill is my fault. I can't let Zac deal with this pain all alone. C-A-N-T can't.

"Wait," I call to Zac. "I want to help."

Zac looks at me with an incredulous face. "Help? You want to help?"

"Yes," I reply, defensively. "I would like to help you … not be so hurt."

"Uncle G, I don't think there's a single thing you could possibly do to fix this, unless you can find a way for Jill to un-dump me."

"There's one person who can get Jill to change her mind."

"Who's that?"

"Shoelace, of course. It's time we hashed everything out, the three of us, like men."

"We don't even know where he is. He disappeared."

"How much do you want to bet? Come with me."

Zac follows me to the car and we head for the Healing Lodge, where we found Shoelace before. It only take a few minutes down the Trans-Canada to get to the log cabin, but there's no ultracompact hybrid in the driveway, just a beaten-up pickup truck. Zac looks at me, hopeful, tears dried.

He follows me inside the lodge.

"Holy shit," a man's voice cackles, "is that Gibbers?"

The man has a ponytail now, a puffy nose and a pot belly that matches mine, but I'd never forget his face: Bruce Wapiti.

Bruce, the kid from Maple Lake who I crossed the racial divide to play alongside, bussed to school from the reserve every day until he was old enough to skip the bus. Then he hitched a ride to high school with his friends. I drove him a few times in Grade 12. All his friends did.

And then, at a bush party one weekend, Bruce showed up, and when he told me he thought fondly of Luanne, I had no choice but to throw myself at her before Bruce could.

Bruce takes my hand and shakes the hell out of it.

"I didn't know you were back. Why haven't we gone for a coffee to catch up yet?" He laughs with his tongue sticking out, making the laugh wilder and a little bit irreverent.

Bruce is now a councillor at Maple Lake and runs the band's economic development corporation. He's cleaning up the cabin, taking measurements and pictures for planning purposes. Apparently, healing and teaching lodges aren't that lucrative, and so Bruce has decided to explore other uses for it, like a bed-and-breakfast or call centre. I think we'd still be close if I hadn't left town.

We ask if he knows Shoelace.

Bruce laughs. "Do I know Shoelace? Of course. He's the biggest pain in my ass, Gibbers. Total preservationist, eh? Doesn't see the point in progress."

"Do you know where he is right now?"

"I think he said something about a farm and some deer?"

Zac and I exchange an "anyplace but there" look.

"Dearheart Farm. Let's go," I tell Zac, not believing the words as they leave my mouth. I am the man in the movie who suggests that, in the murderous midnight woods, we should all split up.

"Give him wings and he'll help you fly," Bruce says.

"What did you say?" Did he appear in my Prairie Caribou vision? Was he there that night?

"I said we should do that coffee sometime, catch up," Bruce says.

I nod and smile. "It's good to see you. Maybe we could," I tell him, and we make our way to the car.

"Are we really doing this?" Zac says.

"I believe we are. For the love of all that is holy, I believe we are."

We pass Karl on the way, trudging along the shoulder of the Trans-Canada, back toward Greatness. We find the nondescript turn-off and zigzag through dirt roads. The bobbing pumpjacks give way to farmland, and soon we arrive at the telephone pole gate with the two-hearted deer emblazoned on it. I stop the car and grip the steering wheel, hesitant to go any further.

"Look—by the farmhouse," Zac says. It's Shoelace's car. I take a deep breath, steel myself, and drive us across the threshold.

Misty comes out of the house to greet us, her sundress bearing sunflowers this time, and a sunflower in her blonde terrifying locks. Thankfully, she wields a dish towel this time instead of a hatchet. But her look is still enough to fill me with fear. My fingers tighten their grip on the Cadillac's steering wheel.

"Oh God," I shudder. "Help me Zac, I am afraid."

Zac opens his door, then stops and looks over at me. With a disapproving look, Zac doesn't say a word. He just leans back into the car, pries each of my fingers off the steering wheel, one by one, then the thumbs, and then steps out of the car.

"I'm glad you're here, Pegg," Misty says to me as we reach the bottom step of her porch.

"Why's that? You planning to have us for dinner?" Zac elbows me. "Sorry. We're just looking for Shoelace. We mean no offense."

"Well I think maybe I owe you an apology. Sometimes I get a wee bit protective, especially about my wife. Maybe you sensed that."

Zac and I look at each other in puzzlement. "Nope, didn't sense anything like it," we tell her.

"Well I've been talking a lot with Shoelace, and I realize I'm crushing the butterfly when I squeeze too tight." That sounds like something Shoelace would say. "People make mistakes. I shouldn't have said Beth is out of your production, especially when Beth herself had no chance to express to me what she wanted. Nope, that's crushing the butterfly."

I'm baffled to the point of stammering.

"I mean you know what it's like to love something that much, right?"

Do I?

"I'll go get Shoelace."

No Escape from Greatness

Misty goes back inside and we haven't even climbed up the first step.

I take a deep breath to steel myself. Zac runs his fingers through his unthinning hair, turns and nods at me like a prisoner ready for the firing squad.

Misty comes back out. Then out comes Shoelace, ducking to get through the doorway.

"So I talked to Beth and she says she would be all right with working on your movie again," Misty says. Shoelace glares down at us, his eyes eleven feet above us.

"We ... can discuss it," Zac suggests, and I wholeheartedly agree.

"Yes," I add, "at a later date we can arrange something." I feel like a cockroach skittering across the kitchen floor as Shoelace turns the light on.

"Wait," I say, taking that first step up the porch stairs. "The truth of the matter, Misty, is that ... the production is finished. My (I shudder at the word) *comedy* troupe is reuniting and I will be leaving as soon as I am able. So, for now, it seems *Descent into Greatness* is on hiatus."

Shoelace booms his voice at us like a bazooka. "Why are you here? You need to say something to me?"

I take another step up. "Shoelace, I know you have feelings for Jill, but you're treating her like chattel, and it has to stop. She's too talented to stay here—you and I both know it. You said it yourself, Shoelace: don't let history colour her future. You need to let her go, set her free, and let her figure things out for herself. Who knows what she is capable of out there, and who are you to keep her from it? You can't treat her this way and you can't bully my nephew because of your unrequited love."

I've done it. I've confronted the two people in Southwestern Manitoba most likely to break my legs, and now they both stare down at me. Relieved, and resigned to my fate at the same time,

I clench my jaw and prepare for some form of diving attack, or flying drop kick from above—instead, I see Zac's face. He's smiling at me. I think that may even be pride I see in his eyes, but there's no possible way I could positively identify that look, because I've never seen it before.

After a moment, Shoelace sighs. "You're right. I'm crushing the butterfly." Shoelace looks down at the cast on Zac's ankle. "Sorry about that. I lost my head."

"Sorry I broke into your house," Zac says.

"If it makes Jill happy, then it's what she ought to do. Be kind to her and help her, or I'll find you. And if the investigators ever come …"

"… if the investigators come, tell them she's chasing the Canadian dream."

Shoelace smiles at me. "Good one," he says. Zac and I return to our car and pull away. Beth comes out and embraces her wife. The three of them watch us drive away.

"Thanks, Uncle G," Zac says to me as we pass through the gate. "I can't believe you did that."

I did that.

I can feel my grip ease around the steering wheel as we get back into the Manitoba oil patch and closer to home.

31.

The other members of Erratic Automatic—JD, Gord and Snorri-Stein—turn up the next day, each flying in to Winnipeg, meeting up at the Hotel Fort Garry for a pint at the Palm Room, then renting a car to make the three-hour trek to Greatness. They arrive in a brand-new subcompact.

JD—who was often known as "the oddball" or "the French one"—was living in sin with a guy in Calgary. You can't live in Calgary without a driver's license; and JD had one, which was fortuitous for Gord and Snorri-Stein, neither of whom had a license, what with Gord living in Vancouver and riding his bicycle everywhere, and Snorri-Stein's almost compulsive obsession with cabs and their drivers. JD could chauffeur them until someone offered a tour bus or limousine. Perhaps Snorri-Stein's lineage included a ferryman; perhaps the one who paddled across the River Styx. Anyone who met Snorri-Stein would consider that a distinct possibility. At any rate, Gord (the giant redhead with a Hebridean temperament and blood pressure to match, known as "the indignant one" or "the big one"), Snorri-Stein (the Icelandic Polish character man known to us as "Goolack," a clever amalgam of two ethnic slurs, such brilliant comedic wordsmithing we were capable of!) and JD the oddball roll up to Shane's hotel as the sun reaches its peak over Greatness and the rusty sewer pipe smell finds its zenith.

Shane takes them to my house and greetings are exchanged. Some awkward embraces. I feel happy to see JD, at least, and then suddenly I have left myself. It's not unlike the Prairie Caribou vision quest. I'm here, but not here. I am doing this, but it's not me touching my old troupe-mates. It's not me bringing them back to my hometown so they can rescue me.

"Scene of the crime, eh?" JD says as he looks around at Greatness. I nod, but it's not me who nods.

Zac is introduced to the group, but he keeps his distance and doesn't smile much. I am taken to the Welsh Community Theatre. We rehearse, all day long. Townsfolk pop their heads in to get a glimpse of us, but they are shooed away or beat a hasty retreat once they are discovered.

We rehearse the one sketch that is easiest for us to pick up on short notice. The one sketch whose structure, like an insipid pop song, just gets sung over and over again, different lyrics but the same song, over and over, and is familiar to everyone but lost its thrill for us long ago. We still know how to fake the energy, and we are satisfied after a couple hours that we can sing this old song again. The worst song I ever wrote. Beloved by millions.

The beeping of a cube van going in reverse heralds the arrival of Luanne and a bank of blue portable toilets. Like cockroaches when the light is turned on, the boys scurry to the four corners of the church, pretending to examine the walls or contemplate quietly or whatever. I just stand there and take the look of murderous betrayal as Luanne directs two guys to wheel the potties up to centre stage. Her arms never unfold. Her jaw never unclenches. Her gaze never veers from mine. She's like

No Escape from Greatness

a crystal-eyed tiger in the bushes, and I'm the gazelle in the meadow, looking up from my feeding because something is there, but freezing in the hopes that it will not pounce.

Until this morning, Luanne's hatred for the other men in Erratic Automatic, especially Shane, was unrivalled. Now I suspect all of that hatred has been refocused, like five accusatory laser pointers being refracted straight into my eye socket. And I can't blame her. Really, this whole salvo is about finally setting her free from me, not the other way around..

Without words, she levels all her anger at me. It starts to weigh me down and I can feel my shoulders starting to buckle. After an eternity, the labourers finally set the portables down from off their dollies and we have a bank of three, in a tidy row, so Luanne has no further reason to stand here and wrap us up in her cilice of "you took him away from me" or "you took you away from me" or the thousand other hairshirts she could foist upon us.

The afternoon goes by and I say the lines, from inside the latrine and out, and behind, and in front, and the guys fall into their characters and even chuckle nostalgically, but I don't. I'm floating around in the theatre, watching my body go through it but never really going through it.

Zac turns up around five o'clock with computer equipment and cameras. As soon as he passes through the doors, he notices the blue plastic array on the stage and nearly drops his travel case. But he sets up our streaming equipment all the same, silently, keeping his judgements to himself. He brings in a lighting rig and sets that up so the toilets are in perfect view for the internetting audience.

At six o'clock, a kid from the *Brandon Sun* shows up, and ten minutes after that, the *Greatness Advance-Empire*'s owner/operator arrives with a microcassette recorder. The kid from the Sun mentions his story will definitely get picked up by the *Winnipeg*

Free Press, and maybe even the *CP* Wire. We are news again. Zac tells Shane that their UStream account has already got thirty-five thousand people logged in ahead of the scheduled streaming time, and *Deadline Hollywood Daily* has "tweeted out the earl." I must assume that tweeting earls is cause for excitement.

The other guys look nervous as we make our final preparations for this sketch, which will be in front of a live audience greater than any we've performed live in front of before. Shane disappears and reappears with something on a hanger beneath dry cleaner's plastic: it's a black topcoat and tails.

He brought the costume.

JD smiles and tells me to put it on, but I hesitate. Gord gives me an openhanded slap across the back of my head, and a cursive "do it," and I get dressed.

Zac gives us the cue to take our places. As though someone opened the floodgates, we see everyone from Greatness enter the theatre at the same time: Tom, Carol and Karl, China Joe, Misty and Beth, Jill and her Four Winds Truck Stop people, Daniel (who can't bear to miss an opportunity to watch me humiliate myself), Shoelace, Dr. Karen Ross, the town fathers and other Shriners, Destiny and Hope, the teacher that Toon broke, the boxercise instructor, Bruce Wapiti from Maple Lake, and a hundred others.

Zac drops the curtains so we can't see everyone enter. We can hear the rustle of the crowd drowning out the opera music Zac's playing as people take their seat. I can only wonder if Toon and Luanne have arrived. The smell of PVC plastic, chlorine cleaner and the irascible aroma of raw sewage begin to pool up on the stage. These are newer thrones, but they aren't new.

As is our ongoing tradition, Erratic Automatic gathers in a circle, shoulder to shoulder, and it is as though I am watching it from above. Snorri-Stein puts his hand into the centre of the circle, and we all follow suit. He wishes us the best show. There's

No Escape from Greatness

no comedy to it. Just as he did hundreds of times before, Snorri-Stein puts all of his most serious energy into his intention now, as though forcing us to entertain people through single-minded power of will. Shane goes through his pre-game ritual of flashing his smile as widely as he can, like cheek calisthenics, "turning on the pretty" we sometimes call it. Gord loosens himself up, which looks a little like a bull shuffling the sand before it charges. JD mouths his lines to himself at top speed, his eyes raised to God. I shuffle myself over to the middle Port-O-Potty, open the door, sit inside, and slide the locking mechanism so that it is halfway between the red of "occupied" and the green of "available." I straighten my top hat, slide my pants to my shins, sit atop the seat—which is only as sanitized as much as it can be—and try not to breathe in all the disgusting contaminants that pool up inside these places.

I hear the roar of applause.

INT. WELSH COMMUNITY THEATRE - DAY

Thunderous applause from the standing-room-only audience. TOON and LUANNE lean against the back wall, not applauding, but begrudgingly there to watch the biggest thing that ever happened to Greatness.

The curtain RISES suddenly.

HOWLS of acknowledgment sweep through the crowd as they see the bank of Port-O-Potties on stage.

GORD and JD enter from stage left.

> GORD
> This folk festival is the greatest.

> JD
> But where ...

JD breaks on purpose. Gord sees it too and attempts to look like he's also stifling a laugh.

> JD
> Do we go ...

JD raises his hands up, encouraging the crowd to say it along with him. Dozens do.

> JD
> (with audience voices)
> To do our bizness!?

> GORD
> Did you hear those voices man? Trippy.

A few laughs.

Gord pulls on the leftmost door, despite the red "occupied" sign being in clear view. It's locked, but from within:

> SNORRI-STEIN
> (falsetto)
> Occupado!

No Escape from Greatness

Sparse laughter. JD walks to the second door.

                    JD
          This one's unlocked. See?
          Green.

He whips open the door and

SHANE, standing, leaning against the wall of the Port-O-Potty with an elbow, using the toilet paper like a long corded phone.

                  SHANE
          But I don't have any more
          quarters, operator. Can you
          make a collect call? No,
          a collect call, I know the
          number is correct. Area code
          204 ...

Cheaply acquired applause.

Shane looks at the toilet paper like he may have just realized that he is talking to toilet paper.

Then Shane taps the blue wall.

                SHANE (cont'd)
          Hello? Hello? You're
          breaking up.

```
JD closes the door.

                        JD
            I think he may be a while.
```

Here they come. My cue is next. No turning back.

This blue prison and its polyurethane squalor welcome me home. It's not the chemical offgassing that makes my eyes sting to the point of epiphora. A thin film covers them, but I can still make out Gord's silhouette as it splashes across the blue plastic wall, lit from overhead theatre lights. I nearly forget to use my proper Englishman's voice: in the beginning I knew immediately that he needed a proper English accent, because he needed to be as dignified as possible in order to make the indignities hysterical.

Comedy is about status. It's about the little man making fun of the elite. I've always known this, but I've been such an elitist jackass and then wondered why I was such a joke. It never occurred to me that I was comedy itself.

```
                  PROPER ENGLISHMAN
            Hello?

Hoots and hollers of acknowledgment from
the audience.

                  PROPER ENGLISHMAN
                  (cont'd)
            Can someone kindly assist
            me?

JD and Gord look at each other.

A beat.
```

No Escape from Greatness

          GORD
Look, he's half-green, half-red.

          JD
Hey buddy, are you in or out? We have to go.

          PROPER ENGLISHMAN
Well, you see, that is my quandary, my good man. It appears that I am ... caught between closure and vacancy.

          GORD
Is that potty humour?

          PROPER ENGLISHMAN
It's no joke. Regrettably, I am unable to leave, while also, and quite ironically, I might add, the anxiety of having the door partially open leaves me unable to ... do what I came here to do.

          JD
Look there's plenty of trees around here, I'm just gonna —

JD tries to exit, but Gord arm-bars him.

>   GORD
>   Hey man, we're gonna help
>   you, okay? I'm going to push
>   on the door, and you try
>   sliding the lock.

Now the humiliation begins. Apa Jack told me that what I make sometimes isn't for me. I know that.

I do this for them. The audience. Because it's what they want. I'm letting go.

Even though the audience can't see it, I double over, my arms tight into my stomach, my tuxedo pant legs around my ankles. It's precarious because my head must remain perfectly upright in order to balance the top hat. If the top hat isn't perfectly aligned, it isn't as funny.

I call out in my Proper Englishman voice: "Sadly, I suffer from cramps and am unable to rise to my feet to attempt an adjustment of the door latch mechanism."

I let the tear just fall where it wants because the fight is gone.

INT. WELSH COMMUNITY THEATRE - DAY

> ZAC makes adjustments to the computer equipment. On the USTREAM page, it reads 750,000 viewers.
>
> Zac looks over at JILL. She looks down at her lap, like her life-force energy has completely abandoned her body.

No Escape from Greatness

ON STAGE

> JD
> Well what do you want us to do, then?

> GORD
> Yeah bud, how can we help you?

> PROPER ENGLISHMAN
> Help me to alleviate my cramping so I can stand up, then I can slide the door latch mechanism and vacate.

> JD
> Help you vacate so we can help you vacate, non?

> GORD
> Good one! Ha ha!

Gord and JD wait for Gabriel to deliver his line.

And wait.

Someone in the audience laughs nervously.

> KARL
> (heckling)
> He needs cue cards!

Gord shoots a scolding look to the crowd.

>   JD
>   (whispers)
>   Come on Gabe.

Snorri-Stein opens his door.

>   SNORRI-STEIN
>   (from Toilet #1)
>   Help him to relax already!

They all share a fake break, pretending to fall out of character.

>   GORD
>   Good idea, toilet number
>   one.

>   JD
>   Ha ha.

>   GORD
>   How do we get you to relax,
>   proper English gentleman?

I missed my cue and the guys are fudging around it. I exhale hard and try to compose myself. My chin won't stop trembling but the show must go on and it's too late to stop. It's like the knife is halfway in. It doesn't matter if it goes all the way in, now.

I feed them the line that gets us back on track, in my English accent: "Would you be so kind as to help me …"—here it comes—"think of England?"

I hear laughter. Familiar laughter. A few people joined me in chorus. This laughter used to reassure me, and let me know that everyone out there had seen me on TV and were so happy to watch me replay exactly what they had seen, like a living rerun. It was like a down blanket, or two fingers of something warm on a cold day.

But no longer. Now it's the knife.

Gord tries to play the snickers up into guffaws—"Think of England?" he bellows to the crowd. It does merit a couple of whoops. As he has a thousand times before, JD throws his line out and is accompanied by a couple of old fans. "Close your eyes and think of England!" They shout at me.

"I can't do this," I say, without accent.

IN THE CROWD

```
TOON looks up at her mother.

                    TOON
          This is brutal.

                    LUANNE
          It was funny in the
          nineties.

Gord is clearly agitated. His freckled skin
reddens as his blood begins to boil.

                    GORD
          Oh, but you can do this, and
          you will. You want us to
          help you think of England
          because you miss your home,
          right? The placid meadows!
          Pea soup fog!
```

> JD
> Tie me kangaroo down, sport!

> GORD
> No. Just ... no.
> (to the Port-O-Potty)
> How do we help you think of England?

No sound from inside of the Port-O-Potty. My face is buried in my hands.

> KARL
> (heckling)
> Let's go, Port-O-Potty Guy!

DR. ROSS shushes Karl.

> SHANE
> Don't make me come down there!

> JD
> Look, everyone, it's ... Her Royal Highness, the Queen!

Gord immediately pantomimes a stately walk.

> GORD
> (as the Queen)
> Ola! I've come for a royal tour of the Toronto

No Escape from Greatness

> International Folk Festival.
> Oh, how I love the
> dominion and all its quirky
> hinterlands.
>
>   JD
> Your majesty, we've got
> a retentive Englishman
> occupying a stall here, and
> he's asked us to loosen him
> up,
> right ... Port-O-Potty Guy?
>
> A few cheers emanate from the crowd.
>
> Gabriel is silent.
>
>   JD
> Port-O-Potty Guy.
>
>   GORD
> (As the Queen)
> What did you call him?
>
> More laughs — that's supposed to be Gabriel's line.

It's my line but I don't care. The sketch is taking a nosedive. A tailspin is beginning. I have to hold on to the altitude stick just a little longer. I have to lean in to the knife for a beat or two more and then I'll have killed him. I have to pick up the line that Gord tried to pick up. Too late to go back. "What ... what did you call me?" My accent is adequate, my voice broken but recovering.

Jeffrey John Eyamie

IN THE CROWD

The wave of relief upon hearing Gabriel is palpable as it crosses the room.

Zac looks down at the laptop — 1.1 million UStream viewers. Luanne and Toon look glassy-eyed as they watch Gabriel flail inside the vulgar humiliation.

                JD
      Port-O-Potty Guy, man!

            PROPER ENGLISHMAN
      I'll have you know that
      I am the fourth duke of
      Gruntleshire, and one of
      London's foremost actuaries!

              GORD
      Port-O-Potty Guy is what you
      are.

Gabriel, an errant tear glimmering on his cheek, emerges, in the classic Port-O-Potty Guy stance: pants around ankles, hunched over, tuxedo tails covering most of his bare buttocks.

The audience roars its applause, the loudest it has been.

No Escape from Greatness

> PROPER ENGLISHMAN
> Just use another latrine!

The Proper Englishman curtsies to the Queen.

> PROPER ENGLISHMAN
> (cont'd)
> Your majesty.

Like a cavern in an earthquake, things rumble and fall, crashing into one another. I am on autopilot now, completely lost to the Port-O-Potty Guy. Gabriel Pegg is dead. Inside Gabriel, there is no more Gabriel. There is only what I made myself into and could never escape and what everyone wanted all along. There is only a humiliated Brit in a topcoat and tails, who can't seem to move and can't let go, and despite his horror, he is the butt of all the septic humour.

People are proud. I look out at their faces and they're proud of me, because I'm one of them and I did something notable.

We exchange the jokes mechanically and I run around the bank of potties, whoring for laughs and occasionally getting them. These blue sewage tanks are home now; these men who profit from Gabriel's pratfalls and plaintive moans are family now; all there is and all there will be is Erratic Automatic, or shells of what it once was, like an eroding seashell the mollusc must cling to, coming soon to a concert hall near you. The thing inside me that moves my legs suddenly short-circuits. I slump behind the Port-O-Potties, back to the audience. The earthquakes inside me send a tsunami to my eyes. I am feeling too much. I bawl like a child.

Snorri-Stein is the first to arrive. "Dude, what the hell," he hisses.

"I did this," I wallow. "I created this and I can't escape."

Shane says, "Oh man, Karen told me he was fragile. Jeez."

Snorri-Stein looks back at Shane and then throws his hands up at me and spits, "Get up, asshole!"

"Someone help me," I murmur. "Someone please help me. I'm sorry." I start to rock back and forth.

IN THE CROWD

Shoelace stands up.

Zac presses a button and the lights on stage go dark.

The crowd murmurs.

>   KARL
> Hey, it was just getting good!

Laughter.

>   SHOELACE
> (yelling, his voice
> rattles the stained glass)
> Ladies and gentlemen of
> Greatness.

Zac turns on the spotlight and it illuminates Shoelace as he rises.

Complete silence.

No Escape from Greatness

> SHOELACE
> And all of the people watching over internet, and through various other forms of media. If you want to see this awful series of degrading scatological jokes, and enjoy a bit of disgusting nostalgia, go find the originals on YouTube.

The other members of Erratic Automatic twist around the Port-O-Potties to catch a glimpse of Shoelace. They're saving me. Zac and Shoelace, together.

"Thankfully for us all, Gabriel is announcing his retirement from sketch comedy."

"You are?" Shane says to me.

I am.

Shoelace continues: "Gabriel has begun a new project which will demand all of his considerable insight and creativity."

I wipe my face and chuckle. I know what I need to do—I need to give someone else her wings. Quickly, I rise up and walk to the front of the stage. I find a warm strength in my belly that I haven't felt in a long time.

"Thank you, Shoelace. Thank you, everyone. Sadly there will be no reunion of your favourite comedy troupe. However, let's not waste this spotlight." I look over to Zac, whose face registers nothing but dread. He has no idea what I'm getting at.

"Zac, play some opera," I urge him, and he twigs in.

I call for Jill to take the stage. Reluctantly, she does, after everyone from Greatness encourages her, urging her to the front and to the spotlight. "Please, Jill," I tell her, "share with the world the special gift you have."

The opening strains of "O Mio Babbino Caro" play.

It takes her a moment, but finally Jill sings. Everyone is moved. I watch her and listen to her angelic voice and realize that this is what true purpose is, and it is one in a million. If only we were all so fortunate. She sings eight bars and that's all it takes for the world to love her.

That's why they call it a gift.

32.

Many pats on the back and embraces for Jill, as her song comes to a close and she realizes, for better or worse, she has just made a name for herself in front of millions. TMZ immediately phones the diner and has someone on the next plane from Los Angeles. A trip from Los Angeles to Greatness would involve at least one stopover, in either Vancouver, Calgary, Denver, Chicago, or Toronto, then a three-hour drive from Winnipeg to town. Factoring in the layover times, missed flight connections, car rental mishaps, the traffic on Lincoln Boulevard to LAX, and you've got yourself a 24-hour trip.

I stand in the front of the stage, pants haphazardly pulled up over my waist, and I applaud in sincere admiration of Jill's talent. Everyone was dead on. She is the most delectable vocal talent to which I have ever had the privilege to listen. Such soulfulness. It is so obviously her purpose to share this talent with the world.

Even though I can feel the eyes of Shane, Gord, Snorri-Stein and JD boring holes into the back of my head, I leap from the stage and press toward Jill, as so many others do in the crowd, trying to touch her as though she's just become an image of the Virgin Mary burnt by the sun into a terra cotta wall.

Jill pushes the throng as she tries to move to her right, toward Shoelace, who is busy with handshakes and pats on the back from townsfolk as well.

I look back at Zac, who sits at his computer area still, observing everything, watching Jill, pride salted with something bitter in his eyes. He points at me, and mouths "Thank you," and I mimic clenching my heart in both hands.

Then I point back to him and say, "This is for you."

I'm going to set things right with Jill; and Zac is going to get what he deserves, which is the heart of this young woman, and all the laughter and chaos and tears and surprises and scars and tickles that come with it.

I knife my way through the throng, from the back, through row upon row of new Jill disciples, just as Jill makes her way through Shoelace's admirers to Shoelace himself. I put my arm on Jill's shoulders and call her name, but she's busy.

She wraps both arms around Shoelace and pulls him in tight.

It surprises the behemoth. He closes his eyes and grins gently, pressing Jill's head into his solar plexus.

The jostling around us stops. Onlookers stop reaching for them and simply witness this moment. I can feel Zac's heart turning into an ashtray, fifty yards behind me. I know what damage can be done to a heart when it breaks. I refuse to allow it to happen to my nephew. Not on my account.

I prepare to challenge Shoelace to fisticuffs and tell him he's crushing the butterfly, but before I can, he takes Jill by the shoulders and looks deeply into her eyes. I feel a consummative kiss coming, and I clench my fists.

I'm wrong. Instead, Shoelace smiles at Jill and softly says, "Go." Everyone hears it, like a distant vibration of thunder.

No Escape from Greatness

Shoelace turns Jill around to face Zac. People make a corridor fifty yards long, with Zac and Jill at opposite ends and me caught in the middle.

Jill is uncertain. She stands at the other end of the corridor, unable to move.

"Go. Be a star. Be happy," Shoelace says, and with a gentle push, he launches her toward Zac, through the corridor. I nod and smile at my friend Shoelace as I step aside and let the lovers return to each others' arms. I get out of their way.

I believe I have learned to get out of my own way, too.

EPILOGUE

There is no escape from Greatness.

It's insidious because, like the mind-controlling nanoparticles cats embed in their owners, Greatness embeds itself within you. Even if a Greatnessite sips an iced tea in the sweetest smelling garden, halfway across the world, there's that tinge of rusty sewer pipe that never quite escapes your nostrils.

Erratic Automatic thought they could get me out of here, but Greatness wasn't ready to give me up quite so easily.

I tried to ride a Caribou out of here, but Greatness wasn't ready to let me go.

I pushed and pushed, wore disguises, became apoplectic.

I hid inside a Port-O-Potty.

Didn't matter. There is no escape.

And so, after Greatness very clearly saved me from very certain doom, I give in.

I say goodbye to Zac and wish him a comfortable ride on the coattails of his shooting-star girlfriend. I'm sure she will entertain many people, just as I'm sure that she will be back to visit.

TMZ is joined by *Entertainment Tonight, Entertainment Weekly*, and even a team from Japan. Erin calls me, no doubt looking to represent Jill, but I don't answer. Zac can be Jill's agent. Between tabloid entertainment interviews, Jill books four shows in one day, and a record company offers her a recording contract, but it looks shady. Zac suggests that she bide her time, and Shoelace agrees, and so she does. Jill and her agent/manager/boyfriend drive to Winnipeg in a convoy with all of the rental cars and share the same flight from Winnipeg to Los Angeles.

At home, I take all of these bits of screenplay that I've dashed off, put them in a pile, and study each page. There's a story here; perhaps it isn't an Oscar-winning smash or an artistic tour de force, but there's something. I consider turning these pages into a novel or memoir. I'll need to clean up a lot of the vulgarity, and find a way to make the narration more honest, but this is my story, five and a half decades in the making: the story of how there is no escape from Greatness, and it needs to be told. It's no cautionary tale, but it's no tale of victory, either. It simply is what it is, and ambition need not come knocking any longer. I am neither too big nor too small to be here, and now, maybe for the first time ever, I am here. Purposeless and present.

I begin to laugh a different laugh. A last laugh. A laugh at myself.

The pages feel different from anything I've written before, because my heart is in the spaces between the letters. I don't care if people love it or hate it, I am it and it is me. It is the story of my life, as small and as gargantuan as my life itself. If others can see themselves in it, then maybe I'm beginning to understand people. I realize, though, that this story isn't *for* me.

On a writing break, I scuffle through the snow down to 7th Avenue and the dollar store that used to be Robinson's. People nod hello as they pass me by in their pickup trucks, that casual hand-lift that never changes. I make my way over to Lions

No Escape from Greatness

Cemetery. My toes are nearly frozen by the time I get there, with the snow melting on the tips of my shoes and then permeating right through to the socks. Winter is nature's way of telling you to stay the hell inside and do some writing. I take note of this.

I wipe the snow from my mother's tombstone so I can see her name. I take my three-foot-tall arrangement of plastic flowers: fake white daffodils, some purple daisy-like things I don't recognize—they even sell a fake version of the blue wildflowers any yokel could pluck from the ditches around here at springtime—and I rest them on her grave. She hated flowers.

"No one gets it all. I see that now," I say to her. "But I think I know how to be happy."

When I get back to Jimmy's house, there is a for sale sign on the lawn.

No eviction notice comes, but my money has run out. As consuming as my writing work has become, I need to feed myself. I need a job.

If you need a job and you're in Greatness, there's only one person to talk to.

I find Luanne at the Four Winds Truck Stop Diner, which is no small doing, as I had to comb Greatness on foot in the new-fallen snow. She's alone when I arrive, eating an English muffin and drinking tea. Shoelace sits in the diner, reading *The Atlantic Monthly*, and we nod silently to one another as I pass. A couple of people from town smile hello to me, and I smile back. Their kids look up from their *Yes & Know* books, see that it's me, and return to their games.

Luanne clocks me coming in and never breaks her stare. Let's call it icy, though perhaps it's more steely.

"He told me you'd be coming to see me one of these days," she says, pointing at Shoelace. Shoelace turns the page on his magazine, pretending not to overhear.

"I need to ask you for something, Luanne."

"Should I be calling my lawyers to attend this breakfast?" Luanne says. "Are you going after custody now?"

"I'm staying," I tell her. "For a while."

"Well you can't stay in the house. I need to sell it. I need it to … be someone else's."

Luanne looks defeated. I shouldn't be surprised that losing control of this whole situation has left her in pain; she needed the control to keep herself protected, safe from harm. I think her need to run things used to make me angry. As my sludgey coffee arrives, it occurs to me that it is a quite sad way to live one's life.

I get on with it. "I'm here to ask for a job," I say, realizing that if I were to become Luanne's employee, she would have all sorts of control over me, and a thousand ways to abuse her authority, and maybe, just maybe, that would make amends for hurting her.

"I've applied to rent a place at Roscoe Apartments, over by Centennial Park. But they want me to write down a reference and an employer. I was wondering if perhaps you could be both."

Luanne freezes mid-bite, her teeth visibly lodged in the marmalade. Her eyes bulge like a wolf's when the wolf realizes it just bit its own tail. She unsticks herself from the English muffin, applies her paper serviette deftly to her lips, places it down flatly on the table, spreading her fingers across it to smooth out the folds.

"No," she says. She doesn't offer any passion or explanation.

This is the point where we would always argue, perhaps even to the edge of violence—or worse, romance—and then would both emerge with unresolved arguments and more deep-seated regrets. It's our dance, like two prizefighters ready to be put to pasture, muscles sagging and midriffs thickening, but knowing nothing but this dance, rematch after rematch, familiar and harmful, there is no champion.

No Escape from Greatness

I refuse to dance. Instead, I sip what they call coffee in this place.

"I can't offer you a reference because I own the company," she says. "In terms of a job, I can think of a couple of possibilities. I could use a caretaker at Roscoe, so that cuts your rent in half. And ... this isn't my idea, but with Gopher Trails growing our population by maybe fifty percent, we need someone to act like an ambassador for the town. We asked Shoelace to do it, but he says that you're the perfect fit."

"You want me to be the Welcome Wagon? For the town I have decried, publicly, for so long? How is that a perfect fit?"

"If someone else had suggested it to me, I would have laughed in their face. But it wasn't someone else. It was him. I don't see why it's a good idea, but if Shoelace says it's for the best ... I would be your direct supervisor, and if I catch you alienating or belittling any of the new oil people that move into town ..."

"I can do it," I tell her, and offer a handshake.

She studies it. Then, instead of taking my hand, she looks more deeply into my eyes and asks, "What are you going to do about Toon?"

Oddly, behind my back, I can feel Shoelace's smile grow as he buries his face in a stodgy current affairs periodical.

Later that day, I walk with Toon through the new-fallen snow (which does, by the way, season Greatness with a crispness and freshness that can be quite invigorating) to The Clayton Marvin, where Joe from Elkhorn mixes us a couple of Shirley Temples with extra cherries skewered by colourful swizzle sticks, shaped like swords.

I tell Toon that I am not going to leave here for now.

I also tell her that I am not going to leave her, ever.

I tell her that I will be her escort and guide on great adventures, around the world and around town, through her loves and defeats and shattered dreams and maybe even show the world how talented she is at being Toon. Maybe I can help make that happen. But if I can't, I'll find the bubble wrap.

I tell her that anyone who thinks they have some type of divine purpose is full of shit.

She laughs at me and says that's wise like Yoda.

I tell her that I want to be her Dad, but if she won't let me in, then I will be her Yoda. I tell her I'm here and I'm not leaving, even if I go away. She once said I can't be her father, but no one tells Gabriel Pegg what he can't do, because Gabriel Pegg can do anything. Gabriel Pegg can even try to make amends.

We order some perogies.

Toon challenges me to a swordfight with the neon plastic sabres. As she attempts to parry and thrust her plastic blade into my flesh, our fighting hands, ever so slightly and oh so intentionally, brush.

FADE TO BLACK.

Acknowledgements

Thank you

To you, for your time and intellect and sense of risk-taking. Whatever your reason for reading this, thanks. I appreciate you!

To Sharon, Jamis, Michelle and Sara of Turnstone Press, thanks so much for your hard work and belief. I hope that I have reflected your belief in me with an equal amount of belief in you and what you are doing.

To my amazing wife Tiffany and dynamic daughter Sophie: I love you both to infinity. You give me wings. I don't dare try something like putting a book out there without your faith in me. You help me to be a little less Gabriel, every day.

Special thanks to the cast and crew who volunteered their time and talents to my dramatized book trailers: my co-director Roger Boyer, Ross McMillan, Shannon Jacques, Aaron Merke, Lauren Cochrane, Aaron Hughes, Luther Alexander, Eric Neufeld, and Nicole Staats, Adeline Bird, and Kirk Ferland, who helped us a ton!

Thanks to Mark McKinney for showing me what storytelling at the highest level looks like; thanks to Miriam Toews for the same, and for your encouragement and kindness.

Thanks to Pamela Davies and David Borutski for giving me my happiest happy place to write, at Victoria Beach; thanks to the fantastic writer Jeffrey Solmundson for your storytelling eye and wisdom, and a second thanks to Sharon Caseburg for grooming this book into something people could (I really hope) love.